I0536396

BOOK TWO OF THE
CLAN NOVEL:TREMERE TRILOGY

By Eric Griffin

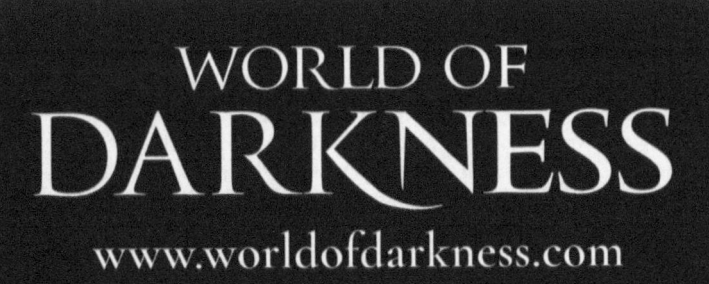

For Linda,
And those we love in common.

Wipe your hand across your mouth, and laugh;
The worlds revolve like ancient women
Gathering fuel in vacant lots.

— *Preludes*, T.S. Eliot

Preface

This note is something of both a foreword and an afterword. Three months have passed since I penned the final (perhaps, prophetic) line of this volume. (No, don't flip ahead. It reads "I was a fool ever to have left it.")

And so now I find myself—after long and uncomfortable absence—once again, sitting down face to face with an old intimate. After some awkward catching up, I can't help but feel that she has changed in some way that is not easy for me to put my finger on at first.

Intellectually, of course, I know that it is not she who has changed, but something else. The entire context of our conversation. But it is easier to pretend that the fault lies with her. Or even with me. Far better that one of us should have grown distant, colder, than to admit that something more fundamental has changed.

As I sit down to streak this page with words and doubts, exactly one week has passed since the tragic events of September 11, 2001, when a series of terrorist attacks upon New York City and Washington, DC shook the ground that all of us stood upon.

"And even in our sleep, pain that cannot forget falls drop by drop upon the heart, and in our own despair, against our will, comes wisdom to us by the awe-filled grace of God."

—Aeschylus

2 / Eric Griffin

These are the opening lines of *Widow's Walk*, the first book of Clan Novel Trilogy: Tremere, which was released this last April. As many of you are aware, this book revolves around a bombing of the Empire State Building. I've been sick about this issue since the events of last Tuesday.

I am still very much grappling with horror and doubts that these atrocities have summoned up. I am currently writing the final book of the series and recent events have raised some serious questions as to how I might hope to proceed. Somehow stories of fictional inhuman monsters pale beside the atrocities of actual human ones. And the last thing we need right now is another horror story about New York.

One of my first reactions to this crisis was to take my web site offline for the week, leaving only a message of sympathy for those caught up in these attacks.

After receiving numerous emails from concerned readers, I have now restored the site and put together some thoughts there on the crisis that I hope may answer some of the anxious questions that have come in.

Emotions here are running high right now. I think many folks are moving past the initial stunned disbelief and anxiety over further attacks and have moved on to grief and a roiling anger.

There is no doubt that this will be the worst disaster in US history. The people of New York have suffered an unspeakable tragedy—one that none of us will find ourselves able to forget.

If there is one positive aspect of all this that has struck me these last few days, it is that although some terrorist group has managed to mobilize about 50 suicidal fanatics for an act of destruction, the city of New York spontaneously produced thousands of people—normal civilians—who were willing to put their own lives on the line just to help sift through the wreckage and pull the wounded from the rubble. There is a magic of scope and of intent there that is very reassuring.

Thank you all for your kind notes.

For all of you who lost friends, colleagues and loved ones in this crisis, I wish you peace and solace. Know that you are constantly in our thoughts and prayers.

—Eric Griffin, St. Columcille's, September 18, 2001

Chapter 1
Widow's Walk

Antigone landed hard and skidded toward the edge of the rooftop. She teetered upon its edge, knowing an uncharacteristic moment of cold panic. She flailed, caught herself and spun, bracing herself for signs of pursuit. The circle of artfully arranged glass shards that she had emerged from was empty. There was still time.

With one foot, she swiped angrily at the diagram, clearing a wide swath from the pattern. That ought to keep anyone from following her through.

Then a more disturbing thought occurred to her. A determined pursuer might not be frustrated by the closing of this one means of ingress. She had reason to believe that the Astors were nothing if not determined. If this doorway were closed to them, they might open another.

Swiftly, Antigone stooped and began methodically rearranging the delicate glass mosaic—repairing the damage she had done here, altering a supporting glyph there. She was working from memory, reconstructing a pattern she had only glimpsed in the crypts below the Chantry of Five Boroughs. And even she had to admit, it was a pattern she only imperfectly understood. A protective circle, inverted.

She was still bent over the scattered slivers of glass—trying to recall the correct conjugation of the rune of elemental warding—when Stephens stepped through. Crouched before him, Antigone threw up her arms in front of her face, nearly tumbling over backwards.

Stephens must have been running when he hit the portal. He erupted from the diagram, crashing into the outer ring of wardings. His features contorted into a cry of pain and outrage as he rebounded and fell heavily to the concrete.

As terrified as Antigone was, she could not help thinking of a gull who had flown straight into the old bay window on her house in Scoville, when she was only a girl. Right now, she felt very much like a small and terrified girl once again.

Stephens rose like a squall, angry and foreboding. He towered over her, mouthing silent words, entreaties, threats, but no sound penetrated the barrier. Antigone plonked down backwards on her palms and backside. She could feel the cruel shards of glass penetrating her hands, but still she could not tear herself away from the demand in his eyes. It held her there, pinned, wriggling, under glass. She could neither move nor speak beneath the weight of his expectation.

"Brava!"

The voice came from directly behind her, startling her out of this paralyzing fascination. Antigone craned her head around, bracing for some new attack from an unexpected corner. She could make out little more than the vague outlines of a figure creeping towards her.

Antigone was suddenly conscious of the indignity of her position. She was about to die; she had little doubt on that score. The Astors were here. She had assaulted one of them. And now she was surrounded. Yes, she knew she was about to die. But strangely, instead of this conviction deepening her despair and paralysis, it liberated her. If she were going to die, she at least was not going to die like this—sprawled ungracefully amidst the debris, staring up helplessly at the doom descending upon her.

Slowly, deliberately, she brushed her hands upon the front of her robes, dislodging a gentle rain of glass slivers. Then, gathering what dignity she could muster, she straightened regally and turned to face this new threat.

Her eyes widened and her resolve nearly faltered again. "You!" she accused. "How long have you been…"

"Easy, little one," Sturbridge replied, coming forward out of the shadow of the service elevator. "Long enough. I saw your razor's rite earlier and now this. Very impressive."

Sturbridge circled the diagram, the prisoner's eyes following her every move. She pointedly ignored him. "May I?" she asked Antigone.

Not really knowing what to expect, Antigone nodded mute agreement. Sturbridge bent and rearranged one of the supporting glyphs, muttering under her breath. Antigone caught a snatch of something that sounded a bit like a chant in some harsh, guttural tongue.

At the caress of her words, the tiny pinpricks of moonlight reflected in each shard of glass caught life and blazed. Squinting against the blinding glare, Antigone saw Stephens' visage contort in a howl of pain and frustration. An instant later, he vanished entirely.

Smiling, Sturbridge turned to Antigone. Something in the novice's expression took her aback. She had expected to see relief, perhaps even gratitude in Antigone's face. But in spite of herself, only concern was apparent in the novice's unguarded expression. "He's not…?"

"No, he'll be fine," Sturbridge said. "I've just taken him out of harm's way for a little while." She studied Antigone's features, watched as acceptance, belief, and then finally, the long-expected moment of realization and relief played out in turn. She was safe now. She knew that.

Sturbridge circled the diagram again until she stood squarely between it and Antigone. Best to get the unpleasantries out of the way immediately, she thought. She did not know how shaken up the novice might be from her recent run-in with the Astors. She did not want to take a chance on Antigone doing something stupid.

Like trying to destroy the diagram again. That would be very bad for Mr. Stephens, and Sturbridge still had some rather pointed questions she wanted to put to the over-zealous inquisitor.

Or worse, Antigone could decide to leap in after him, in a fit of remorse or revenge. Stephens would be safe enough where Sturbridge had sent him—tucked away in the labyrinth of crypts beneath the Chantry of Five Boroughs until she had further need of him. She could not say that Antigone would fare as well, alone with him.

But there was no gain in sheltering the novice from the full consequences of her actions. Sturbridge forced the death mask of her face into what she hoped was a calming expression. He tone was quiet, unhurried, speculative. "You know," she said, "that particular confinement diagram you caught him in, it's not an overly pleasant one. Believe it or not, there's a perfectly good reason that the Convention banned its use back in the fifteenth century. This is the point in this little history lesson where I mention that you are officially under censure for invoking a *verboten* dark thaumaturgic rite."

She watched Antigone's jaw drop, but pressed on before the full import of what she had said could sink in. "Still, it was very neatly done, and pulled off under duress, I might add. Quite remarkable. I myself would be inclined towards leniency, but the gentleman in question would be well within his rights to insist upon the full penalty prescribed by the law. By law, you should burn for it. A friend of yours?"

Antigone started to protest. She tried to speak, found herself unequal to the task and then began again. "But, Regentia! I didn't know...I didn't mean to... Oh, Regentia, he is an Astor!"

Sturbridge accepted this new assertion without challenge. "Hmm. That does rather complicate things. These Astors tend to be very...letter-of-the-law. I don't suppose he has any compelling reason for wanting you alive?"

"He...they wanted to ask me a bunch of questions. About the ambassador and about Eva and about you. That, and they wanted my security codes."

Sturbridge looked disappointed. "Not quite the skeleton in the closet we're looking for here, I'm afraid. And I don't know if we even have a proper burning stake anymore. Well, if they're going to condemn you for this, we can at least make sure that they can't just hush it all up. They may close down the entire chantry by tomorrow night, but that leaves us an evening to set right what we may. Please kneel."

"Regentia?"

Sturbridge, not waiting upon the assumed compliance, closed her eyes and began to recite in a dead tongue. Her voice had the hint of reverence usually reserved for scripture or poetry.

Confused and flustered, Antigone did as she was bid; she slumped to her knees before Sturbridge. Her mind was filled with images of the headsman's axe. She tried to look composed, resigned, but she could feel moisture pooling up in her eyes. She told herself that she was not going to cry, that—if nothing else—she wasn't going to die with blood streaking her cheeks like cheap mascara. Then the full force of her predicament hit her at last, and she realized that no one was going to notice a few blood-red tears when her head was lying face down in the congealing puddle of her spilled lifesblood.

Sturbridge reached out a hand expectantly, palm upward. It was empty, which only confused Antigone. She was still expecting to see a gleaming blade. Then she realized what was expected, and placed her hand within the regent's. She knew she should do something, should say something. But the only thought that crossed her mind at the moment was hoping that her superior had not noticed her hesitation.

Steeling herself, Antigone braced against the inevitable blow. She felt the firm pressure of Sturbridge's grip, but there was no warmth in it. The flesh felt piscine—rough, chill, damp. It reminded her of the brush of pudgy bluish fingers from a recurring nightmare.

Antigone promised herself she would not flinch. But despite her pledge, the slightest of whimpers escaped her lips as she felt flesh part. She cursed herself for her show of weakness. Her eyes burned with shame and she felt the tears come at last, pulsing in time to the warm flush of vitae that surged down her arm. She watched it run over the hump of her wrist and stream between her fingers in long, viscous tendrils. She clamped her eyes shut and stifled a betraying sob.

Sturbridge was speaking again, that same guttural monotone, but Antigone could no longer pick out the words, much less their meaning. Something hot and wet splashed against the side of her face and she recoiled, twisting away from the point of impact. Almost against her will, her eyes flew open, only to see the next blow already descending.

Sturbridge's cupped hand slashed downward again. The blow fell this time upon Antigone's right side—the fistful of her own vitae broke upon her collarbone like a wave. Its hot spume washed up and over her jaw line, a mirror image of the previous blow.

Uncomprehendingly, Antigone gazed up at Sturbridge as if she saw, not her familiar regent, but some macabre avenging angel. In Sturbridge's eyes, however, Antigone saw no trace of malice, of righteous retribution, of justice served. There was only solemnity, and a strange hint of pride.

Antigone could not hold her regent's gaze. Confused and frightened, she cast her gaze down. Her attention was captured by the two angry red weals—painted, she realized, in her own spilled lifesblood—upon the front of her robes. The bloody swaths began at her shoulders and met at a point between her breasts. It was a yoke of blood.

A slow apprehension was nagging at the back of the novice's mind. A dim awareness of having seen these sanguine markings before. The contrast between the stark black robes and the livid band of color at the collar...

Sturbridge smiled down at her, extending both hands to draw Antigone to her feet. Taking the novice's forearm, Sturbridge tenderly raised it to her lips and ran her tongue over the wicked slash of the open wound. It closed at its master's touch.

"This is usually the point in the ceremony when you would partake of the Blood of the Seven. It is a reminder of your Oath of Initiation into this noble order. A rejuvenation of that first fiery idealism. It is also a renewed pledge of dedication to the Pyramid that seals your promotion to the Second Circle of the Novitiate. Given the events that await us tomorrow evening, however, such a pledge seems somehow out of place. Inauthentic. We will improvise."

Sturbridge laid open her own wrist with one fingernail.

"I...I don't understand," Antigone stammered.

Sturbridge smiled. "If you can work a truthsaying and subdue an Astor—in a single evening, no less—you are a Novice of the First Circle no longer. I will put through the necessary paperwork tonight, when I return to the chantry. There will be time enough. What you have done here this evening will be part of the record of our people before any report the Astors might bring against you."

The blood was flowing freely now. Sturbridge stretched out her arm. "I will not abandon you, Antigone. Even if the Pyramid itself should fall upon you."

Hesitantly, Antigone took Sturbridge's arm in both hands and bent over it. "I don't know why you're doing this. *Especially* now. When everything seems to be teetering on the brink. You don't have to. To anyone else it couldn't make any difference. A hollow and useless gesture. But not to me. Whatever else will come of this, I thank you. I am, as always, yours to command, Regentia." She drank.

Sturbridge stroked Antigone's hair gently, in time to the electric, ecstatic spurt of the blood flowing between them. If anything, she held the embrace too long. Until her own awareness was no more than a dim flutter.

"My child," she crooned softly over and over again to herself, "my beautiful little girl."

Antigone sputtered and choked upon the sudden mouthful of stagnant, icy water. She broke away, consumed in a fit of coughing. Doubled over.

Sturbridge slowly came back to herself. The flow of blood from her forearm had ceased entirely. Instead, the wound seeped a chill dark water. The pink, puckered flesh around it had taken on an unmistakably bluish tinge. Self-consciously, she smoothed her sleeve down over it.

She thought of Eva, of the ambassador, of her own little girl. Of all the children who had gone before them into that dark well. All the recriminating stares that awaited her there whenever she closed her eyes. "It is time," she said aloud.

Antigone staggered to her feet, taking one hesitant step toward her. "Regentia, I..."

"I know, little one. But the night has grown long and you must fly now. It is not safe for you to return to the chantry. You are a dangerous fugitive. A dark thaumaturge. You understand this?" She smiled, but Antigone found nothing reassuring in the gesture. Perhaps Antigone was still lightheaded from the exchange of vitae. Sturbridge's eyes seemed to her to be too large, too glassy. The eyes of a corpse that had been many days beneath the waters.

Antigone shook her head and, when she looked again, the unsettling impression was gone. "Yes, but...but where will I go?" she asked.

Sturbridge was quiet a long time. She stared hard at Antigone, but her vision was haunted by shadows. She kept seeing, not her novice standing on that precarious perch, but another. A fledgling prince restlessly pacing the battlements. Leaning far out over the Widow's Walk. Trying to pry from the city spread out below its secrets.

"You will go underground," Sturbridge said at last. "To the Nosferatu, to Calebros. You will tell them I sent you and that they are to keep you safe, at all costs. You may tell them they will do this for the sake of the bones that lie beneath the regent's blood. They will not refuse you sanctuary. Do you have that? Repeat it back to me."

"For the sake of the bones that lie beneath the regent's blood," Antigone said. "But what does it mean?"

"The Nosferatu, they will know what it means."

Antigone shook her head. "Sanctuary." She laughed nervously, thinking of her own caged bird, Mr. Felton. What would become of him now that she herself was a fugitive? "I understand," she said. "I will go into exile and willingly, Regentia. But there are still things I have to see to, back at the chantry. Our guest, he is my responsibility. What will happen to him once the Astors find out he's...? Oh, Regentia. I can't just leave him to the Astors. And you know I can't very well take him with—"

"An exceptional idea," Sturbridge said. "He will go into hiding with you. It will give the Nosferatu something to debate about. They do so love a good moral dilemma. Being bound to protect the very assassin whose blood they have been hunting these last nights. Yes, it is a dilemma worthy of them. Don't be afraid. The Nosferatu know the value of a favor, a debt unpaid. They will keep the both of you safe enough. Now, no more arguments, and no long good-byes. It is better this way. The shadow of the Pyramid is long enough..." She began the traditional words of leave-taking and then broke off.

"That one more might shelter beneath it," Antigone finished, realizing that, for the first time in seventy years, she would not be shielded by the protecting bulk of that pyramid. She suddenly felt very alone, almost exposed. She clutched at the front of her robes for comfort, but her hands came away bloody.

"In this case, far beneath it." Sturbridge smiled. "Good-bye, Antigone."

Antigone's voice was soft, subdued. "Good-bye, then." Slowly, she turned and began walking. She had no particular destination in mind, but her feet sought out the path of least resistance — the place that they were most comfortable. The very edge of the precipice.

She seemed to gain in confidence with each stride. There was now a hint of purpose in Antigone's measured step, although her course remained exactly as before — picking her way silently and methodically along the very edge of the abyss.

The prince's mistake, she thought, was that he had forgotten about the catch platforms. Or perhaps he had misjudged their reach. It was not enough to just slip over the side, merely to step out into the arms of the abyss. These things required a certain boldness, a certain abandon.

Reaching the corner, she saw the lights of Broadway spread out below her like ships' lanterns swaying from the prows of boats tied up along a quayside. They flickered, bobbing in time to the lapping of unseen waves. There were sacred galleries hidden there, she knew. Pockets of air nestled just below the docks, silent chambers defined by the rows of tarred wooden pilings sunk into the seabed.

She remembered them well. Back home in Scoville, as a girl, diving by night beneath the chill waters and the crowding hulls of moored fishing boats, one might win through—break the surface *below* the docks, in the sacred chamber ringed with wooden obelisks. The pillars were carved with the names and signs of the faithful. There they might exchange secrets, schemes, or covert kisses—in the darkness, shivering and treading water.

Antigone slipped from the cumbersome black robes—long the symbol of her novitiate, of her failure. The bloody badge of her final triumph was still fresh upon the breast. The coarse and awkward second skin she had worn these seventy years slipped to the scarred concrete.

She stood poised upon the very edge of the precipice, naked and radiant in the moonlight. She drank in the cool night air. Her arms stretched upward as if she would catch the moon in the net of her outspread fingers. Her body arced, taut and youthful. Deceptively so. In that single unselfconscious gesture it belied a century of memories and responsibilities.

She bounded high, flashed in the moonlight—like a fish breaking the plane of the water and, for a moment, soaring. At the crux of the arc, she bent perfectly double, fingers touching toes and then unfolding like a straight razor. Then she succumbed to the gentle tug of the earth. Calling her name, calling her home.

There was a rushing of wind in her ears, billowing her hair out and back. She dove through it, beating powerful strokes, trying to fight deep enough that she might win through—might make it all the way under the keels of the moored boats and emerge in the pillared recess beneath the docks. That she might emerge, shivering and gasping burning lungfuls of life, in the hidden sanctuary of the watery tomb.

Chapter 2
A Domain of Wind and Vertigo

Sturbridge rushed to the edge of the parapet, but already it was too late. Her hands knotted around the twisted remains of the guardrail. The metal squealed and pulled farther away from its concrete anchors as she leaned far out over the abyss.

She ignored its obvious warning. *Too late!* Sturbridge raged. She knew that Antigone had been frightened. The mere presence of the Astors here certainly posed a threat to Antigone—to all of them, for that matter. As a leader of the chantry security team, Antigone would surely come under scrutiny for the string of suspicious deaths that had plagued the chantry. But in the final reckoning, Antigone's share in the responsibility would be proportional to her place in the Pyramid. She might be stripped of rank, but she had little to lose on that score. She might suffer a forced relocation to another chantry. But this?

Antigone's encounter with the Astors had changed everything. She had been shaken, that much was obvious. Panicked enough to attempt a rite she should have known better than to invoke. Sturbridge still did not know how the novice had managed to pull off the ritual that had imprisoned Stephens. But Sturbridge did have a pretty good idea where Antigone had seen that *verboten* dark thaumaturgic diagram. It was the inverted hermetic circle that Eva had inscribed in the crypts deep beneath the chantry.

Eva, Sturbridge thought. *Another of my failures.*

She forced the thought aside. Eva had struck her own dark bargain. She had sought to destroy the Children Down the Well, the reproachful nightmare visitations that were the dark obverse of the thaumaturgic blood arts. The attempt to sever the nearly limitless power of the blood from the price it exacted from its wielders had proved misguided and, ultimately, Eva paid for it with her life. Sturbridge's own suffering seemed incidental to Eva's lofty design.

In mimicking the trappings of Eva's forbidden rite, Antigone had earned herself a death sentence. But Sturbridge had given her a way out. The life of an exile—a fugitive from the Pyramid—was no easy path, but it was far preferable to being staked out to meet the sun. Surely Antigone had seen that. Surely Sturbridge had been able to make at least that much clear.

She had thought the matter settled when Antigone had agreed to go into hiding among the Nosferatu. The novice had even made arrangements for her saboteur-prisoner-*cum*-coconspirator, Mr. Felton, to go into hiding with her.

So why, then, did she do it? Why did she jump?

By the time Sturbridge had realized what Antigone was up to, it was already too late. The regent had been powerless to stop her, even to cry out. In the end, all Sturbridge's authority, all her years of experience manipulating the elaborate Tremere hierarchy, all the dark secrets of her blood magics, all the superhuman reflexes and instincts of her unaging predator's body—none of these had been sufficient to save even this little one.

What hope, then, did Sturbridge herself have against the reckoning that was now at hand?

Craning far out over the parapet, her eyes raked the abyss. But if she hoped to catch one final glimpse of Antigone as the novice plunged toward the pavement over a hundred stories below, even this small mercy was denied her. The expanse of sky that so suddenly separated the two them—severing the lifeline that bound them, a tenuous cord of stolen Tremere blood—was too vast to take in. Sturbridge felt as if she herself were falling, drowning within that domain of wind and vertigo spread out below her, brim-filling the world from horizon to horizon.

So why did it feel as if the greater gulf of emptiness was inside her? Sturbridge felt hollow, as if something essential had just been wrenched out of her.

She clung to the railing, but without conviction. A leaf clothed in winter black, clinging to its branch more from habit than from hubris. She was distantly aware of a section of metal railing, somewhere off to her right, peeling away and careening musically off the side of the building before surrendering itself to the long fall. Sturbridge paid it no mind. From her position and the way her whole body heaved convulsively, wracked with sudden and senseless loss, she might have been mistaken for some old derelict retching over the rail. Certainly she felt as if she could not keep it all down—could not swallow what had just been done here—to Antigone. To Sturbridge herself.

Only her long straight black robes gave the lie to the impression that she was merely some unfortunate drunk on an improbable perch. Her unusual ensemble gave her the aspect of a hollow marsh reed bent beneath the coming storm.

Why did she have to jump? Damn it, she could have made it! If she could have just won her way through to the Nosferatu, Antigone would have had a chance. A real chance. They would have kept her safe, if nothing else for Sturbridge's sake. She had come to the aid of their prince when there was no other hope for him. And of all the Kindred, the Nosferatu knew the value of a favor owed. They would have kept Antigone safe within their warrens. No one—not even the most determined Tremere inquisitor—would dare violate the prince's private domain in search of a fugitive.

Or the Nosferatu could just as easily have smuggled her out of the city. Send her somewhere no one would think to look for her. Somewhere Antigone could have started over. The shadow of the Pyramid was long, yes, but it did not eclipse the entire world.

Then why? Sturbridge muttered over and over again to herself, clutching the bent metal strut, wringing it with white-knuckled fists, curling her whole body around it. *Why?* She rocked slowly back and forth.

She thought of all of the novices she had failed. Of Antigone who, fleeing the reproach of Vienna, hurled herself from this lofty perch. Of Jacqueline who poked her nose too deeply into the affairs of the first wave of infiltrators from the Fatherhouse—and lost her head for her troubles. She thought of Chessie, Dorfman's attaché from the Washington chantry, whom Sturbridge had, in a vulnerable moment, personally ushered across the threshold of the undying, only to abandon her to madness, hunger and solitary peril in war-torn Baltimore. And of course, she thought of Eva. Sturbridge's own protégé and hand-picked successor had also proved her betrayer.

They had all been Sturbridge's own special charges, her own little girls. And now they were, all of them, beyond reach. Beyond touching. Beyond redemption.

Sturbridge's thoughts spiraled in upon themselves. A vague, wavering image rose unbidden in her mind. Its features were those of another little girl, one who—for Sturbridge—was always implicit. The model on which all of the others were based.

To a shrewd observer, the face was almost a composite of those other faces. It shared Antigone's raven hair and storm-creased brow. There was something of Jacqueline in the high, regal cheekbones, the almost predatory avian angles of the face. The defiant jut of the chin could have been Chessie's own, or the sudden smile that flicked on like a light switch and seemed to eclipse the entire face. And she had Eva's eyes, a child's eyes, alternately burning with curiosity and laughter.

There was a name lurking, somewhere just beneath the surface of that face. Etched into the very bones of the half-concealed skull. It was the name of Sturbridge's own beloved daughter, separated from her now by the breadth of one hundred years and a single death. She was the first victim of Sturbridge's predatory existence, this monstrous parody of life everlasting that she had bargained away her own life for. And the life of her daughter.

The name rose unbidden from the depths of memory, from that special cell she had lovingly wrought to keep that most precious recollection safe against the cruel edges and casual indignities of this monstrous adult world.

Maeve.

With a broken cry, Sturbridge tore herself away from the edge of the parapet and stumbled half-blind over and through the ruins of the observation deck. She had been unable to save any of them. Not a one. Not her mortal daughter, nor her immortal childe. Not any of the long string of special charges she had hand-picked, studied from afar and so cunningly drawn under her protection.

She couldn't save them. She couldn't redeem them. It seemed that all she could do was gather in their bodies. Hers was a macabre collection of identical little china dolls, pretty maids all in a row, with cracked porcelain faces.

No, she thought, that wasn't precisely correct. That wasn't all she could do. Someone would still have to sweep up all the bone-white shards and put them somewhere safe. Somewhere

where no one could harm them, ever again. She could still do that at least.

And then, of course, she would see to it that someone paid for all her delicate little broken things.

Chapter 3
Dreams of the Father

"You were quite right to, ehm, come to me, Adepta. Quite right," Himes assured her. The special operative from Vienna sat rigidly upright in the metal folding chair. If he felt any discomfort at these commandeered arrangements, he gave no outward sign of it. Helena, the chantry's Head of Security, sat directly across the long table from him, her back to the door that led to the Hall of Daggers and Mirrors. She looked bone-weary, as if she personally felt the entire weight of the tons of rock and earth poised above their heads. She found her gaze flickering wistfully over her shoulder towards the overstuffed armchairs in the formal sitting room just below the dais. Right now, she would like nothing better than to relax within the layers of rich cinnamon upholstery and just sink from sight. She shifted uncomfortably on her metal perch.

Himes did not so much as glance up at Helena, although barely three feet separated the pair. Instead, his attention was fixed on the piece of stationery in his hand. Helena stared as well; not at the note, but at his hands.

They were long, delicate and precise. The nails were meticulous. Those hands were far more revealing than the Astor's impassive face. Helena studied them with the intensity of a palmist, as Himes reread the note for perhaps the third time. She noticed that they trembled slightly.

The paper was badly crumpled—a result of Helena's own ill-concealed emotions upon first reading it. She had immediately repented of her outburst, but her best efforts to smooth the note out flat again had proved ineffectual.

The note read:

> Helena,
>
> Perhaps I phrased that poorly. All is well. As well as can be expected. Perhaps better than can be explained.
>
> Eva is dead and beyond harm. It seems the rest of us may not have been as fortunate. I think it will be quite some time before we can fully grasp, much less begin to heal, the injury she has inflicted upon us. Even as you slumber, I can feel your hurt. I can smell your blood upon you and I know what it is that you suffer. This affliction that is upon me, it has much the same source.
>
> You were much closer to the truth than I was ready to admit when you insisted that I had eaten our dead. I know that sounds monstrous but there is no other way that I can say it or understand it at present. Not physically eaten them, of course. That would be merely ghoulish. But I have devoured them—the Children, the nightmares, les Tremeres. Swallowed them utterly.
>
> I am watching you now, as you slumber. Do you see them still, I wonder. The Children, the reproachful, self-incriminating dreams of the Father. Or do they belong to me and me alone now? One thing is certain, Eva wanted to be free of the nightmare. In this she succeeded beyond her wildest expectations. Within the walls of this

chantry, she may be condemned a murderer, but beyond? It may be that to those who will come after us, she will be hailed as the hero, if not the redeemer, of our line.

I must go. Too much has been left undone for too long. Know that I forgive you. But do not be here when I return.

—A.S.

P.S. The security clearance hierarchy is a wreck. Casualties. Please update.

"And you say, ehm, Adepta..." Himes mumbled. "May I call you Helena? You are very kind. And you say, Helena, that Regent Sturbridge wrote you this note?"

"Yes, I—"

Without waiting for anything more than her nod, Himes pressed on, mumbling apparently to himself. "Yes, this is her hand, certainly. I went to some pains before our departure from the Fatherhouse to familiarize myself with the regent's handwriting. To be quite frank, some of the dispatches coming out of this chantry of late have been—how do you say?—suspect."

Helena kept her gaze lowered, studying the slight predatory curl of his fingers. "I am pleased," she said carefully, "that the intent of those missives was not lost upon our brethren back at the Fatherhouse. You understand that I could not openly set down my concerns about the regent's health...."

"Just so," Himes said. "Just so." One of those fluttering avian hands reached across the table and patted her own three times, reassuringly. Then he grunted and pushed himself up suddenly from the table, nearly upsetting the chair. He took up a restless pacing behind his side of the table.

After a few minutes, Helena became half-convinced that the old man had forgotten her. He seemed intent on mumbling to himself, but Helena only caught scattered words amidst the low hum. She cleared her throat softly.

Himes glanced up, startled, and then shaking his head he returned to his pacing and grumbling. For a brief moment, Helena considered just getting up and retreating from the chamber. It had been a mistake to come here. These Astors, they were not from around here. Not even from this country. Hell, not even from this century, it seemed. How was she supposed to make them understand what was going on? Helena wasn't entirely convinced that she herself had managed to grasp all the finer points. It was just so monstrous. But she had to try. There was no other way she was going to get either herself or Sturbridge out of this one if she didn't at least make the attempt.

"Look, all I'm trying to say is—" she began.

"That we have you, yourself, to thank for those, hmm, subtle communiqués?" Himes had shed his absent mutterings and come to the point of attack with a disturbing alacrity. Helena gaped at him.

In her moment's hesitation, he read all he needed to know. He smiled and resumed his doddering manner, taking off his brass-rimmed spectacles and holding them up to the light.

All right, Helena thought. *Fair enough. First blood to you. But now you've shown your steel, old man, and you can be sure you won't catch me off guard a second time.*

Himes frowned at the lenses. He set the crumpled note down gingerly upon the table—as if half afraid that she would snatch it away again—and extracted a handkerchief from his breast pocket. The motion reminded Helena of a spindly waterfowl dipping its beak into the shallows. He rubbed patiently at some invisible mote on the lenses.

"Yes," Helena admitted. "I've had to take over most of the chantry's official correspondences in the regent's absence.

Someone had to step in to maintain the routine functions. The regent was unwell. I think both the contents of her note and her current absence would bear out that point."

"We will come back to the question of Sturbridge's whereabouts presently," said Himes. He held the glasses at arm's length and frowned. "But I am curious. Why this charade? Why did you feel it necessary to keep up the appearance that all was well? That Sturbridge was still at the helm? That the ambassador was still—how to put it delicately—among the living?"

"I knew that the discrepancies would be noted," she said without hesitation. She had spent nights playing out this encounter in her thoughts—ever since it became clear to her that things had gone too far and that Vienna would have no choice but to send in its inquisitors. It was always unsettling when she actually arrived at such a long-dreaded confrontation. The details never quite matched the elaborate settings she had constructed. She had always pictured that her interrogation would take place in a more private venue—in the regent's sanctum, or perhaps the security control room. She had never anticipated sitting face to face with her inquisitor over a folding banquet table erected on the dais of the Hall of Audience.

But, for that matter, she had never anticipated an inquisitor quite so disarming as Mr. Himes, an old-school cavalier who gave the impression that he had nobly suffered the indignity of witnessing the death of a more genteel age. He was a relic, a slightly embarrassing anachronism that had no place in this time, but no time of his own to go back to. A White Knight without a Wonderland, pressed into a service that ill-suited his temperament.

Helena had to keep forcing herself to remember who he was, why he was here, and how much of her future hung on convincing him of her painstakingly constructed story.

Yes, she admitted aloud. It was true enough. She had known that she would not be able to maintain the deception. But what else could she have done? With Sturbridge wavering between torpidity and madness, Helena could not write to them openly. Could not give them the direct answers they wanted. She did not know those answers herself. And what she did know had to be carefully couched. Surely they could appreciate how tenuous her position had been. And what great lengths she had gone to bring them here.

She had recited these exact words a hundred times before, and never had she reeled them off with such precision and conviction.

Himes, it seemed, did not share her opinion of the performance. He regarded her skeptically and gave up on the lenses in frustration. He slid the glasses down onto the table between them. Helena, her eyes locked on those hands, caught the nearly imperceptible irritated flick of the fingers. The clack and slide of the brass frames was clearly audible in the silence that hung between them. "Ah," he said. "You deliberately falsified those reports."

"Knowing that they would send up a red flag," Helena said. "And that someone at the Fatherhouse would send help."

Himes slowly refolded his handkerchief and tucked it back into his breast pocket, without ever looking at either. Helena doubted that, even given a straight edge and a half hour to work at it, she could have achieved the crisp precision of that angle of linen jutting from the pocket. Its exacting geometry, she saw, was a rite in itself. A glyph, a warding. A protective diagramma interposed between the two of them.

Embarrassed, she realized she was staring. She rushed on to cover the uncomfortable pause. "If the chantry had suddenly gone incommunicado—and in the midst of the battle to liberate the city—you would have feared the worst. It would have caused panic," Helena said. "In that case, you and I would not be having a reasonable discussion of these concerns. Vienna would have reacted to a perceived military threat. They would not have dispatched investigators, but a strike force. New York is just too volatile right now to allow even the perception of Tremere weakness."

Himes sighed and folded his hands before him on the table. "You have marshaled your arguments most carefully, Helena. But the fact still remains that you forged chantry communiqués. You lied to your superiors and you covered up at least one brutal murder. Surely you can understand our position." He looked very sad, and one hand fidgeted absently with the spectacles laying on the table. "The position of my superiors. We can ill afford to suffer such deceptions, much less from within our own ranks. You had been entrusted the security of this chantry...."

"I fully understand the seriousness of this matter," Helena said. "I have done only what was necessary to protect my regent and to preserve this house. It has not been easy for me, and if there is a further price to be paid for these decisions, I am prepared to pay it."

His avian hands pecked out an agitated staccato on the tabletop. "Yes, yes. Very noble sentiments. But we have little use for sentiment here. What I need from you is, ahem, information. You have done well to come to us of your own free will, to present this...evidence. Your prompt surrender of your clearance codes and your cooperation in restructuring the chantry security hierarchy speak to your credit. Things may yet go well for you, Helena. But we will need someone we can rely upon here, within the chantry, to help complete this investigation quickly. Before anyone else is hurt or killed. I trust that we understand each other?"

Helena could only nod.

"Excellent, then I have some basic questions. I would like for you to answer them as truly and as completely as you can. Shall we begin?"

She nodded again. "I'm ready."

"Helena, do you know why we, my colleagues and I, are here?

Horror stories of the "liquidation" of the Tel Aviv chantry flashed through Helena's mind. Tales of the Astors ruthlessly purging the chantry house with fire and the stake. She selected her words with care.

"You are here to restore order," she said. "This house has been under a *maledictus* these past weeks. We have been afflicted with murders, fire and madness. The chaos has to stop."

"The chaos will stop, Adepta. Have no fear on that account. The Chantry of Five Boroughs has been the jewel in the crown of our operations on this continent. But of late, this gem has become...murky. With deception. So much so that the crown itself has become corroded. We will restore its luster. But first, we must understand why things have degraded so far. You will assist us in this inquiry."

"I understand," Helena said.

"Things need not have come to this. Some weeks ago, the Council saw fit to send an official representative to this house. This legate was entrusted with assisting you in putting the affairs of this house back in order, *before* things took a more dramatic turn. When this legate failed to report in as scheduled, the Fatherhouse received—how do you say?—unsatisfactory explanations. So I will ask you directly, where is the ambassador?"

"He is dead," Helena admitted. "We found his remains in the crypts, at the bottom of the well. He had...fallen."

Himes cocked an eyebrow. "Fallen in battle, do you mean? That was the explanation that we received. But surely, if the chantry house itself had come under attack, that would have been mentioned in dispatches?"

"You misunderstand," Helena said. "He had fallen. From a height."

Himes scrutinized her as if looking for an opening in which to best insinuate a knife. His tone was incredulous. "And this, this is another example of your having altered official correspondences in order to summon help?"

"As you say. The reports were inaccurate."

"The reports were lies!" His composure cracked, his fist smashing down upon the table, sending the spectacles skittering away. Slowly, deliberately, he forced his hands to unclench, fanning his fingers flat on the tabletop.

"They were necessary inaccuracies," Helena countered, her eyes never leaving his hands. "I did what could be done to safeguard the regent and this house."

"I am not interested in your rationalizations, Adepta. For the present, we are conducting a factual inquiry. You will reply accordingly. Tell me, what do you know about the ambassador?"

Helena glared at him, but did not rise to the bait. "He called himself the *Logos Etrius*, the Word of Etrius." Her tone was precise, formal. "He identified himself as a legate from the Fatherhouse. He said he had come to put an end to the string of murders and to restore order."

Helena trailed off and let that thought hang between them for a while. It wasn't exactly a threat, but her meaning was clear enough. These Astors were not the first to undertake this fool's task. And the last person to do so had come to a bad end.

"I am aware of his mission," Himes replied. "That is all? Did the ambassador not confide in you anything about his identity, his home chantry, his lineage?"

Helena shook her head. "No, that's about all I knew of him. We were not on more personal terms. He was not exactly what you might call approachable."

"How *would* you characterize your relationship with the ambassador, then?" Himes asked.

"Formal. I didn't have much opportunity to deal with him at all, except when he had certain demands to make of me in my role as head of security. Mostly he dealt with Sturbridge. He didn't give me the impression that he was in the habit of fraternizing with those of lesser rank."

He considered. "And this was true of his relationships with the novices as well? As far as you know?"

"Yes," she replied. "It wasn't just me. I can't recall seeing him spending time with any of the novices."

"And Regent Sturbridge?" he asked. "How would you describe the regent's relationship with the ambassador?"

Helena took her time in answering. "Sturbridge was the very image of the gracious hostess."

"But she was not *really* a gracious hostess. She was just the 'image' of one." It was not a question.

"That's not what I meant, Mr. Himes—"

"Nevertheless, that is what you said. Would you say that Sturbridge felt threatened by the ambassador's arrival?"

"Threatened? No. There was never any question in my mind that the regent could handle him. No, I think she took his presence as more of an imposition—a distraction. Like being ordered off to that Camarilla war council in Baltimore when she obviously had pressing problems to deal with here at home."

"So Sturbridge was resentful of those orders?"

"Not resentful, just…"

"Inconvenienced?" he pressed.

Helena felt flustered by this barrage. And getting flustered always made her angry. "Yeah, you could say 'inconvenienced.' If it were me, I would have told them where they could stick those orders. Damn it, people were dying here. Novices! You can't just demand that someone drop everything and go traipsing off to Baltimore when her people are dying."

Helena broke off and fumed silently, realizing perhaps that she had gone too far.

Himes let her wind down. After a time, he picked up the dangling thread of conversation. "So, it is your considered opinion that an ideal regent would be resentful of such a summons. Is that a fair statement? And the fact that Sturbridge was not outraged would clearly indicate…"

"I never said anything against the regent."

"Of course. But I can follow a logical inference, Adepta. Clearly, at some point you came to believe that Sturbridge was no longer capable of making command decisions. I am just trying to ascertain at which point. Now, if I may resume…. Sturbridge did not express any dissatisfaction with her orders? Perhaps with the agenda for that meeting?"

"I really don't know anything about that agenda," Helena said coolly. "But her place was here. She should have been getting to the bottom of those murders before anyone else got hurt. If she were, maybe none of this would have happened."

"Would it surprise you to learn," Himes interposed, "that those orders came directly from Pontifex Dorfman?"

Helena was not sure if the question were meant to chastise her, to remind her of her place. Peter Dorfman was Sturbridge's superior and well within his rights to decide for himself what was best for Sturbridge and for this chantry. "No, I guess that doesn't surprise me," Helena said. "I know Dorfman has a vested interest in clan politics. That emergency Camarilla war council in Baltimore sounds like something that might fall under his domain."

"Do you think that Sturbridge was resentful enough that she would undermine Dorfman's efforts in the council?"

"What are you saying?" Helena accused. "That Sturbridge went to Baltimore and undermined the Camarilla war effort because she felt she had been somehow inconvenienced by Dorfman's summons?"

"I'm not saying anything. I'm asking whether or not Sturbridge was resentful enough to undermine Dorfman. Just to hold back a bit. Not to push his agenda as hard as she might. Maybe even make him look bad before the council?"

"Ridiculous!"

"Why ridiculous?" he countered. "Did you never know Regent Sturbridge to thwart someone here at the chantry who proved a nuisance to her, an inconvenience, an embarrassment?"

Helena waved aside his concerns. "I'm saying that Sturbridge doesn't sacrifice Pyramid goals to settle personal grudges."

Himes sat straight up as if he had been slapped. "Are you saying that Pontifex Dorfman is in the habit of sacrificing Pyramid goals to settle personal grudges?"

"What? I wasn't talking about Dorfman, I was…"

Her genuine surprise seemed to mollify him. But Helena was aware that something she said must have hit a nerve. It seemed that there were more dangers in this interview than the obvious ones.

"Never mind, Adepta. It seems I misunderstood. Where is Eva?"

Helena was slightly taken aback by this sudden change of gears. "Eva? She's dead. Well, officially she is still missing in action. We found her outline burned into the floor of the crypts. There has been no further sign of her these past weeks."

"How would you say she died?" Himes asked. "Another fall?"

Helena gave him a hard stare. "No. I can't say for sure how she died. Sturbridge said something about her being 'burned by the light of truth' or something like that. Whatever that means."

"So Sturbridge saw Eva die?"

"I think so," Helena said after some consideration. "Although the regent has not been herself. I'm not sure how much stock to place in…"

"So noted. You tell me what was said. You can leave me to puzzle over how much stock to place in it."

She could have hit him. She refrained. Already she knew that he was going out of his way to get under her skin, to force her into unguarded comments. The worst thing she could do at this point was to give in.

"Was Sturbridge present when the ambassador died as well?" he asked.

"No. Well, I'm not sure. Neither Eva nor the ambassador should have been able to access those crypts by themselves. Security clearance. I think that Sturbridge must have gone down there with them."

"Helena, do you think that Regent Sturbridge killed Eva and the ambassador?"

Helena shifted uncomfortably. "I…I don't know."

"Is there any reason to believe that she did not kill them?"

"She says she did not kill them. I only wish…"

"Yes?"

"I only wish I could be more confident that she were in a right state of mind. But I know the regent. I have lived and worked and studied with her for decades. I find it hard to believe that she could suddenly have become a callous, calculating…" She broke off.

"Killer?" Himes asked. "Well that's not really at issue is it? We're all killers, now, aren't we? But tell me about the dead novice. Eva. Were the two of you close?"

Helena shook her head. "No. The neophytes don't have a lot of free time, and Eva spent most of that in orbit around Sturbridge. I think the regent looked on her as a kind of protégée. I certainly can't believe that the regent would just..."

"Did Eva confide in you anything about her identity? Her home chantry or her lineage, say?"

Helena thought a moment. "I never heard her speak of it. But that wasn't so unusual. She came to us just like all the others do. Pressed into service. The Chantry of Five Boroughs is a war chantry. The only way we can keep our numbers up is through a steady stream of 'volunteers' from other, more peaceful sisterhouses. That means we tend to get the problem cases, the novices that other regents didn't want to deal with. It never really does to pry too deeply into a new transfer's background. There's always an unpleasant story there somewhere and pressing them on it just builds resentment."

"So you would say that Eva was a 'problem case'?"

"I don't know. She was one of the better ones. Never got into much trouble. Nothing so dramatic that they had to call in the security team...." Helena hazarded a smile, but the effort was wasted on Himes. He still wasn't even looking at her. He had resumed his distracted pacing.

"Never got into much trouble?" he mused aloud. "That is a strange assertion, don't you think? Given the present circumstances. Let me make sure that I understand you correctly: Eva is dead, found within the crypts. And the ambassador, he is dead as well. And like Eva, he is found within the crypts. And you tell me that it was Sturbridge who brought them there. And Sturbridge who witnessed their deaths. And Sturbridge who has written this monstrous confession, admitting to eating the dead. And, I cannot help notice, Sturbridge herself is, even now, among the missing. You must admit, things look rather bad for Ms. Sturbridge."

Now it was Helena who could not meet his gaze. She knew what she would find there. The condemning certainty of an inquisitor, a hanging judge. She could see it in the predatory curl of his fingers.

The Astor had already made up his mind that Sturbridge was to blame. And perhaps, Helena admitted miserably, the regent *was* to blame. Helena simply didn't know anymore.

All she knew was that her words would be the pyre on which they burned her regent.

She was only vaguely aware of Himes' persistent litany of questions. She heard the rise and fall of his inflections, but the words held little meaning for her anymore. She felt as if she were imprisoned within the confines of her skull, looking out through the high barred windows of her eyes. She answered his questions woodenly, aware that she could do little more than watch as the gallows took form outside her prison window.

Chapter 4
The Pool of Suicides

Antigone broke the surface to find herself treading the icy waters of a subterranean pool. She could hear the lapping of water against marble. The obelisks that bordered this hidden chamber were of not of tar and wood, but of carved stone. Their markings were clearly of an older order, hieroglyphs both ancient and authentic.

She paddled to the edge of the pool and pushed herself up. Water streamed from her lithe form as she walked dripping from the silent waters. The marble was cool against the soles of her feet.

But what was this place?

When she was back on the Widow's Walk, everything had seemed so certain. So right. All that was necessary was the proper resolve, the proper conviction. A leap of faith.

She had pulled off the trick before, many times. Her dramatic leaps between life and death had become ritualized, almost theatrical. It was now something of a disappearing act. Now you see her, now you don't.

True, she had never played her game of ledges on such a grand scale before, but the height should not have mattered. Even the epic scale of the plunge from the observation deck should not have proved too great an obstacle. If anything, the heroic scope made her stronger, larger than life. And, she hoped, larger than death.

But something had gone amiss. She should not be here. She should have awakened in some hospital bed, broken in body but triumphant in spirit. She would smile up at the attendant through the bandages, her most winning smile, and express her hope that she hadn't worried them.

That was the best part of the act. The look on their faces, it was priceless. It was all the applause she craved. That one look made it all worthwhile, worth coming back again and again. To be needed. To be somehow essential. So much so that it seemed life itself simply could not bear to go on without her.

Death was not big enough to hold her. It never had been. It always disgorged her, deposited her back here, under the sterile glaring lights.

"Worried us? Jeezus, lady, you're lucky to be alive."

He would have been half right.

The sound of a footfall in the darkened tomb ruined her moment. It jerked Antigone out of her reverie. She froze, instinctively dropping to a fighting crouch at the water's edge. The *plish* of water falling from her body and striking the floor boomed in the darkness. It pinpointed her position.

A torch hissed to life, momentarily blinding her. When she had blinked her eyes clear, she saw that the brand was held aloft by a huge ebon claw. Beyond it, she could make out only a hulking shadowy form that swelled in the torchlight, filling the room from corner to corner. Her eyes squinted, but the only detail of it she could make out was the glint of light off wicked canines. A mocking Cheshire Cat smile.

The voice was gentle, but vast as the sea. It filled the tiny grotto and caught her up in its undertow, nearly sweeping her feet out from under her. "You are shivering, little one. Come closer, into the light and warm yourself."

She was suddenly aware of her nakedness and vulnerability. She wavered there, both afraid and ashamed to approach the light.

"Suit yourself," the voice washed over her. "You will probably catch your death of cold. But perhaps that is not so grim a prospect for you as it once was. Some manage to make themselves quite comfortable here, at the water's edge. Some linger for years without ever daring to approach the light."

Something brushed past Antigone's shoulder. She wheeled to confront her unseen assailant, but found she could barely budge. She was caught, wedged in a great press of bodies, all crowded here at the water's edge. She felt as if she were trying to draw breath, but she could not. She could not even remember why this might be important.

She tried to twist free, but only found herself pressed face to face with the man next to her. The top and back of his head had been violently blown outward. His eyes widened in recognition, but when he opened his mouth to address her, the only thing that emerged was a wash of blood from the gaping hole in the roof of his mouth.

Antigone tried to push free of him, to spin away, to lose herself in the press. She reached out, groped blindly and latched onto something firm. A hand in the dark mass of flesh. She tightened her grip and pulled herself closer. A face swam towards her through the sea of bodies. For an instant she saw her look of relief mirrored in the other woman's face. Then, just as suddenly, the look dissolved into one of horror and repulsion.

Antigone could not hold the other woman's stare. Her eyes dropped to their clenched hands and for the first time she saw long, exaggerated shreds of flesh trailing from the other's forearms. They dragged the floor in her wake.

She would not scream. Antigone clenched her teeth over the rising panic and revulsion and cast about for some way out of the throng of bodies. The pool! She fought her way back towards the sound of lapping waters, lashing out indiscriminately.

With a cry of relief, she picked out the outline of the pool's edge. A bloated blue hand burst from the waters and groped at her ankles. She kicked out at it, backing away as it splashed heavily again into the water. It was not the pudgy, bluish fingers of the drowned child that repulsed and alarmed her. It was the sheer volume of bodies clamoring and clawing their way out of the Pool of Suicides.

Desperately, Antigone cast about for the only other landmark she knew in this vast landscape of flesh—the torch. She could barely pick out the flicker of the distant light. Unless she had totally lost her sense of direction, it had moved since she had last sighted it. Step by step, she fought her way forward. "I am coming!" she shouted. "Don't leave me here."

She saw a momentary opening in the press of bodies and immediately dove towards it, twisted and rolled. She could feel hands snatching at her, but they could find no purchase on her wet, sleek form. There were no trailing robes for them to get a grip on, but she felt handfuls of hair tear away. She came to her feet, bleeding from a dozen small wounds. But she could feel the stirring of a draft on her face. She had broken free and there was only open space ahead of her. With all of her remaining strength, she sprinted away from the clinging hands of the damned.

She stumbled and came to an abrupt halt against a pillar. At least she had thought it was a pillar. Looking up, she saw the blazing glow of the torch directly above her. In the light it cast, she could see that the "pillar" was covered in a coarse black fur.

"Here you are, little one." The familiar laughing voice wrapped around her like a blanket. But there was no warmth in it, only the whisper of the wind through exhumed skulls. "I had hoped you would find my company preferable to that of your peers, and here you are at last. But you are trembling! Where is the pelt that I gave you at our last meeting? Surely you have not left it behind? A pity. You seem even to have shed your skin—you are all pale and moist and wriggling. Hold still a moment."

"But I don't know how...I don't know how I got here," Antigone said miserably.

"Shh. Easy now, little one. Let us see."

She felt his great soft paws close over her. As she sank into their warmth, she curled in upon herself. He rolled her in his palms like a ball of pliable clay.

It was as if her arms had gotten tangled up in her legs and she couldn't quite get them all sorted out again. She tried to cry out, but her words came out muffled as if her head were wrapped in layers of thick cloth.

"There, that is better. It is much as I first remember you."

As the comforting darkness of the great paws peeled away, Antigone found herself faced with the indignity of being dangled upside down by one heel. She batted at the tangle of long black skirts that hung down over her face.

"Set me down," she managed to choke out.

"Or almost as I remember you," the Jackal amended. The room suddenly righted itself and Antigone found herself once more upon solid ground. As she smoothed the trailing skirts back into place, she was struck by the contrast between her slightly ridiculous position and the solemnity of the ensemble. The long black dress was formal, but simple, almost shapeless. She felt as if she were sheathed in rustling layers—a pale reed girded dark against the marshes. The somber gown even smelled musty, of mothballs. It reminded her of desolate places—of moors, of gardens in winter, of churchyards.

There was no mistaking its function. It was mourning dress. Widow's weeds.

Even as she realized this, Antigone was struck with the similarity between this gown and her novice's robes abandoned on the Widow's Walk. Had it been only a lifetime ago?

It was not so much a visual similarity as one of feel, of purpose. But her old robes were a badge of her years of servitude to House Tremere and her hopeless struggle against the monolithic and impersonal stasis of the Tremere Pyramid. It was not a burden she was eager to take up again.

She found her hand straying, as if by habit, to where the interior cache pocket was on the novice vestments. She was startled to find a familiar shape there, nestled beneath the layers of fabric of her new garment. It was the outline of an ancient straight razor. Occam's Razor. It too should have been left behind, abandoned on the precipice.

"Now, no more running," the Jackal smiled down at her. "The way you flit between places is extremely distracting. It is a wonder you ever manage to finish a thought. Now, sit here at my feet. No arguments. I will be only a moment."

Far overhead, the torch swiveled, leaving Antigone in shadow. The light revealed a set of stone shelves recessed into the wall of the tomb. Fragile clay vessels lined the shelves — canopic jars — each one stoppered with a lifelike sculpted animal head.

The Laughing Guardian of the Dead ran one hand absently along the row of jars, as if reading off their labels, searching for a particular one. "Ah, here we are," he called, removing one of the vessels from its perch. "Antigone, Canis Aureus."

He cocked his head at her curiously and smiled. "Yes, we are of a kind, I think, you and I. Canis Aureus. Jackals by nature and temperament. Worriers of the dead. But I am flattered nonetheless that you should take my name." He smiled down at her and for a moment, she allowed herself to hope that he had forgotten whatever grim purpose he had been about.

"Come along now," he said at last. "You have wasted time enough already with your splashing about."

"But I don't understand. What am I doing here? What the hell is this place?" She shivered involuntarily and self-consciously crossed her arms over her chest, feeling very lost, alone and exposed.

"Nothing so prosaic as that," the Jackal said. "This is merely a crossroads along that path. Do come along." He started off without waiting to see if she followed. He hadn't gone far before he heard the slap of wet footfalls hurrying up behind him. He smiled his death mask smile.

Chapter 5
Only Fever and Torment

F rancesca Lyon emerged from the Greyhound station into the oily evening rain. She tugged angrily at the hood of the camouflage-patterned poncho, but her efforts did little to interrupt the steady stream of water running down her nose and cheek. The poncho was streaked and stained with ruddy patches from prolonged periods of kneeling in the red clay of excavations along Virginia's Tidewater peninsula.

Back in DC, she had been a graduate student in colonial archeology at Georgetown University. But she supposed she had thrown all that out the window when she boarded that bus. She had not bothered with purchasing a return ticket. She was not sure that there was any going back at this point.

She slung her rucksack over one shoulder, lowered her head, and struck out into the rain. Her other hand was shoved deep within the poncho's warm belly-pouch. It was balled into a fist, clutching the note. Sturbridge's note. It read simply:

> Come to New York.
> Delay will bring only fever and torment.
> You are not alone.
> —A.S.

It was only three lines. Fifteen words. But those words had become an all-consuming obsession in the weeks since Sturbridge's visit.

She had tried to fight it off, of course. The sickness. The ravenous hunger. The dark stirrings. She'd tried to convince herself that this wasn't all happening. She needed to talk to someone, to tell somebody about what was going on. About what had been done to her.

She couldn't very well go to the police. The DC police had enough real monsters to worry about right now. The gangs, the addicts, the rapists, the murderers—all the broken people that usually preyed upon the residents of the less-savory stretches of the city were now largely ignored, left to go about their business. Little fish in a big pond. The police had real problems on their hands now.

In the wake of the riots, the Mall in Washington, DC, had assumed the aspect of an armed military encampment. A vast tent city, overflowing with refugees and emergency workers, stretched unbroken between the Capitol and the boarded-up windows of the White House.

The Washington Monument jutted erect and defiant from the press of canvas and unwashed bodies—a finger pointed accusingly at the heavens. Upon closer inspection, however, it was obvious that that the concerted efforts of innumerable vandals had taken their toll. As if sensing the prevailing wind, FEMA workers had at last overcome their awe and reluctance, erecting a makeshift scaffolding in order to paint a bold red cross on each of the obelisk's four sides.

The news broadcasts all carefully avoided the crux of the issue. No one wanted to admit that the nation's capital was now under martial law, and that even this extreme measure was doing little to restore order.

The police would only laugh at her. What would she say to them? That ever since she had driven a visiting professor in archeology to a conference in Baltimore she had been having these...cravings? They would think she was some kind of pervert. Not the kind they dealt with, of course. Hell, she had seen some of the unclean hungers of that mob in the Mall. If the police were not willing to step in to stop the butcherings and the roasting of human meat on the front lawn of the burned-out White House, they certainly weren't going to listen to some coed who says that she's acquired a taste for blood.

Chessie thought she might well be having a breakdown, or maybe even going all-out bull-moose insane. She wondered what that would feel like, to go insane. Was it something that happened all at once, or did it creep up on you gradually, in stages? Could you see yourself going insane? Could you sit back and look at it objectively and think that yes, it is certainly worse today than it was yesterday? Could you document the changes, perhaps keep a journal? That way you might flip back through the pages and trace the inevitable and damning course of your own collapse.

Did you even know it when you went insane? Did you realize that something was wrong—and that that 'something' wrong was with *you*?

She wanted to go to Dean Dorfman. He had always been there for her before, even when no one else had. He was her advisor. He would know what to do.

Dorfman's specialty was in early American secret societies, but almost nobody on campus knew that. Most of the students gave him a pretty wide berth. Not because he was some kind of troll or letch or anything. But mostly because the administration only sent Dorfman the hard cases. The folks already on their third strike—the ones who were about to get booted out of school altogether. Yeah, Dorfman got all the winners: the folks so caught up in the drugs or the drink or the sex that they couldn't find their way back out by themselves anymore.

But Dorfman wasn't there now. Hadn't been for months now. He was away on sabbatical. To Vienna, lucky bastard. And there was no reason to believe that he would be returning home before the start of the next term.

And that left her on her own.

Come to New York.

She didn't even know why she was here. After what Sturbridge had done to her the last time, Chessie couldn't imagine the professor would be glad to see her again. She would probably refuse to see her altogether.

Chessie had thought of little else these past nights. She wasn't even sure she would like what might happen if Sturbridge *did* agree to see her. But she had to talk to someone. Someone who knew what was going on. Someone who could tell her why she was having these...feelings.

She thought briefly of going home. Not home to her family, that would be really stupid. But back to the mountains. It was the only place she had ever felt she had things in perspective. The only place she ever felt that she could get away from the pounding words, the clink of bottles, the clumsy scrapings of the key at the lock.

Maybe the madness didn't have anything to do with Sturbridge. Or with what she had done. Maybe it had been there all along, lying dormant, hiding just below the surface of the skin. It could have been there for years, waiting patiently for someone or something to scratch through.

Her father would know, if anyone would. But she was damned if she was going to put herself within his reach again. Not even to find out the truth about what had happened to her.

Maybe it was all heredity, the dark hunger. A family heirloom. Her birthright. Maybe what Sturbridge did only drew it out of her, brought it welling to the surface.

Maybe, she thought, Sturbridge would know how to put it back. And to lock it down deep so that nobody ever saw it again. So that it couldn't hurt anyone else.

Or maybe Sturbridge would laugh at her too. Chessie kicked angrily through a puddle, crushing her own reflection. There was no one else to go to now. Resignedly, she set her steps towards Barnard College. She had the feeling that Sturbridge might be in the habit of keeping late office hours.

Chessie shuddered, feeling the first rough caress of the dark hunger rising up within her. With a shudder, she shifted the rucksack to her other shoulder. She curled beneath it, trying to make herself very small. So small that the hunger might not notice her. She closed her eyes and pulled the poncho up tightly under her chin. Her lips moved with silent prayers that it might go away, if only just for tonight. She would be good, if only it would go away. But already she could smell its sickly-sweet breath.

She whimpered and sank further into the shadowed recess of the shop doorway. Where the rain, at least, could not touch her.

Chapter 6
The Empress of India

As Sturbridge crossed to the circle of artfully arranged glass shards, her face composed itself into a dispassionate death mask. She straightened regally and smoothed down the worst of the creases in her robes.

A few arcane passes were all it took. Stephens stood before her once again, summoned back from the depths of the crypts where she had banished him. To the inverted circle that was the twin of this one. His face was still twisted with the same look of indignation. He was mouthing the same curses and threats. It was as if he had never been away.

He raged on for some while silence, his words unable to prevail against the barrier of the mystic diagramma. He soon realized the futility of it and fell into a brooding stillness.

Sturbridge let him wind himself down. She let the silence hang between them, let the moment stretch until she saw his first uncomfortable shiftings—until she was sure that he realized that he was at her mercy.

When she at last spoke, her tone was short, clipped, a voice accustomed to decades of command.

"You are an intruder in my house. You have killed my novice. You will answer for these trespasses."

Sturbridge bent to shift a jagged shard of glass, rearranging one of the diagram's supporting glyphs. This gesture breached the dam that had held back his words and they came tumbling out.

"...That young lady has a lot to answer for! And she's not the only one. What do you mean by keeping me imprisoned here?" Stephens demanded.

Sturbridge ignored his ranting. "You will, no doubt, be pleased to learn that Ms. Baines is no further threat to you. I am not so pleased. Now, you will tell me who you are and why you have killed my novice."

Stephens was having none of it. "Enough of this. I didn't kill anyone, as you well know. You and your 'novice' trapped me in this damned diagram." He took an experimental step forward. His hands impacted the line of the outer wardings and he snatched them back again, cursing and rubbing at his wrists.

"I am Aisling Sturbridge, mistress of this house. You will answer my questions. Then I will decide whether or not you should be set at liberty. I asked who you were and why you killed my novice."

Stephens considered throwing some weight against the wardings and thought better of it. His strengths did not lie along those lines. He changed tack. "We just wanted to talk to the girl," he said, a conciliatory note creeping into his voice. "My name is Stephens. We're here on an official inquiry, from the Fatherhouse. I never even touched your novice and she was certainly still among the living when you messed with this diagram and sent me spiraling down into those catacombs. Look, I'm just trying to do my job. Can we go back to the chantry and discuss this? If something has happened to the girl, we'll help you get to the bottom of it." He gave her what he hoped was a disarming smile.

"Just doing your job? You would have me believe, then, that you are an assassin by trade, Mr. Stephens?"

"Now just wait a minute. I never said anything like that. I'm an investigator, Ms. Sturbridge. From the Fatherhouse. In Vienna. Surely this doesn't come as a surprise to you…."

"You may address me as Regent Sturbridge. And please do not think that you will evade punishment by sheltering behind this flimsy pretence. You are no investigator."

He opened his mouth to protest, but she cut him off sharply. "At this point, you are not even a representative of the Fatherhouse. If you were, you would have formally presented yourself to me upon your arrival—as all emissaries from the Fatherhouse are bound to do by the charter granted this house. Since you failed to do so, you are an intruder."

"I assure you, Ms. Sturbridge, that we are exactly…"

"But let us say that you had presented yourself as was your duty," she interrupted. "And that I were satisfied with your presumed credentials—and that I were, for some reason, inclined to request your assistance in an investigation. Then, and only then, I might choose to confer upon you the title of 'investigator.' Or I might just decide to call you 'the Empress of India.' To be quite frank, an Empress of India with my blessing is going to command a lot more clout in this house than someone that a Vienna bureaucrat may or may not have once called an 'investigator.' Are we clear on this so far?"

"I understand your feeling on this, Ms. Sturbridge, but our credentials are quite authentic. It would be my pleasure to present them to you formally, if you would just be so kind as to…" He gestured encouragingly at the confinement diagram.

Sturbridge's gaze was unyielding. "If it is easier for you to appreciate your situation in terms of your confinement, Mr. Stephens, that is also acceptable. Either way, the fact remains that you have no official position here. You are caught, quite literally, between two places. You are suffered to speak only at the mercy of my justice, to answer for what you have done. You are suffered to exist, I am afraid, only at the mercy of this admittedly treacherous diagram."

"Are you threatening me, Ms. Sturbridge? Surely you know that to hinder the course of an Astor's inquiries in any way is itself a criminal act. Brothers have met the sun for merely attempting to withhold pertinent information from us. To actually threaten the well-being of an investigator…"

Sturbridge smiled. "Ah, you misunderstand me, Mr. Stephens. I do not make threats. It is not, after all, I who am keeping you from your business. It is this thrice-damned diagram. If it were up to me, I would attempt to free you immediately. But I understand this diagram only imperfectly. I am afraid that if I attempted to free you now, I might—inadvertently, you understand—actually do you lasting harm."

His face stiffened. Sturbridge could see that he had taken her point. But he rallied for a last desperate attempt. Locking their gazes, he said, "But I think you do know how to free me."

All the force of his will and training was channeled through the tenuous invisible conduit between their eyes. Power crackled just beneath the surface of the innocent-seeming stream of syllables.

Sturbridge held his gaze. Her voice was as cold as a knife thrust. "Shall I make the attempt then?"

His confidence wavered, but he was not about to back down now.

"Do it," he commanded.

She nodded slowly. "Kneel, then."

This took him off guard. He regarded her questioningly.

"The only way I can think of to free you is to carry this ill-conceived rite through to its conclusion. If you want to be free, you have to help. Or I can just scrub the attempt now, destroy the diagram and you can take your chances with the backlash. Your choice."

He knelt.

"Now you will acknowledge me as the lawful regent of this house and you will pledge yourself to abide by my rules for so long as you are a guest here."

He smiled and shook his head, laughing softly to himself. Gathering what dignity he could, Stephens rose slowly to his feet, brushing at the ash and soot covering the knees of his suit. "Very good, Ms. Sturbridge," he said. "You had me going there for a minute. Help you complete the rite…"

"I am very serious Mr. Stephens. What I am asking is no more than the basic courtesy due me as your hostess. If you are not willing to grant me this, we have nothing more to discuss."

He decided to try one more time. Maybe she could be made to see facts. "Look, you know I can't do that, Ms. Sturbridge. My oath is to the Order. And my duty may very well compel me to do some things that, frankly, a lady such as yourself should not have to tolerate in a houseguest. We're here to stop a series of brutal murders, Ms. Sturbridge. This is not something we take lightly. We're going to do whatever it takes to make this chantry safe again. And if that involves stepping on a few toes and dispensing with a few social niceties—well, then I'd consider that a very small price to pay."

"I see," Sturbridge said at last. "You then will understand when I say that the risk of your death is far too high a price for me to pay for the luxury of having you at liberty. I cannot, in good faith, attempt to free you from this diagram, Mr. Stephens."

"Then it would seem that we are at an impasse," he said. "You cannot set me free—for fear of killing me, as you say. And we certainly cannot just remain here, glaring at one another until sunup. Any ideas?"

She did not return his smile. "Are you sure you will not reconsider? I offer you the opportunity to place yourself under my protection. You will go free and no harm or reproach will come to you while you remain within my house. And you will also be freed from the indignity of being forced by your peers to do anything that might…weigh upon your conscience."

He shook his head sadly. "Nothing personal, Ms. Sturbridge. But I'm not sure what my promise to be on my best behavior would be worth to you, if I had to foreswear myself in order to make that pledge."

"I had not taken you for such an idealist, Mr. Stephens. Of course, if it is your wish to place yourself outside of my protection, I cannot be accountable for…"

"Would you prefer that I be more pragmatic, Ms. Sturbridge? Frankly, even within the walls of your chantry, your 'protection' doesn't have much of a track record. And if it comes down to either you or Vienna, I know where the smart money is."

Now it was Sturbridge's turn to look taken aback. "I appreciate your honesty, Mr. Stephens. I see there is no changing your mind on this issue. And that is a pity. Things would have been so much easier—for both of us—if you had agreed to pledge your support. Now, I'm afraid, we're out of options. You're going to have to return to the crypts for a while. Tell me, are you well regarded among your colleagues, Mr. Stephens?"

Stephens shook his head at the sudden change of topic. "I'm not sure I follow you, Ms. Sturbridge."

"Well, it occurs to me that your 'life'—for want of a better word—may well be the only thing of value that I might bring to the negotiations with your companions. Tell me, Mr. Stephens, would your fellow investigators find you more valuable alive or dead?"

His self-satisfied, businesslike demeanor was back. "That's not going to work, Ms. Sturbridge. The Astors are not going to negotiate with any hostage-takers. You start talking like that and they'll just cut you down where you…"

She shrugged. "Pity. I suppose the best thing, then, would be to arrange an accident right here. Oh, don't bluster so, Mr. Stephens. Despite fanciful tales to the contrary, I am not in the habit of killing novices and houseguests. I only mentioned it because I would like you to think very hard about my offer during your confinement."

He started to retort, but she waved her hand dismissively and his words cut off abruptly. He continued to mouth words of condemnation as she bent to the diagram and banished him to the crypts once more.

After his image had flickered out, she carefully unmade the diagram, sealing all hope of egress. She wondered how long it would be before he was missed. Then she set about reestablishing the portal link with the Chantry of Five Boroughs.

Chapter 7
The Scales of Anubis

"The last time you were here," the Jackal-headed Warder of the Dead called over his shoulder, "I could not get you to sit still. Do you remember? My silly little bird. But now, now you hang back. Why is that, I wonder? Surely you have not come to fear me?"

Antigone stiffened. "I am not afraid," she said quietly.

He did not contradict her. "The problem then becomes one of what we should do with you, little one," said the Jackal. His torch had guttered out long ago. Their journey through the cool subterranean passages seemed unending. He led the way forward holding the canopic jar up before him like a lantern. A diffused ruddy light emanated from it. It did not so much light their path as throw the surrounding shadows in sharper relief. Carefully, Antigone picked her way between the outcroppings of shadow, fearing a misstep in the dark.

Ahead of her, Anubis had emerged into a vast chamber, a formal audience hall. The dim red light gleamed on burnished gold, picked out a set of standing balances at the room's focal point. The delicate device stood easily as tall as she did. *A hall of judgment*, she thought. The idea did not comfort her.

An unsettling quiet hung over the court. Its only sounds were scattered scratchings, as of rats within the walls. The slow but unstoppable gnawing of the forces of decay and corruption.

"Here we are at last," her guide said with obvious enthusiasm. "Please make yourself comfortable. I shall not be a moment."

Antigone hung back in the entryway. She strained to pick out the slight telltale sounds from within. The scrape of a stylus from the room's far corner might signify the presence of an unseen scribe recording the proceedings. The persistent clatter of claw upon stone surely indicated the restless pacing of some great beast along the wall opposite. There was no indication, however, whether it awaited judgment, or if it were a judgment awaiting someone else.

"That's very considerate of you," Antigone called. "But I really won't have you going to any trouble on my account. It would be a kindness if you would just show me the way back. Then I will be on my way. I would not dream of inconveniencing you further."

Her host crossed to the scales at the room's center and began adjusting the mechanism. "Not at all. It is a delight that you have returned to us. But you have put your finger precisely upon the problem, my dear. You did not think to provide for your return ahead of time. You are now left to negotiate at something of a disadvantage."

"But nothing like this has ever happened before," she stammered. "I mean, each of the other times, there was never any question of getting back again. There was never anywhere to return from. I would just wake up, in bed, listening to the doctor confiding unpleasantries in hushed tones. There was never any of...this. What is this place?"

Anubis grinned but did not turn from his task. "Look around you, little one. You are no stranger here. You know this place as you know me. It is enough. And we know you as well. You and your little balancing act, your game of ledges. Did you really think you would be able to escape us indefinitely?"

Antigone frowned and retreated a step up the corridor. "I don't understand. I know you. But you don't belong here. This is *my* rite. The dance along the precipice. It is something personal, something private, something *intimate*. And you are not a part of it—never were a part of it. You shouldn't be here."

"Ah, but here, in fact, I am."

Antigone shook her head stubbornly. "No, this isn't right. You are a product of a different time in my life, a later dynasty. Why, it wasn't until I had learned the ways of the Pyramid that I even knew of your existence."

"Is that the problem?" He shifted his attention to the other side of the balances. "You cannot unlearn the ways, little one. You know this. I am with you now and always shall be. *Selah*."

"The rite cannot change," she insisted. "It's mine. I created it. Only I can alter it. And I didn't alter it. Nothing has been changed—the sloughing off of the old skin, the taking up of a new name..."

He stepped back and examined his handiwork with a critical eye. "Quiet now, little one. You are correct; the rite has not changed. Where you are mistaken is in thinking that it somehow originated with you. It is older than you are, far older. It is as old as the magic of the pyramids, this journey from one life to the next. Did you really think that you were the first? To play at your lethal game of knives and herbs and ledges? To flirt with self-annihilation and then to dance back away from the brink of the abyss? Surely the ceremonial trappings have changed—you now have guns and pills and gas ovens at your disposal. But the game is essentially the same, is it not?"

She braved his mocking grin. "No, that's not what I meant at all. I know there have been others who have...who have taken their own lives. But I was talking about my rite, my *personal* rite. It's brought me through before. It's got to work. I can't be just plain..."

"Dead?" he asked. "Is that such a terrible thing? Why, look at you! You are trembling, little one. Come here."

She had already taken a step forward towards the comforting blanket of his voice before she realized it and dug in her heels. "No," she insisted. "There is a way back. There's always a way back. The trick's not over until they put me back together again. Until I wake up to find the doctors pumping me full of polysyllabic elixirs and wrapping me in pristine white bandages…"

He chuckled low in his throat. "That, little bird, is the oldest magic of them all. Do you not recognize its trappings all around you? It is no matter. All that need concern you is that the rite was given into my hands, long ago. And you must do the same—place yourself in my hands. It is enough. Be still, now. The pyramid is an integral part. You have taken powerful oaths, oaths of blood. You can no longer work your trick of flitting from one life to the next without going by way of the pyramid now and by following its rules. And perhaps you never could. But that is another matter. We are bound together, you and I. It would be best if you were to resign yourself to this fact now."

"But that's just it. I'm not a part of the Pyramid any longer," she insisted. "They turned me out, declared me a renegade, an outcast, a—"

"A jackal?" he interrupted, flashing that persistent grin. It was not quite mocking; it was more *knowing*. As if he already knew her thoughts before she could give them voice. But perhaps all thoughts that would be spoken had already been spoken here. Perhaps all thoughts that could be spoken. Antigone found that grin infuriating. She kept picturing a jagged hole the size of her fist piercing the gleaming row of teeth.

"You are always running," he said before she could even deny the previous charge. "It is the single defining act of your existence. It makes me dizzy to watch you."

She shifted uncomfortably under his accusation, but caught herself and forced her body to go rigid. To hold its exact position. "That is not what I was talking about and you know it," she said. "I meant that it is silly to insist on holding me accountable to the traditions of my people if they themselves have turned their backs on me. They have severed me from that tradition in no uncertain terms. If they find me, I will burn."

The Jackal waved dismissively. "You run from life, you run from death and now, it seems, you must flee even your own people. Why can't you just be still? It is as if there were some great emptiness in the world and you must personally fill it up—with words, with frantic motion. If you will insist on wasting what little time remains to you, I might suggest that you at least apply your efforts a bit more strategically. You might, for example, attempt to bargain for your freedom. Many do. This might, in fact, be an ideal time to do so. Once the judgment has commenced, we will have little opportunity for such pleasant exchanges."

At his words, an apprehension crept the length of Antigone's spine. She was not eager to face the test of the Jackal-god's scales. "Bargain? What do I have that you would want?" Antigone asked guardedly.

"The first sensible question you've put to me since your arrival. The suicides are always so self-involved. It would surprise you how few of them actually bother to pose that most pertinent question. What do you have that I would want? Let me see. Already I have your heart." He placed the canopic jar upon one side of the balances. The scales dipped noticeably and the Jackal-god frowned.

"What's wrong?" she asked anxiously. *What does he mean, he has my heart?*

He shook his head sadly. "I will not conceal from you the fact that I am not optimistic. Your heart, I fear it is too heavy. You may have chosen an inauspicious time to die."

"Inauspicious?! You mean there's a *good* time to die?"

When he spoke, he was no longer addressing her, but crooning over the tiny clay vessel. "Certainly, child. It is good to die when the heart is unburdened. In the Weighing of the Heart, it is imperative that it balance precisely against the feather of Ma'at—what you would call Truth. I fear you have come back to us too late. Your heart is full of discord and self-doubt. You have forgotten how the ancient trick is played, little one—the game of death and names. When you were yet a child, you knew. When you were yet a mortal, you knew. Now? Now, you have grown heavy with years. It is better this way. You will go to the Devourer and life may begin anew."

There was an eager gnashing of teeth from the prowling beast in the darkened corner of the Hall of Judgment. She felt, rather than saw, the great bulk of it stalking closer. She could catch only the vaguest hint of its blasphemous outline—like a cross between a lion, a hippopotamus and a crocodile—the three most feared ravagers that dwelt along the banks of the Nile.

"What are you talking about?" Antigone crowded closer to the scales and farther away from the encroaching beast. "I'm not going to any Devourer. I'm going home. Tell me what you want from me, what I need to do to get home."

Anubis circled the balances. Arriving at the far side, he turned towards the shadows and received a single black feather from a shallow beaten-copper dish. Antigone could not make out how he had come by it. She had a fleeting impression that it was placed in his hands by a woman whose bared wrists were so pale as to be almost ethereal. She did not know how they bore up the mass of the crude copper dish.

As the grail withdrew again, Antigone found herself squinting into the shadows, trying to make out its enigmatic bearer. Just before the vessel vanished, Antigone had a fleeting impression of a dark-maned apparition. The pale woman was all severe angles—shoulders, elbows, nose, jaw, all razor sharp. Her ceremonial robe seemed to be a patchwork of alternating tomb-dark and sepulchre-white diamonds—a harlequin magus.

"You stand at the fulcrum, the very crux," the Jackal's voice intruded upon her thoughts. "There are only two ways you may go from here. The first is by way of the Devourer. This path will not carry you home, but you will be freed at least from the Rota, the Great Wheel. And often that is enough. The second way, well, I don't think we need concern ourselves with the second."

Without ceremony, he placed the feather in the opposite side of the balances. The scales never budged.

The jackal turned his ebon claws upward, apologetically. "It is as I feared," he said.

"Now wait a minute. *That's* your test? The damned clay jar weighs more than that feather! There's no way those two are ever going to balance out." She stalked angrily up to the scales.

"I assure you, my adjustments were exacting," he said. "And they took into account the weight of the vessel. I am your patron here, Antigone. Your advocate. But the scales do not lie. We must all abide by their verdict."

She glared at him. There was a sound of something large dragging itself forward across the stone floor. Antigone could not bring herself to look in that direction. "All right, you want to weigh my heart against Truth? We'll weigh it against Truth. But it's going to be against my truth, not that of some dusty old civilization that vanished from the face of the earth thousands of years before I was born. What kind of test is that?"

Her hand was knotted into a fist within the pocket of her robes. She drew out the wicked straight razor and flicked it open, she brandishing it against her self-appointed judge.

He made no move to protect himself, but looked slightly disappointed at this display.

"Occam's Razor," she said, casting it disdainfully into the balances—adding its weight to that of the feather.

The scales sagged noticeably.

"Or how about we pile on Diogenes' Lantern? Or a volume of Aquinas' *De Veritas*? That one ought to tip the scales in my favor; it's got some heft to it."

The Jackal stood unmoved before her outburst. "You act as if they were all interchangeable, little one," he said and smiled.

"Damn it, I want to be judged by my own peers, by the standards of my own people and culture. Not by some moldering old half-forgotten—"

"Have a care, my dear. In my house, words cannot be unspoken. And names, once they have been uttered, cannot be revoked."

She fumed in silence, ashamed of her outburst, but not about to go gently into that good night.

"But seeing that you have chosen to respect my request," he continued smoothly. "I shall honor yours. You are quite certain you would like to be judged by the standards of your own people? Of your own Pyramid?"

At the word 'pyramid,' Antigone's head jerked up. She could feel the noose tightening, but a retrial—any retrial—had to be preferable to the alternative. "I think I'll take my chances among my own kind."

"So be it," the Jackal intoned. "I will forestall the judgment of this court. You will have the opportunity to go among your own people. We will see what sentence they shall bring to bear upon you. But know this. Your reprieve is for a brief time only—no more than the blink of an eye in the final reckoning. When you next return to me, then you will face the sentence handed down by this court. Do you understand?"

Antigone could only nod. "Thank you. The Lord of the Dead is nothing if not just."

"One thing more, little one. Do not think you will escape me. You will return to me, sooner or later. And what is more, you shall choose to return to me. I know you. Better perhaps than you know yourself. You cannot resist your little game of ledges. It is the only way you assure yourself that you're are still 'alive,' that you are still vital. You are, in the grand scheme of things, only a little bird. Nothing more. And a little bird cannot resist making its perch among the ledges and cornices."

Antigone made to interrupt, but he forestalled her with a raised finger. "In the meantime, you may return to the judgment and censure of your own kind. I do not envy you it, but you have chosen. Now, fly away home, little one."

Fly away home.

At the foot of the Empire State Building, David Foucault, Channel 11 News, spilled his coffee, sputtered and nearly choked. "Jeezus! Look at that. Jack, grab that damned camera!" He wiped at the long wet coffee stain that ran the entire length of his front. He leaned way over backward—as he had a moment before, trying to get at the last drop of tepid coffee— now craning up towards the observation deck.

"Where?" Jack challenged. He had been the brunt of Foucault's little jokes before.

David thrust an angry finger skyward, jabbing at the slight but unmistakable silhouette framed against the disc of the moon.

"Son of a bitch! How the hell did that idiot get up there?" Jack scrambled for the camera. In one single motion he popped the lens cap and thumbed the roll-tape. The focus whirred even before the rig settled to rest on his shoulder.

"Damned if I know. Stairwell's buried in rubble and I've seen the remains of that elevator car. You getting all this?"

Foucault demanded. He looked around nervously. Already the initial pounce of discovery was giving way to a gentle apprehension. He was not a slow man, and the inevitable question of the point of impact and an understandable concern for his own safety were fighting their way to the fore.

"Not getting a damned thing yet," Jack grumbled, squinting through the eyepiece and trying to blink free the moon-shaped retinal after-image. "You still got a bead on him?"

"Listen!" Foucault's whisper was sharp, imperative. A low whistling rush of air bore down upon them. "Shit." He began scrambling hurriedly around the van, toward the shelter of buildings across the street. Jack held his ground a moment longer. Two. Three. Then broke away under his partner's barrage of profanities.

"All right, I'm coming." He bent low, nearly double, cradling the camera beneath his chest. As if he would rather take the blow on his head than on his footage. He braced against the imminent impact.

Nothing.

"Real funny, asshole." Having reached Foucault's bunker, the doorway of a shop opposite, Jack punched his partner ungently in the shoulder.

"What the hell?" Foucault said. He walked out from cover, scanning the skies as if for an expected downpour that had suddenly failed to materialize.

A sudden breeze ruffled his seven strands of comb-over, but the only feature he could pick out in the inscrutable face of the night sky was the outline of a solitary night bird pulling out of a long dive. Struggling for altitude. A piercing mournful cry, and gone.

Chapter 8
Old Wives' Tales

Cordelia careened around the corner of the Science Building and reeled out onto the quad. Her ears were singing with the heady rush of blood. She felt *alive*. More alive than she had felt in years. More alive than she had any business feeling.

Her whole body thrummed to a sort of low electric tone. She had to move—to keep moving! Running, pouncing through puddles. Anything to give it outlet. If she stood still, tried to keep it all bottled up, she knew the power coursing through her veins would turn upon her. Twist her, curl her fingers, bend her back. So she ran, abandoning herself to the ecstatic communion of the night.

The rain stippled the open ground between the ponderous academic buildings, but Cordelia was oblivious to the steady drizzle. If anything, it made a comforting counterpoint to the molten fire that surged within her veins. She skidded to a stop on the slick paving stones and pushed her hood back with one hand. Throwing back her head, she savored the plish of the icy droplets on her face, the chill seep of the rain burrowing under her collar and down her back.

Long, inky strands of hair plastered themselves across the shoulders and back of that ridiculous mud-stained poncho. She shook her head from side to side, feeling the wet slap as her hair beat against the cheap vinyl rain-slicker. She felt like singing or shouting or crying or giggling. It didn't really matter which. Cordelia opened her throat to the moon and the sound that escaped her was more animal than human.

And all the while, the stolen blood surged within her, rendering even the most mundane sensations—the squeak of damp plastic skidding across flesh, the smell of wet hair—into something ethereal.

It was better than she ever dared hope it would be. Now she knew the reason behind all the horror stories, the dire warnings, the outright threats. *This* is what it was all about. What they were meant to be—the ultimate predators. This was her birthright, her legacy. And now that she had a taste of what that meant, she would not go back to feeding upon mere human chattel again.

How could she go back? To feel the blood of another of her own kind within her! To feel the stranger's very *life* inside her—it awakened feelings she had though lost to her. Long ago.

It was more than just the hot rush of the vitae, surging through her, wracking her body with its power and dark majesty. It was intoxicating jumble of all of the other's thoughts, her memories, her feelings. All of them, swallowed utterly.

Cordelia thought that if she could only keep still for a moment, she might—even now—reach out and touch those memories. Turn them over in her mind like jagged multi-colored shards of glass. Artifacts sifted from the sands of time and memory. She imagined herself piecing them together like a jigsaw puzzle, painstakingly reassembling some snapshot of the life she had so suddenly and brutally taken.

The very thought that the other was inside her still, trapped there, sentenced to await Cordelia's whim, to subsist on the scant crumbs of attention she might lavish on her or withhold as it pleased her—it was sublime.

She would do it again. Oh yes. In a heartbeat. Tomorrow night, perhaps. And the night after that...

The sight of Millbank Hall brought her up short. The administrative building was the most public point of ingress to the subterranean Chantry of Five Boroughs, Cordelia's home these last eight years.

She had spent each of those years under the shadow of what her sisters called the Sabbat Occupation. More old wives' tales to keep the novices in their place. Seldom were Cordelia or her sisters granted leave to venture out into the big, bad city alone. There were monsters and bogeymen there, lurking in the shadows of alleyways—monsters that hunted young novices for sport—or for their very blood.

Yes, Cordelia thought. *For their blood. I can see that now.*

Tonight, Cordelia had not asked anyone's permission to venture out. The chantry house was in chaos. Everybody was running around like a head with its chicken cut off. The talk in the novice domicilium was that some big muckety-mucks from Vienna had arrived and that they were going to clean house. And sweep the floor with Regent Sturbridge and anyone else who got in their way.

Screw them. Cordelia wasn't about to get in their way. The best thing, she figured, was just to get out from underfoot. To let the worst of it blow over. And anything had to be better than sitting around the hen-house fretting with the fluttering black-robed poultry.

So she had set her mind on going out and getting drunk, rip-roaring drunk. She could still do that, if she put her mind to it, if only indirectly. Alcohol literally tore holes through her stomach at this point—ever since the Embrace. Her few experiments along those lines had proved disastrous.

But she could still catch something of the buzz secondhand. She could haunt the bars at closing time, pick out the marks who were much too sloshed to make it home unaided. And make sure they never got that aid.

So she had gone out tonight to hunt. She was going to kill somebody—maybe more than one somebody—and drink him bone-white. Her plan hadn't been any more ambitious than that. She had no intention of even reaching for, much less tasting, the forbidden fruit. Honest. That part just sort of happened.

It had been so easy. That was the thing that stuck with her. Last call had found her in Antoine's down off Broadway and 117th. The place tried just a bit too self-consciously to be a sports bar and never quite pulled it off. Its Manhattan address and clientele never entirely cooperated with its plebian vision.

She had been settled in for a while, people-watching, and had already scoped out the three or four most likely contenders, folks who probably should have been cut off by the bartender some time ago. She made it a point never to get her heart set on any one of them.

She was acting *in loco fortunae* here—the self-appointed stand-in for the fickle finger of fate. It wouldn't be fair to make her decision based on personal preference. She wouldn't choose based on which of her potential victims she found most attractive. She seldom had to reminded herself anymore that she wasn't out shopping for a hookup, but old habits do die hard. Nor would she choose based on which was the most belligerent. As tempting as it might be to assume the role of self-appointed avenging angel, that was not her place either.

No, she would be patient and pragmatic. The ideal mark was the one that played along with her gameplan, unwittingly, but of his or her own volition. She had a simple formula she had worked out for it—a test that went into effect as soon as the barkeep bellowed, "Last call!"

It was simple, really. Most of the herd took that announcement as their cue to order another round. The mark she wanted, however, was the one who pushed himself back from the bar and took his leave at that point.

For one, that meant he was usually leaving alone. For two, the early departure gave her the opportunity to give the mark about a minute's headstart. She didn't do this out of some cavalier sense of sportsmanship, but because this precaution was preferable to having someone see you follow him out. It was rare that a chance mortal bystander could make any serious trouble for one of her kind, but it wasn't unheard of.

In this case, her caution reaped an unexpected windfall. As she watched, a shadow near the doorway detached itself and followed her mark out into the street.

Although she was intrigued, she forced herself to count off the seconds, to give the pair a comfortable lead. To put them off their guard. She knew it would not be hard to find them again. It never was. She had already gotten the rhythm of the mark's heavy, reeling gait. Her keen predator's senses would have little trouble picking it out again out in the mostly deserted streets.

Now, however, it was no longer so much the mark that interested her, as his pursuer. She could tell in a glance, in the brief instant before he vanished out into the night, that he was one of her own kind. It was more than the pasty complexion, the slight telltale reek of the grave that hung in his wake, the inhuman speed of his movements. These were all part of it, of course, but only part of it. There were a dozen small but distinctive clues that all added up to give him the aura of one who was no longer among the living.

Cordelia had become quite adept at reading these holistic auras in even the briefest of impressions. She was no Sherlock Holmes, able to trace labyrinthine threads of deduction from the scantest of evidence. Sometimes she was hard-pressed even to reconstruct what the specific details were that led to her sweeping assessments. But she had learned to trust her instincts and snap judgments.

She still had no clear picture of what she was about to do when she caught up with them in an alley not two blocks from

Antoine's. The footfalls had turned from a drunken rambling to a quicker, apprehensive stride, and then had broken into a run for a few paces before falling silent. In the end, it was not the sound of footsteps, but a hushed ecstatic moan that had led her to turn into the alley.

She found the pair locked together like young lovers. The mark leaned heavily against the wall with his shoulders and one foot pushing back against the bricks. His bent knee was caught between the thighs of his pursuer, who leaned across him. The two ground together slowly, cyclically, in time to the spurt of blood between them. The dark pursuer's head was buried in the hollow of the mark's throat and it was difficult to discern which was the source of the muffled moans. Her unnatural perceptions told her that the sound somehow arose from both of them—that at this moment, they were little more than a single conjoined being. A very vulnerable being.

As she watched, a feeling stirred in her. She tried to ignore it, to push it down before it could distract her from what she must do. But it was already too late. She had recognized the emotion welling up within her. It was envy.

She could not strike now. Not while the motivation was personal. She would not. She was no murderer, she told herself and then repeated it—as if the repetition alone could summon conviction. She was no murderer. She did not kill out of anger, or vengeance, or envy or even pleasure. If she allowed herself to begin killing for her own benefit, where would it stop?

Quietly, she edged backwards out of the alley. The journey took exactly three steps and one lifetime, but by the time she had reached the street, she was in control once again. The dispassionate agent of fate and nothing more. And if, this night, fate had decreed two deaths instead of one, who was she to contradict it?

It would have been so much harder if she had recognized him, she thought as she pulled loose a slat from the broken pallet that leaned against the alley's mouth. If he had been someone she knew or, worse, someone from the chantry. She did not know if she could have summoned up the necessary detachment to do the deed right, without her becoming a murderer, a monster.

She winced at the sound of the long wooden spike wrenching free. Her gaze darted apprehensively to the couple in the alley, but the noise failed to intrude on their ardor. She kept her gaze lowered as she approached, her eyes riveted on the small patch of ground just before her feet. At last, when she could no longer ignore their coupling, she lashed out.

The improvised stake struck true, pinioning the squirming eight-legged creature. Cordelia threw all her weight against it, felt the spike jarringly hit brick, and then twisted. Two voices raised themselves in a single scream, then choked and fell silent.

It was the heady aroma of the blood that brought Cordelia back to her senses. Both of her hands were covered with hot, sticky vitae. The savor of it filled her head and staggered her. One finger found her mouth, and then she was anxiously lapping at both hands, front and back, tongue darting between her own fingers. Trying to cram both hands into her mouth at the same time. Before a single drop could be lost.

When at last the shadow of the bestial hunger withdrew from her senses, she found herself trembling and slumped over the drained corpses. A restless energy wracked her body. She had to move, had to run, had to give some outlet to the potent vitae that surged within her. Before it tore her apart.

Chapter 9
Blood, Favors and Ready Cash

When Antigone came to ground at last, she found herself alone, frightened and unsure of where to turn. Her strange sojourn in the underworld had left her deeply shaken. The surreal experience certainly seemed as real to her as her nightmare plunge off the observation deck of the Empire State Building. By all rights, she knew, she should be dead.

She forced herself to her feet and set off at random. The important thing now was just to move, to assure herself that there was still life—or some semblance of it—within her. It was a brisk quarter of an hour's hike later before she succeeded in convincing herself that all this was real and not some further delusion.

Only then was she able to ask herself the pressing question: Where to go? Antigone knew she needed to get out of sight, and quickly. Once word spread at the chantry that she was wanted by the Astors, so much as being seen by one of her former Tremere brethren would be as good as a death sentence.

She needed to see the prince. That much had stuck with her. Even the Luciferian fall had not jogged Sturbridge's parting words from Antigone's head. *Seek sanctuary among the Nosferatu,* Sturbridge had said and, *Tell them they will do this for the sake of the bones that lie beneath the regent's blood.*

Antigone had no idea what that cryptic pronouncement might mean, and furthermore, she was quickly coming to realize that seeking out the Nosferat prince and finding him were two very different matters. She certainly did not know the location of the Nosferatu's subterranean warrens, and the thought of aimlessly wandering the miles upon miles of sewer or subway tunnels in the hopes of stumbling across him was not appealing.

Aside from the handful of defectors from the prince's camp that had joined up with the Conventicle, Antigone didn't think she even knew any Nosferatu. And although the renegades might welcome an opportunity to betray Calebros' confidences, they would most likely ask some rather pointed questions about what Antigone planned to do with that information. Questions that might compromise their working together in the future.

She wasn't entirely sure she even knew anybody who knew the prince. Aside from Sturbridge, of course. But Antigone couldn't very well go back now and ask for directions. That was when she thought of Johanus. Of course! The adept had been away from the chantry for weeks, working closely with the prince's own men to coordinate efforts to integrate the floodtide of refugees and opportunists pouring into the city in the wake of the Camarilla victory. Surely Johanus could at least get her in touch with someone who could get her in touch with the prince. But would he help her?

If there was one thing working in her favor, it was that Johanus had been so out of the loop of chantry events lately that it might well be weeks before he heard the first whisper of Antigone's new outcast status.

That is how Antigone came to find herself elbowing her way through a crowd of undead refugees packed into a high-school gymnasium. The fact that the high school was closed for the evening did not seem to have any impact on the throng of newcomers that had come to present themselves to the prince. Prince Calebros himself was not, of course, on hand personally. That would have made things far too easy.

In his stead, the swarm of displaced Kindred supplicants faced a small, haggard corps of representatives-cum-relief-workers who tried desperately to assist the descending horde of newcomers in finding safe haven and feeding grounds—that they might at least survive their first few nights in the city without inadvertently encroaching on the territory of others.

Even under ideal circumstances, there was an upper limit to how many Kindred a city—even one the size of New York—could hope to support. It was not just a matter of the number of warm bodies walking the streets. The mortal population had to be large enough not only to provide for the Kindred's nocturnal predations, but also to conceal them. It was not enough that there be an abundance of victims, but rather that there be an abundance of victims that would never be missed.

The game of concealment was both ancient and pragmatic. The Kindred took this time-honored Masquerade very seriously. But in the past weeks, things had been stretched to the breaking point. The relief teams had documented the arrival of close to one hundred and fifty additional refugees pouring into the city.

These were the people of the aftermath. The Sabbat offensive had swept the entire Eastern Seaboard, toppling cities, slaughtering scores of Camarilla Kindred, and uprooting countless others from their havens. The floodtide of refugees had surged into New York as the last bastion of Camarilla strength on the East Coast.

No one was prepared to deal with the consequences of that floodtide. The city's Kindred population had doubled within a single month's time. And even the most staggering population estimates did not include the unguessed masses who had simply decided not to present themselves formally to the prince upon arrival, as prescribed by Camarilla tradition. The actual numbers could be a full order of magnitude higher.

Antigone pushed her way through the throng and up to the nearest station. It consisted of two folding banquet tables side by side with a large aerial map taped across them. The map was covered in strange symbols in Magic Marker—the meaning of which was not readily apparent to her. Over the tables hung a pasteboard sign that read "Manhattan."

"I'm looking for Johanus," she called to the man wielding a red marker. She had to shout to be heard above the tumult. "Johanus!"

He looked up and caught her eye. He had a haggard look, degrading into ill-disguised desperation about the edges. His vague gesturings in response to her question might have been intended to mean "Check over there," or "He's somewhere around here," or even "If you find him, send him over here, quick."

Antigone mouthed a thank you and sank back into the swell of the crowd. Various sensations materialized out of the sea of bodies, vied for her attention for a moment and then vanished again without a trace. She was in turn jostled, prodded and groped. She smelled gunpowder, a sharp accent to the pervasive aroma of dried blood that hung over the room. She heard raised voices nearby, arguing some finer point of precedence in a preposterously thick Bronx accent. She nearly slipped on a scattered stack of twenty-dollar bills that had fallen neglected to the floor. There was the sound of newspaper tearing. A set of keys flashed, changed hands. An indignant young man demanded to see the prince immediately. Another leeringly offered Antigone "more suitable" accommodation for the evening.

Slowly, Antigone came to realize that there was much more going on within this hall than even the prince had ever intended. There was a double-blind here. Sure, she could see the concealed knife peeking out from behind the prince's back. It was expected. He was taking full advantage of the tradition of Presentation to further his own ends, to establish a firmer grip upon his newly-won city. By registering the newcomers and documenting their havens and feeding grounds, he gained critical intelligence. For the Nosferat, knowledge was the coin of the realm. Under less chaotic circumstances, a city's Kindred would never have submitted to such an intrusion into their private affairs.

But there was a counter-movement here as well, lurking just below the surface. A purpose of which even the prince might be unaware. Carried along by the swell of the crowd, Antigone became acutely aware that not all those present in the rising tide of bodies were refugees. Many of the faces in the crowd bore the unmistakable mark of those who were wont to prey upon such newcomers. Under cover of coming to pay homage to the prince, an entirely different purpose was flourishing. A more sinister purpose. It was a burgeoning black market, trading in blood, favors, ready cash, safe haven, thralls, hope, protection, information and opportunity.

Just about everything—and everyone—present had its price. And most were willing to haggle.

Antigone found herself shrinking back from the surging currents of commerce and borne towards the outskirts of the crowd. It deposited her on a far shore, at the base of a cliff of bleachers folded closed for the night. She made her way along it to a thick knot of Kindred clustered before a pair of swinging double doors.

From the center of that knot, a tall man with fiery red hair and beard was trying to extricate himself from the press and the accompanying barrage of questions.

"The prince would be here if he could. No slight is intended. As you say, he could not possibly have known that you would be here this evening. He regrets that pressing matters keep him away at present, and will look forward to greeting you in a more formal venue, as befits your station, later in the month. Now, if you will excuse me." Johanus managed to get as far as putting one hand to the door before he was again forestalled. He patiently heard out this latest inquiry.

"Yes, I'm afraid that is necessary," he replied. Antigone recognized the tone of voice the one-time Master of Novices customarily used in his oft-rehearsed lectures. "That way we can direct other newcomers away from your choice of preferred hunting grounds. It helps prevent inadvertent trespass and, ultimately, messy confrontations in the streets."

There was an indignant outburst which Johanus dismissed with a wave of his hand. "Too intrusive? I assure you, sir, that a few simple questions are far less intrusive than a dozen or so displaced Kindred accidentally stumbling through your territory. And nothing is permanent. The prince is most even-handed. Once the present crisis has passed, I am sure he will amply reward those who have made sacrifices for his sake and for the sake of the city."

Johanus caught sight of black novice's robes fluttering towards him through the crowd. His eyes lit up at the convenient excuse this offered him. "But you gentlemen will excuse me. Here is the courier with the volatiles I requested from the chantry house."

As he beckoned eagerly for the novice to approach, the crowd cautiously edged away. They had no desire for a near brush with anything that the Tremere might consider volatile.

Antigone froze in place like a cornered animal, realizing that it was not her that Johanus was gesturing towards. Pressing forward through the crowd, she could pick out the familiar form of Jervais. Jervais was the personal assistant, or, as he preferred to put it, "second in command," to Eugenio Estevez, the Regent of the Maupassant Chantry. He seldom missed an opportunity to flaunt his lofty position or the freedom it afforded him. The Maupassant Room was one of the satellite chantries that reported to the motherhouse of the Chantry of Five Boroughs. They were, in effect, like individual campuses of the greater university.

Unlike its resident novices, Jervais pretty much came and went as he pleased from the fortified subterranean motherhouse. It was just one other thing he lorded over them. Antigone caught the flash of bright bands of silver at the cuffs of his dark robes—the insignia that identified him as a novice of the Third Circle. Jervais seldom missed an opportunity to flaunt his regalia before the other novices.

Antigone found herself acutely aware that she was out of uniform. After her leap from the Widow's Walk, her own novice's robes had been left in a heap upon the precipice. They had borne the blood-red markings at the collar, the mark of her yearned-for promotion to the Second Circle that she had been so long denied. But she had, quite literally, left all that behind her now.

After her sojourn among the dead, she now found herself more humbly attired. Her simple black dress was worn and a bit frayed about the hems. It was totally without adornment or ostentation, plain, dark, and more than a little bit musty, as if it had been locked away in mothballs for a season. She could not say from which hidden horde of grave goods the grinning Jackal god might have liberated it.

Still, for all that, the costume suited her. She smoothed at the worst of the creases, reflecting that she had just laid her old life to rest. After nearly a century, she had left the familiar confines of the Tremere Pyramid. It was only appropriate that she should wear the Widow's Weeds—the formal mourning dress.

She feared, however, that the plain black dress would not be dissimilar enough from her novitiate robes to prevent her being spotted and recognized. Whatever pretext Jervais had in coming here, he would surely be bringing Johanus news of the recent calamitous events at the chantry. Damn him.

Antigone tried to slip back into the anonymity of the crowd as she saw Johanus interpose his body between the throng and the exit. Swinging the door wide, he gestured for Jervais to proceed him and then quickly followed into the relative silence of the deserted corridor.

"Well that was a timely intervention," Johanus whispered with evident relief, as the door swung slowly towards closed. "What brings you all the way out here to the asylum?"

Antigone watched the door swing to with an admixture of relief and alarm. She had no doubt that, if Jervais were to discover her there, the ambitious novice would not scruple to turn her in—if not to try to apprehend her himself. More likely, he would get Johanus to do it.

Damn it, she needed Johanus' help to get to the prince and safety. Jervais could be, even now, undermining any footing she might have had with the adept. She hesitated, caught between the desire to follow the retreating pair and the consequences of being discovered doing so.

Just then, a hand latched firmly onto her forearm.

A rasping voice whispered in her ear. "It is all set. Tonight, just like you wanted. Don't worry, you've still got about an hour to clear out. Mind you, it wasn't easy. I've gone to considerable risk, not to mention personal expense. But I'm sure we can find some way to make it up to me…."

Antigone wheeled around, realizing as she did so that her opportunity to follow the two Tremere had just slipped away from her. She fixed the stranger with her haughtiest glare. He was short, grubby, with a two-day growth of beard. The butt of a pistol peeked from the top of his belt. It gleamed silver. Where his fingers wrapped tightly around her forearm, she could feel the hammer of his pulse. It distracted her. She realized that she had been through quite an ordeal tonight, and that she was hungry.

She forced the thought down. "You will take your hand from me. Now." she said.

She needn't have bothered to speak aloud. As she turned, he realized his error and immediately let her go. He was already backing away into the crowd and murmuring apologies.

"Sorry, lady. Thought you were somebody else. Stupid of me, really. I mean, you two don't really look anything alike, now do you? Sorry."

Cursing himself, the curious little man disappeared back into the crowd. Antigone stared after him for a moment, less from curiosity than to be certain that he did not reemerge — perhaps to cover up his error by making sure that she could not interfere with whatever deal he had going down that evening.

Satisfied, she turned back to the double doors. She cracked one open slightly and listened for the sound of voices. Her ears could pick out only the echo of distant footsteps echoing down the empty corridor. With one last backward glance to make sure her departure was not noted, she slipped silently from the gym.

Chapter 10
Rendezvous

A small voice directly behind her brought Cordelia out of her reverie.

"Excuse me. I was wondering if you could direct me to the archeology building?"

Cordelia turned upon the newcomer. She was slight, rain-matted and draped in a ridiculous mud-stained poncho. She looked as if she could be a student here. That is, if one disregarded the fact that a student might be expected to know that the exclusive girls' school was not anywhere near large enough as to boast an archeology building. That, and the fact that this pale, shivering "student" was, unmistakably, no longer among the living. Cordelia had a sense for these things.

"I know it's late, but I need to find the archeology department offices," Chessie said. "I'm looking for Professor Sturbridge."

Cordelia almost laughed aloud. It was too precious. She could feel the bubbling hysteria welling up within her, the potent vitae she had drunk seeking outlet. She shifted from foot to foot at the effort of keeping it all in. "Not from around here, are you?" she said, beckoning the newcomer closer.

Chessie shook her head miserably, scattering raindrops on all sides.

"Look, it's probably locked up for the night," Cordelia said. "But it's just on the other side of the quad. If you cut between those two buildings there, you'll run straight into it."

"Thanks," Chessie muttered, pulling the hood of the poncho down more tightly around her face. She turned and plodded her way through the puddles towards the opening between the two leering brick edifices.

Cordelia gave her a minute's head start.

Eugenio Estevez checked his watch for probably the tenth time. Against the blue luminous backlight, the LED numerals stood out in sharp relief. 03:17. His superior was already fifteen minutes late and had, predictably, left him waiting in the rain.

He had called from LaGuardia to tell Eugenio to meet him out front of Millbank Hall. Polite inquiries about the flight in from Vienna had availed Eugenio nothing. Nor had any amount of hinting that a more comfortable reception at the luxurious Maupassant Room would better befit one of the Lord High Inquisitor's lofty station.

"I'm afraid it's business this time, Eugenio, not pleasure. And the sooner we get this unpleasantness wrapped up, the sooner I'll be out of your hair. Now, won't that make everyone rest a bit easier?"

"Nonsense!" Eugenio hastened to protest. "Your presence is not in the least an imposition, my lord. In fact, I have rather been looking forward to..." he said to the dead line. Eugenio smiled and gently replaced the receiver in its cradle. He always smiled when slighted. It didn't matter that no one was there to observe the chivalric gesture. It was a habit that, to his mind, spoke of character in the face of adversity.

He supposed that some might construe standing in the rain for a quarter hour as character-building as well, although it did little to improve Eugenio's disposition. Usually he would leave such unpleasant vigils to Jervais, his aide-de-camp. Eugenio was a man of some standing, after all. He had worked hard to get where he was. As regent of the refined Maupassant chantry, Eugenio was the public face of the Tremere Pyramid in Camarilla-liberated New York City. He had served as host to princes and justicars. High Regent Sturbridge relied upon him implicitly.

Perhaps too implicitly, he thought, peering out from the inadequate shelter of his umbrella. Its silver handle was sculpted in the shape of a caduceus — the entwined serpents of Mercury. The healer and messenger of the gods was something of a patron saint to Eugenio. They shared a common vocation — to bring fractious parties together, to start the slow process of patching up the raw wounds. Eugenio knew that the most efficacious medicines in his doctor's bag were congenial conversation and luxurious excess, and he plied them to dramatic effect.

So why wasn't it Sturbridge standing here, trying unsuccessfully to press herself back under the eaves of the campus administrative building and escape the worst of the steady downpour? Eugenio was afraid he might already know the answer. The very fact that the Lord Inquisitor and his team were here spoke volumes. Something had gone terribly wrong at the Chantry of Five Boroughs. He wondered if that something had happened to Regent Sturbridge directly. He could think of few causes less monumental than the death of a regent that would bring the Astors swooping in from Vienna to restore order. With no advance notice.

The regency was a position of consequence. In the wake of being selected to lead the Maupassant Chantry, Eugenio had immersed himself in perks of his newfound autonomy. Looking back now, he could see that this freedom had made him grow distant from Sturbridge and the motherhouse. It even made him somewhat resentful of efforts on her part to bridge the widening gulf.

If something was wrong, he should have known. He should have been the first to know. He should have been there.

This was no way to find out—a phone call in the middle of the night from Vienna operatives jetting in to intervene. It wasn't right that he should be so far out of the loop. He felt simultaneously resentful and guilty that this could have happened.

Eugenio resolved, on the spot, that he would do whatever was in his power to help ease this crisis and smooth out any ruffled feathers between his brothers from the Chantry of Five Boroughs and those from Vienna. He was already drafting elaborate reconciliations in his head when the sound of spinning tires on the rain-slick pavement brought him up short. The sleek gray Jaguar zipped around the corner and slewed to a halt diagonally across the parking space labeled, in stenciled baby-blue lettering, "Reserved. Assoc. Dean of Interdepartmental Disciplinary Review." The warning covered most of the parking space.

The headlights winked out and receded flush with the hood. The wipers clacked to a halt. The engine revved once and then fell silent.

Eugenio stepped forward to the driver's-side door, extending his umbrella in welcome until the rain ran unimpeded down the back of his starched collar.

Dorfman unfolded from the driver's seat with a nod and a grunt by way of welcome as he accepted the proffered umbrella. "Good to see you, Eugenio. Hope I didn't keep you waiting." With his free hand, he flipped open a cellphone of Finnish contours.

"Not all at," Eugenio sputtered, gazing wistfully at his commandeered umbrella. "I hope you did not have any trouble on your drive in from the—"

"Himes!" Dorfman barked into the cellphone. "I'm right outside. Meet me at the main entrance. You got the security system locked down? Good. You with Sturbridge now? What?! What do you mean you haven't... Shit. Look, just meet me at the front door. Yeah, I'm on my way now. I can see it from here. Yeah, and I've got Estevez in tow."

Dorfman snapped the phone shut on the voice from the other end. "Where's Sturbridge?" he asked without slowing.

Eugenio hurried to catch up. "I take it she's not at the chantry. And that your colleagues already are inside. I wish that you had told me of your itinerary earlier. I could have arranged a more appropriate welcome for you and your..."

Dorfman stopped cold, throwing up one hand for silence. He was peering intently at the shadowed pass-through between the two nearest buildings.

"It's just this way," Eugenio said, gesturing in the other direction, towards the main entrance to the subterranean chantry.

Dorfman hissed at him irritably for silence. Now Eugenio could hear it too. It sounded like a struggle. To his credit, he was already moving, pressing forward to shield his superior from whatever new threat might materialize. It was a noble if ultimately futile gesture. Dorfman was more than capable of taking care of himself.

Eugenio was the first to reach the pair. He recognized Cordelia by sight, of course, although they were only slightly acquainted and he would have been hard pressed to recall her name. He had seen her at formal gathers at the main chantry house.

The other girl, the one in the ridiculous camouflage rain poncho, he did not recognize. The point, however, was largely moot as the novice had obviously just drained her of the last of her lifesblood. The puckered pink wounds at her throat gaped, but failed to surrender even the barest trickle of blood.

"Blasphemous!" He hissed before he could force his jaws to clench tight around the word. Diablerie—the drinking of the blood of another Kindred—was the one unforgivable sin among their kind. To find this odious offense taking place, here, upon the very threshold of the motherhouse—and before the eyes of the Lord Inquisitor himself!—was unthinkable.

All this flashed through his mind in a single moment of revulsion. In that moment, Cordelia wheeled upon the newcomer with superhuman speed. Her avaricious grin was tinted ruddy, trailing long viscous strands of red—the incriminating evidence of her grim feast. She jittered, surged with a restless energy that uncoiled suddenly, cracking like a whip. Eugenio was overwhelmed with the sudden ferocity of the attack. His hands came up defensively, but not quite quickly enough.

He managed to catch her by the shoulders as she barreled into him, but her momentum bowled both of them over backwards, her teeth gnashing for his throat.

It is strange how, in moments of great peril, the most insignificant of details rise up to monopolize the attention, assuming an importance far greater than their due. Eugenio was acutely aware of this phenomenon as he found himself increasingly irritated by the distracting buzz of a gnat about his face.

He shook his head and blew upward to clear the insect from his eyes, all the while seeming only peripherally concerned with warding off the lethal fangs that pressed upon him. Another part of his mind found itself suddenly turning over the strange jumble of words that his assailant spat at him. It sounded surprisingly like, "Stop looking at me like that! I am NOT a monster."

The buzzing in his ears grew stronger as his attacker repeatedly smashed his head into the puddle where the cobbles of the path met. This activity must have stirred up a cloud of midges. He could hardly focus enough to see her face clearly through the swarm. He squinted his eyes into mere slits in the effort to shield them from the horde of tiny stinging insects.

Cordelia could not have been oblivious to this new element either. She batted distractedly at one ear even as they grappled. Her swipe dislodged a sizable spider that had swung down to her shoulder. But that did not seem to lessen her irritation.

Eugenio took advantage of this brief opening to throw his weight to one side, overturning her and reversing their positions. Still, Cordelia clawed at her ear as they rolled. Her nails came away bloody.

Pressed as closely together as they were—for all practical purposes, cheek to cheek—Eugenio could see the tattered remains of the earlobe dangling from a thread of flesh. But that was not what held his attention. Rather, it was the fat, oily, red and black body segment of a worm—as thick around as his thumb—protruding obscenely from the cavity of her ear.

Eugenio found himself caught in an increasingly ridiculous position as his chivalrous nature got the better of him. Having recovered from his earlier shock and at last gained the upper hand, he now discovered himself poised precisely at the crux between trying to bludgeon the girl into oblivion and politely, if rather uncomfortably, pointing out to her that she seemed to have something lodged in her ear.

He resolved the dilemma by deciding to focus his efforts on keeping the girl pinned down so that she could not do either of them any serious harm. With her vitae-fueled reserve of strength, however, this proved no mean feat. He was about to mention the futility of further struggle and offer her quarter, when he became aware of an unsettling shifting of the fabric where he gripped her sleeves. Or rather, an unsettling shifting *beneath* it.

He tried for a better grip but his hands could find no purchase. He suddenly felt a maddening, itching sensation scuttling up the flesh of his hands and wrists. It spread like a fire, racing to his elbows, consuming him. He recoiled from her and lurched unsteadily to his feet, tearing at the exposed flesh of his forearms with his nails.

So involved was he with scraping away the creeping carapaced horde, he barely noticed that he had only narrowly escaped the full force of the cresting wave. The flesh of Cordelia's face—now seen only dimly through the cloud of crawling, scuttling and flying things—streamed, pooled and ran like a liquid until he could see the clear contours of the skull beneath. And once the fleshly barricade was breached, things only got worse. Squirming fistfuls of maggots squelched out from her gaping sockets, and darker things still uncoiled from the ruins of her guts. Eugenio turned away, dry-heaving, pressing a handkerchief to his mouth.

He caught sight of Dorfman out of the corner of his eye. The Inquisitor stood with one hand raised as in invocation. "Damned diablerists," he muttered. "Death's too good for the likes of her. They're rotten, rotten on the inside." He shook his head and crossed to where Eugenio was doubled over. "You okay?" He slapped him on the shoulder, producing another choking cough.

"I'm fine, fine," he croaked. "But that! Did you do—"

"Of course you are," Dorfman said. "You know either of the two stiffs?"

Eugenio nodded slowly, struggling for his composure. "That one is, or rather was, a novice here. The other..." he shrugged.

Dorfman had already turned away and started back towards the main entrance. If he had stopped to examine the bodies, he himself could have identified the other, although he might have been surprised to find her here. He flipped open the cellphone and keyed the speed-dial. "Himes! Where are you? Yeah, I know what I told you, but I need a clean-up crew out front. Now. Yes, two of them. Estevez says one's a novice, so I guess you'd better open a file. *First official termination. Cause: Diablerie. Judgment: Summary execution by order of Dorfman, Peter, LHI at...*" he checked his Rolex. "*03:32 hours.* You got that? Good, log it. We do this one by the book."

He snapped the phone shut, preempting further discussion.

"I don't think," said Eugenio, hastening to catch up with his superior, "that I care much for your book."

"Nobody does," Dorfman said. "That's how I ended up with it."

Chapter 11
Rogue Adept

"I thought you would appreciate a bit of advance warning," Jervais said, glancing at the adept circumspectly. "This development has come as rather an abrupt surprise for many of us. Given your position, I feel certain they will wish to question you personally at the earliest opportunity."

Johanus did not miss the tone in the novice's voice. Jervais wanted to make very clear that he had put himself in a delicate position to bring the adept this news.

"It was thoughtful of you to come to me," Johanus said. "I imagine they would have gotten around to summoning me eventually. I will spare them the trouble and return directly."

"Excellent," Jervais replied. "I'll accompany you, then."

"You won't be missed?" Johanus asked. "No, I won't hear of it. You have done enough already. I won't have you risking formal disciplinary action on my account."

Jervais' mouth was already open, deploying his carefully marshaled counter-arguments. He knew that, with the Astors in town, Johanus would shortly find himself the object of several very pointed inquiries. If things went well for the adept in the arduous interrogations ahead, it would not hurt for him to remember that it was Jervais who had stood by his side on that long, thoughtful trip to face his inquisitors. And if things should go ill, well, then the powers-that-be could surely be made to appreciate the fact that it was Jervais who had brought the "rogue adept" back in. It would quite likely win him an delightfully infamous reputation among the novices.

"It is nothing," Jervais smiled his most ingratiating smile. "They will be so relieved at your return that I will hardly be noticed. We will need a firm hand at the helm to steer us through this crisis."

A look of concern, and something else—guilt?—flashed across Johanus' face. "Then Sturbridge is still…indisposed," he hastily recovered, fearing he had revealed too much. He could not say for certain what had happened to Regent Sturbridge. He knew she had been hurt, deeply hurt, right about the time of the Liberation. Helena told him that Sturbridge had been slipping in and out of torpor for weeks. Johanus knew that details of the regent's condition would be even more strictly kept from the novices. It would not do to promote unease or, worse, opportunism among the ranks.

If Jervais noted the adept's hesitation, he did not comment upon it. "They have been asking after both you and the regent," he said. "Helena has been sequestered all evening."

Johanus filed this new information away. The fact that Sturbridge was unaccounted for was disturbing. It certainly suggested that she might be in the grip of one of what Helena described as the regent's "episodes." Without Helena or someone else capable on hand, there was no telling what harm Sturbridge might do to herself or others. He only hoped that Master Ynnis was attending upon the regent.

"No," Johanus said firmly. "You go ahead; I will follow as soon as I can. That way I can tell them that I was under the impression that you were back at the chantry the entire time. I couldn't forgive myself if they asked me about your absence from the chantry—I would have to report you and then I would be disconsolate."

"Nonsense," Jervais said. "No one wants to be left standing alone at a time like this. Worry, doubt, they burrow inside you and fester. You should know that, whatever happens, there are those of us who will stand behind you."

"Thank you, Jervais. But I have nothing to fear here. I have done nothing wrong. The Astors will be thorough and fair. I trust them to get to the heart of this matter. And I am not it," he added pointedly.

He could see he would need some other way to disentangle himself from the ambitious novice. After some consideration, a thought occurred to him. Clapping Jervais on the shoulder, he said, "But I do have something you can do for me. It is a matter of some delicacy. May I rely upon you?"

Jervais could not quite conceal the predatory flash that lit his eyes. "I am at your service, Adeptus."

"It seems that upon my return to the chantry, I may be immediately detained. I will not have the opportunity to handle certain routine errands that are long overdue. I am particularly concerned about a correspondence of mine that should have been posted some days ago. It is to an old colleague of mine. In Atlanta. I trust you understand my concern."

Jervais nodded sagely. "I do," he said. "Any colleague in Atlanta would be in something of a precarious position." He was not unaware that Atlanta was one of the first Camarilla strongholds to fall before the most recent Sabbat offensive. The Tremere no longer maintained any official presence in the city. Any colleague that Johanus had there must be on a very sensitive—and very covert—mission.

Unless, of course, this penpal were playing for the other team. *Very interesting indeed,* Jervais thought. In either case, he could appreciate why Johanus might not want such an epistle to find its way into the hands of the Astors.

He tried to keep the hint of avarice from his voice. "I would hate to think that your associate might be put in further peril by something so small as a delay in post. I will see that the letter goes out immediately upon my return."

"Thank you," Johanus said. "That is very kind of you. You will find it in my sanctum, in the lowest desk drawer. The address is already on the envelope."

"And the key?" Jervais asked.

"Ah, yes. The key," Johanus said. "The sanctum is warded *interdire confluratorum*. You just have to make quite certain that you have nothing at all of the color black about your person, and you will pass without mishap."

"Nothing black," Jervais parroted, realization and begrudging admiration dawning simultaneously. "Like novice's robes, for example…"

"Yes," Johanus replied, smiling. "That would be a glaring oversight."

"Anything else I should be…aware of?"

"Now that you mention it, I seem to recall some sort of warding on the desk itself. But I'm sure you'll figure it out. You always were such a quick study."

"The adept flatters me. But I would humbly ask that he try to recall the exact nature of the warding on the desk. It would be a great pity if I found myself unable to dispose of…that is to say, 'post,' the letter in question."

"Well, since you have put it that way, let me think. It was something quite incidental. Ah yes, that was it. A fear articulator. On the lower drawer. I find there is always something so cathartic about entrusting one's hand to a dark and enclosed space. You're not squeamish are you? Snakes, fire, that sort of thing?"

"No," Jervais said flatly. He apparently did not find the topic as amusing as did the adept. "Other little incidentals?"

"Not if you don't go poking around. Thank you again, Jervais. If they should ask after me at the chantry, you can tell them that I will be along as soon as I can break away without causing undue alarm."

"Thank you, Adeptus," Jervais said. "You may rely upon me implicitly."

Antigone could make out little enough of the two men's conversation for all the clamor within the gym. The sound of Jervais' footsteps approaching, however, were clear enough. They startled her to action. She silently slipped back into the gymnasium and wrapped the anonymity of the crowd around her like a shawl.

She lingered close enough to the doorway that she could observe Jervais, mark his progress. She needed to know when it was safe to slip past, back the way he had come. She had to catch Johanus before he too struck out for the chantry. Once the adept had returned to the confines of the chantry house, he was lost to her. There was no knowing when or if she might see him again.

Jervais swung wide the doors. In his mind, he was already plundering all the most jealously guarded secrets of the adept's sanctum. His meeting with Johanus had gone far better than he could have even imagined. Instead of merely escorting the adept back to the chantry, Jervais had been given one of those unique opportunities that a man of insight and ambition might exploit to its fullest advantage. He was inordinately pleased with his evening's take.

He had already advanced four or five bold strides into the heart of the throng when he stopped abruptly, as if struck by a sudden thought. Antigone could see his features bunch in consternation. She felt her stomach knot as he slowly pivoted, like a turret, and stared fixedly in her direction.

"Antigone." Jervais' smile was as tight and clipped as his tone. His voice was pitched low, but it cut cleanly through the hum of the background noise and her own muffled curse. He straightened, unconsciously smoothing at the sharp almost military crease in his left cuff. The insignia of his rank flashed silver.

Antigone knew that he had her cornered. There was no way to delicately extricate herself at this point. With the patience of a spider, he descended upon her.

"Jervais," she replied coolly as he drew up in front of her. He hovered uncomfortably close, mere inches separating their faces. It put her on edge. Her mind shuffled through possible outcomes of this unwelcome encounter. She was none too pleased with her options.

Her first instinct was flight, but she stubbornly held her ground. Still, the sooner she could break away, the better. She decided her best chance was to go on the offensive. "It's a good thing I found you," she said. "They were inquiring after you at the chantry. It would probably be best for you to return immediately, before your absence is remarked upon further."

"Thank you for your concern. I am, in fact, on my way there now. There is no need, by the way," he said with a smirk, "for you to bother the adept. He is already aware of the recent developments at the chantry. He will be along presently. Now, don't look so crestfallen. You will have to apply yourself much harder in future if you would steal a march on your betters! But since you are here, you may accompany me back to the chantry. There are certain matters I have been most anxious to discuss with you. Privately."

"Very kind of you," Antigone said. "But I am on the business of the regent and cannot be sidetracked just now. And, as you are expected back home presently—if not sooner—it would be wrong of me to keep you here talking. Another time, perhaps?" She made to turn away and sink back into the crowd.

Jervais caught her by the elbow and fell gracefully into step beside her. "The business of the regent? Why, then you should not be unescorted on such an important errand. What if something should happen to you here among this lot of unsavory characters? I would hold myself personally responsible. And what are you doing here out of uniform, as it were?" His voice dropped to a conspiratorial whisper. "You are not traveling…incognito?"

She smoothly extricated herself from his grip. They had reached the edge of the crowd and stood in the shadow of the bleachers. "I am glad you find this amusing, Jervais. I am sure the regent will find it amusing that you are compromising this mission. Now, if you're quite finished, I've got work to do. And you are cramping my style."

Jervais shrugged off her threat. "I've been trying to catch up with you for the better part of week. Ever since the incident in the novice domicilium. If I didn't know better, I'd think you were trying to avoid me."

At the mention of the novice domicilium, Antigone felt as if she had been hit in the gut with a hammer. A fire had broken out, a warding salamander spirit gone renegade, and Antigone had given the order that had condemned three novices to a fiery final death.

Had it only been a week before? The pain was fresh, but the weight of that decision bearing down on her had become a constant companion—as if the choice had been made a lifetime ago. *Three lifetimes ago,* she thought ruefully.

She emerged from her introspection and realized that Jervais was still speaking, had been for some time: "…Didn't just think we'd all forget about that, did you? Three of us died in that fire! Three of our friends, our brothers and sisters, taken from us. And you pulled the trigger. People are going to want some answers from you, Antigone. And not just the Ast…not just *our guests.* You are a bright girl and I know I don't have to spell it out for you. Whatever happens, things are going to become rather *uncomfortable* for you back at the chantry."

"I did what I had to do," Antigone murmured. "The fire, the defensive system grid down. We were looking at an evacuations scenario. More than three lives would have been lost, Jervais."

"That is your opinion. You will not convince me that it outweighs the lives of three of our brothers and sisters. I seriously doubt you will convince a tribunal of it. Still, it must have been very…gratifying for you. To get to decide who lives and who dies." His voice dripped with undisguised malice.

"It wasn't like that," Antigone insisted, shaking her head vehemently. "You don't know. You weren't caught in the middle of that conflagration. You weren't out there with the emergency response teams…"

"No," he cut her off. "But Marcus was caught in the middle of it. And Clarissa. And Livonia. And now they are dead. And I was, by the way, 'out there.' Working alongside the emergency response team. I still have the burns to prove it. I heard you give that order over the com port. But I did not see *you* there."

Such was his intensity that Jervais did not even seem to notice that he was gathering attention from those nearby.

"Jervais!" Her voice was a fierce whisper. "I don't think that this is either the time nor the place…"

"Then come with me now and we will settle this matter. More privately."

Antigone shook her head. "Look, I don't have time for this. I've got to take care of this business for the regent and I can't break away right now. And your standing here arguing about it is only jeopardizing this mission. Now go. I'll see you back at the chantry."

"I will wait."

"You will not. Besides, this is likely to take a while. Just go."

"I can wait."

"Jervais, it's already looking like I'm going to be here most of the night and the longer I spend talking to you, the longer it will be before I even get started. Now, I hate to have to report people for interfering with chantry security, because you know how Helena gets about that kind of—"

"That will not be necessary," said Jervais smiling broadly. "Helena has been...detained. But do not worry. Our little private reckoning will keep for a while still. You have really been most helpful. You see, I only needed to know that you would be unable to return to the chantry until early this morning."

Slow realization and a cold dread dawned upon Antigone at the same time. "I am not sure why that should concern you," she said carefully.

"It intimately concerns me," he countered. "You see, Marcus was very dear to me. A confidante of mine. And I watched him die. No, don't turn away. I should like for you to hear this. Have you ever seen someone burn to death, Antigone? With our kind, it is actually over quite quickly. Surprisingly quickly. There is the first gentle caress of the flames. And the flesh moans in response, curls towards it..."

"Enough!" she cried. "I am sorry that Marcus is dead. I really am. That decision is something I have to relive each and every night. But I'm not going to stand here and listen to this sick—"

"I wish I could believe that," Jervais mused aloud. "That you are sorry, I mean. That you are truly repentant. That would mean so much to me. That is why I am willing to go out of my way to make absolutely certain of it."

"Is that a threat?"

Jervais raised an eyebrow. "I would like to understand, to appreciate your feelings in this matter. And I would like for you to understand exactly how I feel. Exactly."

"I'm not sure I know what you mean," Antigone replied.

"Only this: that it is no secret that you yourself have acquired a new pet back at the chantry. Oh, do not look so surprised. I myself have dropped in upon your little friend, this Mr. Felton, from time to time. I do not presume to know why the powers-that-be should entrust one such as yourself—a rank novice without notable achievement or distinction of service— to cultivate an apprentice. It is not for me to second-guess the regent. Assuming, of course, that the regent was consulted before your little recruiting effort?"

Antigone could only stare at him in horror as she caught a glimpse of where this was leading.

"I should hate to think that anything might happen to your dear Mr. Felton. Something incendiary, say. Especially when you were away from the chantry. On the regent's personal errand. All night."

He shrugged and turned away from her, pressing his way into the crowd.

"God damn you, Jervais! You touch him and I'll stake your sorry worm-eaten carcass for the sunrise. You hear me?"

He raised one hand in parting salute and vanished within the teeming ranks of the dead.

Chapter 12
A Habit of Half-Truths

"Johanus, I need your help. You've got to—"

"Slow down," Johanus smiled down at Antigone. He placed a steadying hand on each of her shoulders and held her at arm's length, studying her. He was a mountain of a man and tended to treat others with an exaggerated gentleness. As if he were afraid he might break them. "Jervais was just here. He told me all about the trouble back at the chantry."

The adept's patient and patronizing manner only made Antigone more frantic. "You don't understand. Jervais *is* the trouble. He's going to…" She forced herself to rein in. Deliberately, she drew a deep breath. Only after she was certain she was in control did she allow herself to continue. "You've got to come with me."

"All right, easy now. I'm just wrapping up a few last things here and then I'm heading that way myself. You can tell me about it on the way, okay?"

Antigone fumed inwardly, but fell into step beside him, forcing herself to slow down, to match the adept's leisurely pace. Johanus always made her feel like this—awkward, impatient. His calm southern perambulations always managed to bring out the worst in her. Even back when he had served as the chantry's Master of Novices. Antigone could distinctly recall those long, frustrating and humiliating nights—the only fruits of her failed apprenticeship. The parade of evenings when the blood magics simply refused to flow.

"Look," she said. "There is a guest of the chantry, he came to us for sanctuary. It was my duty to protect him. Now Jervais has taken it into his head that if he can get to this guy, he can get to me. He's going to use the confusion of this shakedown by the Astors to cover it all up. I've got to get Felton out of there right away. Tonight."

Johanus stopped before a wooden door bearing a sign that read, "Boiler Room." He fumbled through a ring of keys. "So what do you need me for?" he asked without looking up from his task. His voice was gentle rather than belligerent. "You know that if I were to step in at this point, it would only go harder on you the next time. And there would be sure to be a next time. You've got to find a way to tackle Jervais on your own. To show him he can't mess with you and walk away unscathed."

Antigone shook her head. "That's not it at all. Look, I can't go back to the chantry right now. Sturbridge sent me to Calebros. She said I was not to come back to the chantry tonight, under any circumstances," she said. It was only a half-truth, but she had gotten into a habit of half-truths recently and saw no reason to reform just now.

Sturbridge had said a lot of things. About dark thaumaturgy, about being an outcast from the Pyramid, about seeking sanctuary among the Nosferatu. Antigone thought that sharing any of these complications with Johanus right now would only cloud the waters. She did not know how he would react to the knowledge that she was, herself, now a fugitive, fleeing the justice of the Tremere Pyramid. It was possible that he would try to take her back, to use her to ransom his own life or career. It didn't seem his style, but these were desperate times and she wasn't taking any chances.

Johanus found the right key at last and opened the door. It swung back, revealing a wooden stairway descending into darkness. "So you need somebody to watch over this guy, Felton, until you get back. Is that it?" he asked. "You know that they're not going to give me a lot of leisure time once I poke my head back in at the chantry, right? Jervais says they've had Helena in isolation, grilling her, since their arrival. They're not likely to be real understanding about—"

Antigone interrupted. "Helena's locked up? Then who's with Sturbridge?" she demanded.

Her question took him aback. "How the hell should I know?" he said defensively. "I haven't been back there, remember? You've seen her more recently than I have. But something Jervais said led me to believe that Sturbridge hadn't been there to meet the Astors when they arrived."

Johanus had been about to say something about "one of her fits," but he held back. He was unsure how much Antigone knew about the regent's current condition.

Then a thought occurred to him. "But you've seen Sturbridge tonight," he accused. "She sent you to Calebros. And she wasn't at the chantry."

"No, she wasn't," Antigone admitted. She did not explain further.

"So what's this all about, anyway?" Johanus asked. "Why do you need to see Calebros? Why did Sturbridge warn you to stay away from the chantry? Where is the regent? Nothing's happened to her? You haven't—"

"No! The regent is fine. Or as well as she might be under the circumstances. I needn't tell you that this visit from Vienna bodes ill for her. All in all, I would say that she is taking all this quite well."

"Where is she?" he demanded flatly.

"I hope she is back at the chantry by now. She said there were still some things she had to take care of there."

"How did she...seem to you? When you spoke with her."

"She was fine," Antigone said. Then she became thoughtful. "She seemed sad but resigned. She spoke of things coming to an end here."

Johanus cursed. "I've got to get back," he said. He put one hand on her shoulder and firmly steered down the stairs before him. As she moved past him, he leaned in very close and breathed into her ear. "You are not here to lead them to me, are you? The Astors, I mean. Is that what this is all about?"

Antigone spun upon him with an alarmed expression on her face. "No! Nothing like that, honestly. It's just..."

"Just what?"

"It's just that I think Sturbridge is in trouble. Big trouble. And I'm afraid for her and for Helena. I've heard the nightmare stories—about the liquidation of the Tel Aviv chantry and..."

"It's all right," Johanus said, his natural protective instincts winning out over his suspicions. Distrust did not come easily to him. This was widely regarded as something of a shortcoming in his line of work. "Nothing like that is going to happen here, you understand? Everyone is going to be all right." He drew a deep, steadying breath, as if to fortify himself for the confrontation ahead—or as if trying to convince himself that there was more substance to his words than empty exhalations from the grave.

"Well, that's reassuring," came a voice from somewhere below. "I was beginning to think that we were all fucked."

A moment of panic knotted in the pit of Antigone's stomach. She had not expected that their conversation would be overheard. She found herself rapidly replaying the dialog in her mind, trying to reconstruct exactly how much had been said since they had opened the door to the basement, and precisely how compromising those words might have been.

"Watch your language," Johanus growled back. "We've got company. Ladies present. Umberto, this is Antigone. Antigone, Umberto."

They reached the bottom of the stairway and rounded the imposing bulk of the ancient boiler. There was a blaze of light from the far wall of the unfinished basement. The light came from three huge computer monitors side by side. They formed a bunker in which crouched the bent form of a man.

Umberto craned around in his chair to get a better look at his guests. The motion looked excruciatingly painful and was accompanied by a chorus of spinal poppings and crackings. Catching sight of them, Umberto rose laboriously from his seat.

"'Sa pleasure," he said, shambling forward. "We don't get a lot of visitors down here. Least not the pretty ones. This ugly bastard mostly scares them off." With a jerk of his thumb, he indicated Johanus.

The broken shell of a man wasn't any taller standing than he had been sitting. His features were puffy and bloated; the shape of his head reminded Antigone of a moldy apple perched precariously atop his neck. *Waiting for some ambitious archer to take a shot at it*, she thought.

But despite his obvious deformity, her eyes lit up upon seeing him. He was quite obviously a Nosferat. Already, she felt herself one step closer to the prince and to safety. She accepted his proffered hand and suffered him to raise her fingers to his lips.

"I am very glad to meet you, Umberto," she said. "Johanus was just telling me that you might be able to help me. I have a pressing errand to Prince Calebros from the lady of our house."

"I said no such thing," Johanus mumbled, dropping the latest sheaf of files onto the mound of paperwork that was already overflowing Umberto's desk. But he did not look at all displeased.

"He's really quite perceptive, in his own way," Umberto replied, his eyes never leaving Antigone. "I am always glad to be of service to such a lovely young lady. And if I can service both yourself and your mistress, well, so much the better."

Umberto's hand, which still clung tenaciously to hers, was flushed warm.

"Would it be all right with you," she asked innocently, "if I stayed here with you until Johanus returned? He said he had to nip back over to the chantry and has kindly agreed to escort a friend of ours back here."

"Did not," Johanus called over his shoulder. "And these files aren't in alphabetical order."

"Just leave them on top, I'll get them. And don't contradict the young lady," Umberto said. "I'll look after things for you here while you fetch Miss Antigone's other playmate from the chantry. Go on, now. It's not polite to keep a lady waiting. It's not his fault," he explained to Antigone. "He doesn't get out much. They keep him locked down here most nights. Out of harm's way."

"If this errand is so urgent," Johanus said, "shouldn't you two head out to see the prince right away?" His suspicious look had returned.

"Probably," Antigone agreed. "But I need to know that Fel—my friend is safe."

"Then you can come with me." Johanus saw the look of momentary panic flicker across Antigone's features. He was already waving aside her objections. "Oh, I know what the regent said, about not returning to the chantry tonight. But you can at least accompany me back to Millbank. Once our guests become aware of my return, I am unlikely to break away again. I should be able to arrange to smuggle your friend out the side door, though. You can collect him there."

Antigone was obviously none too comforted by this plan. "Couldn't you send Talbott to escort him back here? Or someone else reliable?"

"The more folks you have involved, the more uncomfortable questions are going to get asked, once your friend's absence becomes noted."

Antigone saw his reasoning and was having some difficulty slipping free of it.

Umberto shifted uncomfortably. "So that's settled then. But you have to promise to hurry back."

"All right," she said. "We will. But you're going to have to let go of my hand at some point."

Embarrassed, Umberto hastily turned her loose.

Chapter 13
Harlequin Magus

Sturbridge finished keying the last of the official reports and pushed back from the monitor with a sigh. It felt as if she were sloughing off the yoke of a burden that she had carried for the better part of a decade. She knew it was over. There was ultimately only one possible outcome of a visit from the Astors.

There must be a final reckoning for what had happened here—for the murders among the novices, for the attacks on the representatives of the Fatherhouse, for her own failures and lapses. She had been entrusted with the care of this house and it was she who would be held personally accountable for what had transpired here.

Not for the first time, she found herself wondering just how much authority the Astors had been given in this matter. She half hoped that their authority extended so far as to permit them to pronounce summary judgment. Even the final death would be preferable to the prolonged indignity of being hauled bodily back to Vienna for some formal tribunal.

She wondered what would happen to them all once she was gone—not only to the novices that had been entrusted to her care, but to those other Children, those who were within her now. Without the fragile vessel of her body, would the nightmare be loosed again? Would the Children be condemned to their restless wanderings once more, searching for someone of the blood to heed their dark whisperings, to give them voice? To give them life?

She felt numb. Sturbridge gazed blankly at the screen and scanned down the list of reports she had just completed. She couldn't seem to focus on the words.

The first report was the confirmation of Antigone's promotion to the second circle of the novitiate. That was the only one that really mattered, now. And that only because of the promise she had made to Antigone on the observation deck. She would keep her word. It might well be all that was left to her after this evening, and she was not about to sell it cheaply.

Sturbridge could not say with any certainty how these final dispatches might be received by her superiors. Most likely they would be dismissed out of hand. Her brethren back in Vienna would be relying explicitly on the results of the Astors' investigation. What Sturbridge had to say at this point could only be of academic interest. Or perhaps it held some small value as evidence of her mindset as she faced the dissolution of all she had worked for.

But she would follow this through to the end. And she would do right by those entrusted to her care. It was a very small gesture, in the grand scheme of things, and one that she knew came far too late to redeem Antigone. It was too late for much of anything, now. Too late to act, certainly, but perhaps not too late to bear witness. So that what they had done here would not be forgotten.

The other reports dealt with one aspect or another of her recommendation that the Chantry of Five Boroughs be formally dissolved. During the long years of the Sabbat siege, there had been a clearly defined need for a single, hulking, fortified edifice that could weather the storm of the Sabbat encroachments. Now, in the wake of the Camarilla Liberation, the war chantry was more than obsolete. It was a liability. It had become not only a drain on House resources, but also an embarrassing reminder of what a peacetime hierarchy must now remember as a "less enlightened" time.

If the Tremere were to remain a vital force in shaping this new frontier, the chantry would have to change dynamically, to become far less rigid, centralized and ponderous. The war chantry had served its purpose, but there was no longer any need for the novices to shelter within the walls of some subterranean bunker. What the House needed now were apprentices of vision who would be out among the Kindred, helping to guide and shape the new order which must now take form.

Johanus would understand. He had, to some degree, anticipated this development. Sturbridge smiled to think of his work among the refugees swarming into the city. It was exactly the sort of thing she envisioned—a non-traditional, dynamic Tremere guiding presence. Working side by side with other Kindred, solving problems, building trust, getting the job done.

It was not easy for Sturbridge, this recommendation. In her brief tenure here, she had come to care very deeply for this house and for those who labored here. She hoped that her superiors would not condemn her recommendations for the peacetime chantry on the basis of her admitted failures with the wartime one.

They had done the impossible here. They had not only held the Sabbat at bay, but they had broken its advance and made possible the liberation of the city and, perhaps soon, of other cities which had not been so fortunate. Their triumph over the external foe had been complete.

But in her single-minded devotion to that cause, Sturbridge had let other things slip. While she had held the front lines against the Sabbat, another, more insidious enemy was gaining ground upon her. An internal enemy. The forces of corruption, betrayal, negligence and conspiracy. The worms that devour a seemingly healthy house from within.

Well, all that was done now. The Astors were here and they would cut the apple open to its core. They would expose the canker gnawing at its heart. Sturbridge hoped that they would carry the operation to its logical conclusion and pare down the ponderous bulk of the chantry-fortress in favor of its satellite houses.

The third dispatch on the screen before her recommended the promotion of Johanus, Adeptus, to the rank of Regent, First Circle, with the specific commission that he develop a new chantry to carry on the work he had begun—to monitor and assist new Kindred arrivals finding their way into the city. This work was critical not only to building strong ties to their new neighbors, but also to promoting a closer working cooperation with the prince. Sturbridge feared that this project might be derailed entirely should Johanus be recalled to Five Boroughs now to deal with problems at home.

Her fourth dispatch was the recommendation for the promotion of Ynnis, Maestro, to the rank of Regent, First Circle, with the specific commission that he develop a new chantry to focus upon research into the apportationist's art—specifically the development of a permanent system of instantaneous travel between regional chantries. Such a system would be a boon to all cooperative projects—especially the sharing of resources and the reinforcement of beleaguered garrisons in the event of renewed Sabbat advances.

Her fifth dispatch was the recommendation for the promotion of Helena, Adepta, to the rank of Regent, First Circle, with the commission of replacing Johnston Foley as junior regent to the main chantry house. Helena had personally designed the elaborate security system for C5B and was the only person qualified to maintain chantry security, stability and, most importantly, continuity during this difficult transition.

The sixth and final dispatch, of course, was Sturbridge's formal resignation as Regent of the Chantry of Five Boroughs.

Sturbridge gazed down the list of reports and clicked the send button on all but the last. Then she pushed herself wearily to her feet and crossed to the antique steamer trunk that already lay open in the center of the room. She began gathering her personal possessions.

Her fingers trailed lovingly along the spines of the ancient volumes overspilling her bookcases. She selected perhaps four tomes from the entire wall of books. Her fingers seemed to stretch of their own accord towards the works that must be left behind.

She paused over a heavy volume bound with her personal seal upon its cover—the flaming sword quenched in a cairn of stones. She whispered lovingly to it and it sighed open revealing, not bound pages, but individual sheet protectors fastened into a three-ring binder. The cover sheet of the manuscript bore the inscription:

> For A.S.—
> Delightful, book, your trip
> To she of night-crowned head;
> A pity it's not you
> That's pining, I that sped.
> —W.B.Y.

Sturbridge had met Yeats in her mortal days—it must have been nearly a century ago, now—through the Golden Dawn in London. The unbound manuscript pages contained his masterwork, his notes for a belief system that would reconcile his life-long fascination with the occult, with his native Catholicism and with the emerging Irish nationalism.

She idly flipped through the familiar pages, tracing the poet's spidery pencil-written scrawl, the impassioned incantations, the hermetic diagramma. Slowly, she let the book fall closed and placed it with great care within the trunk.

She could not bring herself to face the books that she must leave behind. Steeling her heart against their silent accusations, she turned to the mantle. A painting hung there, its jutting angles Pythagorean in their occult precision. Its tones were the aching blue-greens of silent subterranean waters. There was a figure trapped at the painting's center, a harlequin whose body formed the fulcrum of a set of alchemical scales. Even the chantry's newest novices remarked on the figure's resemblance to the regent.

It was a rare novice, however, one with more than a casual expertise in the hermetic societies of the turn of the century, who could actually place the work. The painting was entitled *Adjustment*. It was the original upon which Aleister Crowley had based the Eighth Trump of his infamous tarot deck. The identity of his dark muse, his harlequin magus, was not so widely known. Nor was it realized how narrowly, and by what even darker compact, she had escaped him.

Sturbridge could feel the subtle shifting of those cosmic scales, drawing her inevitably towards a final reckoning. One she had managed to elude for over a century.

But time itself grew thin now, a jumble of sharp angles, its premises and conclusions all slightly askew. Teetering dangerously out of balance. Her packing was not even halfway completed and she could feel the first hint of the dawn returning. She could feel it through the tons of steel and bedrock that separated her from the ancient nemesis—the searing sundisk. The symbol of truth.

She felt sluggish, as if she were moving underwater. Unseen planets careened wildly about her. She could not see them through the ceiling, the lid of her stone sarcophagus. But she felt their unmistakable pull.

She wanted nothing more than to sink into her bed and wrap the oblivion of the daylight hours around her like a shroud. To sink from sight, to sink from memory. To be at rest at the very center of the furiously churning dance of celestials.

No time. She forced her numb hands to gather her belongings, shards of memory. She no longer knew nor cared which, but merely stuffed whatever came to her hand into the trunk. The simple mechanical repetition was a kind of defiance. A blind shouting into the face of the forces of reason that insisted that her cold dead body could not possibly be up and doing what it was doing. Simply to rise each night, to feed, to draw life, that alone was a blasphemous affront against life, against death. It was inevitable, really, that they would seek her out in the end—those two great forces. That they would mark her for their own special brand of retribution.

Still, she was startled when the inevitable summons came. Time.

Chapter 14
The Hall of Daggers and Mirrors

Sturbridge moved like a ghost through the deserted halls, the only sign of her passing the sweep of her long black gown trailing in her wake. *Erasing even my footprints*, she thought. *The last sign of my having been here at all.*

She had carefully laid out her formal robes of office for this occasion, to meet her inquisitors face to face. She had only decided against them at the very last minute. The rich burgundy velvet had always struck her as just a bit much for any but the most formal function. She far preferred the simpler black gown, reminiscent of that worn by the female novices. The ensemble's only concession to her station was the elegant four-pointed star, reminiscent of a stylized cross or sword, that embroidered its front.

Given the circumstances of this visit, she had opted for the more comfortable humility over ostentation.

The chantry was very still tonight. It was as if it had somehow picked up on her mood. Already it seemed to be contemplating her absence, trying the thought on like an outfit that had hung forgotten in the back of the closet for the better part of a decade. It had not yet accustomed itself to the thought of shrugging free of its familiar and well-worn habit. Sturbridge knew, however, that the Chantry of Five Boroughs had managed just fine before her coming. It would certainly survive her leave-taking.

She had come the long way, maybe to give herself time to think, to steel her resolve for what she knew must lie ahead. For what she must now do. As her steps turned the corner into the Hall of Daggers and Mirrors, a jarring note tugged at the edge of her awareness. Preoccupied as she was, she knew that something was out of place. There.

It was down low, about knee height, along the right-hand wall—an unmistakable streak of red marring the pristine sheen of the polished glass. Blood.

Stooping for a closer inspection, Sturbridge saw one long black hair stuck in the razor-fine crevice between the mirrored panes. Carefully, she plucked it from its lodging and it came away, still tipped with the crown of matted blood that had held it in place.

Sturbridge touched the tip of the ebon strand to her tongue, felt the mote of dried blood soften, yield to her. She nodded. Sturbridge knew whose blood this was. She had tasted it just a few hours before. *Antigone.*

Another failing, Sturbridge thought. *Another novice I could not save. Another daughter I could not redeem.*

She took some small comfort in the fact that at least Antigone was beyond harm now, spared the brunt of this inquisition. Sturbridge shook her head. She had done what she could. She knew it was too little and too late. But she had kept her promise to Antigone. That much, at least, Sturbridge had been able to do. She had failed her own daughter, Maeve. She had failed Chessie. She had failed Jacqueline. She had failed Eva. She ticked off the litany of her dead, of the girls who had placed their lives in her hands and who were lost to her now. Beyond help.

Even as the thought crossed her mind, however, she knew that it was not entirely correct. They were lost, yes, but they were with her still. Within her. Not in some sort of mushy, consoling, their-memory-lives-on way. They were among the Children of the Well, now. They had surrendered to the maddening lapping of the dark waters. They had returned to the nightmare from which they had sprung.

If she closed her eyes, she could call them up still, watching anxiously as the impassive blue-tinged faces swam up towards her from the depths of the dark waters. Watching as they broke the surface, their matted hair fanning out like fishing nets lapping at the slick stones of the side of the well. They were her personal accusers, their reproaches far more damning than any charges the Astors might bring against her. The Children knew each of her failings intimately, and the condemnation in their eyes had this edge to it—it was entirely accurate and just.

In the final reckoning, Sturbridge knew, it didn't matter what the Astors did to her. She already suffered under a sentence far more personal and damning than any they could hope to devise for her.

She was ready to face them now. Just ahead, the hulking double doors leading to the Hall of Audiences stood ajar. Usually the sight of them—of their bulk, their solidity, their antiquity—was a comfort to her, a reassurance. Tonight, their solace could not touch her. The icy waters in which she had armored herself rebuffed all contact, whether condemning or bolstering.

But her stoic disposition was not absolute. With a flicker of annoyance, she noted that there was another already waiting outside the doors.

"Regentia! This is an unexpected pleasure. Would you believe that I was just this minute thinking of you? I trust all is well?" Jervais smiled and slid closer to her. He fidgeted with one of his cuffs. A flash of silver caught the light and was echoed back from an infinite number of points all along the mirrored hallway.

Sturbridge felt his proximity like a physical weight, tugging at one sleeve. An anchor dragging her back from the confrontation that she had just managed to steel herself to face. "Thank you, Jervais. It is kind of you to ask. I am on my way to formally welcome our guests."

Jervais leaned closer confidingly. "It seems that our 'guests' are not standing upon formalities. They have already commandeered choice living quarters and premium workspace. Would you believe that I, myself, came upon them rifling through Johanus' study earlier this evening? The presumption!"

He watched her surreptitiously for her reaction to this news, but if he expected some fiery response, he was disappointed. Sturbridge accepted this revelation without so much as a raised eyebrow.

Undeterred, Jervais pressed on. "There must be weighty matters afoot, that you should abandon your research and venture forth from your sanctum. We were told that you were not to be interrupted for any reason. I did not expect to find you, of all people, here at the threshold of our inquisitors. Surely you have not come to present evidence before the Astors?"

"Nothing so romantic, I'm afraid." She caught Jervais' nervous sideward glance towards the open doorway. Sturbridge realized that Jervais certainly was here to see the Astors. But he was afraid. "I imagine our guests will have a few questions for me once they are properly settled in. But there is nothing to worry yourself over. I am sure you have nothing to fear from the Astors."

Jervais shifted uneasily. He studied her face for some sign of a concealed threat behind her words. "Let us hope not."

Sturbridge smiled disarmingly and waved aside all such concerns. "It is nothing. You, all of you, will be fine. Still, we must face up to the fact that there have been some rather dramatic shake-ups here of late and the Fatherhouse, no doubt, would like some assurance that all is back to normal. Our guests will be gone within the fortnight. Have no fear on that account." Sturbridge turned away from him, but Jervais was not to be so easily shaken.

"Regentia!" he implored, falling into step at her elbow. "You can speak freely to me. Give me some slight credit. I think I have an idea of what our guests are about. And if you are not here to give testimony, it must be that someone has been casting aspersions against you. I cannot believe that you would be here to bring suit against another member of this house."

"In that, at least, you are correct. Good evening, Jervais." She reached the open doorway and placed one hand upon the doorpull.

"Then someone has been undermining you and bringing false charges!" Jervais was indignant. His voice rang overloud in the corridor. And also, no doubt, within the Hall of Audiences.

Sturbridge frowned and, taking him by one arm, steered him away from the open doorway and the scrutiny of those within. "If such a thing were true," Sturbridge replied in a whisper, "which is something I can hardly credit, I couldn't think who these mysterious accusers might be. Are there among the novices any who have cause to resent my tenure here?"

Jervais' eyes widened. "Surely not, Regentia."

"Then the matter is settled," she said.

Jervais looked around nervously. His voice still did not rise above an anxious whisper. "Of course. Surely you are correct, there is nothing to fear. After all, what charges could they possibly bring against you? Surely you are above reproach here, within your own house. Surely *someone* must be above suspicion."

She could hear the urgent plea within his voice, but she had no comfort to give him. He was afraid. Whether over some infraction real or imagined, he saw the arrival of the Astors as a direct threat to his position here. She knew that tremor in his voice. It spoke of desperation, of a person willing to go to great lengths to deflect scrutiny from his own affairs.

"It will be all right," she pronounced each word separately and distinctly. "No one, not even these Astors, is going to barge in here and harm those under my care. No one. Do you understand?" Her voice was defiant, but in her own ears the words rang thin and tinny. The evidence of these past few months—the sheer body count—suggested otherwise.

"Ahem, Regent Sturbridge?" The face that peered around the doorway was framed in sparse white hair that hung down perpendicularly. The skeletal lines were clearly visible in the hand that reached up to straighten the brass-rimmed spectacles. "Ah, good, I thought it was you. We are ready for you now."

"Thank you, Mr. Himes. I was on my way to join you. I shall be in directly."

Himes seemed about to say something further, but thought better of it. "Excellent. And if you would be so kind as to draw the doors to as you come?" He did not wait for an answer. His head vanished again behind the imposing oaken portals as suddenly as it had come.

"What a peculiar little man," Jervais mused aloud.

"And Mr. Jervais," called a retreating voice from inside, "you may return to the novice domicilium to await our summons."

Jervais blanched. "What a peculiar little man I must seem to these great personages from the Fatherhouse," he recovered awkwardly, his voice pitched loud enough to carry. "Really, this whole inspection has me quite flustered." Sturbridge shook her head and laid a hand upon his shoulder. "Get some rest, Jervais."

He resumed his urgent whisper. "This is no time for complacency, Regentia. If you are accused of some crime…"

"If someone has presumed to bring formal charge against me, Jervais," Sturbridge said, "I have not yet heard of it. Although I am not oblivious to the rustling of the novices' robes and the whisperings in the corridors. Whisperings of murders, of negligence, of the corruption of novices…"

If Jervais caught the slightly mocking smile, he did not heed it. "Who dares say such things against you? I will see that he has cause to regret his slanders."

"That is quite touching, Jervais. Really. But I will not be requiring a champion tonight. I think I just might manage to get through this initial introduction on my own."

"But, Regentia—"

"No, I won't hear of it. Nor will I listen to you—or anyone else, for that matter—maligning my accusers, real or imagined. These charges we are discussing, they are not frivolous. Whoever had the resolve to bring such accusations must be a man of great character. It requires not only a certain boldness to speak out against one's superiors, but an enviable insight as well. Insight into how novices are properly reared, for example, and how they might be corrupted. And that is to say nothing of the skill it would have taken to ferret out the identities of those corrupters. Yes, my accuser in this matter must be perceptive indeed to have apprehended all these things with so little to go on. I trust the Astors will reward him as he deserves."

Jervais blanched and then tried to laugh off her words and cover his discomfort with a cavalier smile. "Now you are having a jest at my expense," he said. "You surely do not expect me to believe that you approve of these proceedings?"

"But I do," Sturbridge insisted. "Our unknown claimant certainly knows how to make a proper start. He begins with the cultivation of our novices. A good husbandman takes care of the newest shoots first and clears away all that might threaten them. He knows while his present fortunes depend on his fully grown plants, his future will depend upon the youth. But I suspect his plan is even more far-reaching. He will soon, no doubt, turn his gentle ministrations to the elder branches as well. If he continues at this rate, he will be remembered as a great benefactor of our order."

Jervais frowned. "I suspect rather the opposite to be the case. By attacking you, these conspirators are not protecting our neophytes, but merely clawing at the foundation of this house. Trying to drag the whole edifice down around them. In what way do they say that you have corrupted our novices?"

"So, now they are conspirators, instead of a lone accuser?" Sturbridge asked shrewdly. "No matter. The accusations have merit and so it speaks well of our house that more than one of our brethren should have stepped forward."

"Nonsense! These libelers accuse you of negligence and corruption only because they know such charges will fall upon sympathetic ears. I know these 'guests' of ours—or know their type at least. They go about prying into everyone's private affairs until they have found what they are truly after—a scapegoat. Someone they might flay, to offer up his bloody skin before our superiors in Vienna. I have heard the tales. But I will not stand by and watch them mark you for the sacrifice. Let me go with you, Regentia. To stand beside you. They won't dare to—"

"They will do what they must, Jervais. And they certainly will not scruple at cutting their way through you to get to what they want. No, it would be very foolish indeed to cross them, even for my sake. Rather, I would advise silence and patience. And rest."

"No doubt you are right, Regentia." Jervais brooded. "Perhaps I am making too much of this and the whole affair will end in nothing. I cannot bring myself to believe that they could make any charges stick to you. No, I believe each of us will win our cause."

Sturbridge regarded him curiously. "Then you have some dispute as well? I was not aware that you had also been called before the Astors. Ah, but of course, why else then would you be loitering about here. Tell me, Jervais, are you the accuser or the defendant in this matter?"

Jervais would not meet her eye. "I am presenting evidence, Regentia."

"And who is it that you are bringing accusations against?" Sturbridge asked.

"You will think me mad when I tell you, Regentia. It is my own brother, my friend and mentor, the Adeptus Johanus."

"Adeptus Johanus? What possible fault could you find against him? I myself have not even seen him in weeks."

"I left him only a short while ago, Regentia. The charge is one which weighs heavily upon me. I can hardly bring myself to speak it. It is nothing less than conspiring with the enemies of this house," Jervais said.

"That is a very serious charge indeed." Sturbridge considered. "And not an easy one to bring. I take it that you must have some damning proof to bring such an allegation."

"I have." Jervais fidgeted with the cuff of his sleeve. From its recess, he withdrew an ivory envelope, just enough so that Sturbridge could see Johanus' writing upon its face. "It is not a duty which I undertake lightly. Far better for all of us that such charges were to fall upon me rather than upon the good adept. Do you know that he was Master of Novices when I first came to this house? He took me in, looked after me. He may have been the first friend I had here."

"Then it cannot have been an easy decision for you," Sturbridge prompted.

"It is an agony to speak against my brother. But it is a far worse torment to remain silent. By knowingly associating with a traitor, I would become party to his crime."

"I envy you, Jervais, that you should have such certainty, such insight into the nature of loyalty and treason. I imagine many here would be alarmed to learn that you were bringing this charge."

"Some of the other novices will not understand," he agreed. "They will be angry with me. Some will even take their own petty vengeances against me. I can hear them now. First, they will try to tell me that the adept is obviously innocent of any wrongdoing and that I must be mistaken. Then, when the irrefutable evidence is before them, then they will still say that I was in the wrong. That I should have simply pretended not to have known. They may even insist that it was a disloyalty on my part to bring charges against a superior. But surely, Regentia, that is not right. You, of all people, will appreciate the difficulty of this thing I do."

"Your knowledge of loyalty must be very extensive that you are not afraid that their opinion, and the case itself, will turn against you."

"Regentia, you know me. You have known me for many years now. You know I am nothing if not a devoted son of this house. What little reputation I have won for myself here," Jervais fidgeted with the insignia at his cuffs, "it has all been built upon this foundation. What would I have accomplished here—even if I should unlock secrets of the blood magics thought lost for centuries—if I fail in putting my duty to this house and to the Pyramid first? What credit could possibly adhere to such a hollow victory?"

Sturbridge could only shake her head in admiration—for his vehement rhetoric if not for the caliber of his professed loyalty. "You are a rarity, Jervais. Your knowledge of loyalty is such that I think that I should become your pupil. Then, whatever charges these Astors might bring against me, I would cut the ground from beneath them before they could even muster their arguments. I would merely say to them that, as they must surely acknowledge that you are the most loyal son of this house, if they approve of you, then they must approve of me as well and dismiss any wild charges that have been brought against me. But if, on the other hand, they will find fault with my devotion, then they should begin by indicting you who are my teacher—and who will be the ruin, not merely of the young, but of even the old and weary. That is to say, of myself whom you instruct, and of your brother whom you yourself so wisely chastise."

Jervais did not look pleased. "If you will not allow me to speak in your defense, Regentia, I must beg that you at least keep my name out of this matter. I would not like to think of these bloodhounds sniffing too closely around my—or anyone's—loyalty."

"Then, since you have sworn yourself so eager to come to my aid, I hope that you will at least instruct me in the nature of loyalty so that I might make my own defense."

He was aware that he was being baited, but still felt that he must justify his actions. The regent was the hard sell. If he could convince her that his cause was just, then the other novices could hardly hold personal grudges against him for his part in the matter.

"I really don't know what to tell you," he began. "Loyalty, in this case, is merely doing as I am doing—prosecuting the guilty whether he be your brother, your father, your mother. It makes no difference. In fact, I would go so far as to say that to know and not to act would, in itself, be disloyal."

"And this would apply even to the indiscretions of, say, your regent, I should imagine?"

Jervais shifted uncomfortably. "That is not what I meant at all, Regentia. It would be an act of base infamy to bring charges against you, because such accusations have no basis in truth, but only in envy. Here, I will give you a better example of what I am talking about, so that there can be no confusion on this point. The disloyal, whatever his station and no matter how dearly loved, must not go unpunished. Do not the annals of our House tell of how Etrius, the leader of the Council of Seven, brought accusations of treason against his brother Goratrix? And Etrius, if I may say so, is universally regarded as the very paragon of loyalty."

"So he is," Sturbridge admitted.

"And we acknowledge," Jervais pressed, "that he had his own brother expelled from our noble order. And yet when I proceed against my brother, the novices are sure to cry out against me. I will be the first to admit it—as a group, Regentia, we are often fickle and sometimes cruel. And too often our beliefs, even about such fundamental matters as loyalty, remain unexamined and hypocritical."

"A rousing speech," Sturbridge said. "I think you have little to fear from our inquisitors. Your tongue will carry you through all adversity. Unfortunately, my own case now seems more dire than ever. By your words, it seems that either you or the remainder of my novices have fallen into base disloyalty. How can I hope to guard against charges of corruption? I only wish that I had your certainty, to steer the perilous course between these twin perils. Tell me, Jervais, do you really think that these stories—of Etrius and of Goratrix—are true? That our Father's two greatest disciples fought, quarreled, battled and maneuvered against one another, as we are told?"

"I do, Regentia. And there is more I might tell you, if you would like to hear it. I have devoted a good deal of my time to researching what can be known of the problem of Goratrix the Deceiver. I have written upon the topic at some length and my humble monographs on the subject have attracted some slight notice."

"Yes, you must tell me. But perhaps when we have a bit more leisure. Just now, I would prefer to hear from you a more precise answer, which you have not yet given me, to the question of what loyalty is. When I asked you before, you only replied that loyalty was doing as you did, bringing charges of treason against your brother."

"And that is precisely true, Regentia."

"I do not doubt it. You are quite convincing on that count. But surely there is more to loyalty then just exposing the disloyal?"

"Well of course there is, but—"

"I did not ask you for two or three examples of loyalty, but rather to explain to me the general idea which makes all loyal acts to be loyal. That is the knowledge that can save or damn me. Would you say that there is one unifying idea that makes the loyal loyal and the disloyal disloyal? Some criteria I might bring to bear as a measuring stick, for both your actions and my own? If I knew this, I would have some hope of defending myself from these baseless charges."

"All right, then," Jervais rubbed at his chin and began to pace the width of the hall. "Loyalty is doing what is in the best interests of one's superiors and one's house. And disloyalty is the opposite, knowingly doing what is contrary to those interests."

"Well, that's a beginning," Sturbridge said. "That's at least the sort of answer I wanted. But I still cannot tell whether what you say is true or not. Although I imagine you will now go on to demonstrate the truth of your words."

"I will try. What fault do you find with this definition?" he asked.

"Only that we have already admitted that there are often contentions—

some of the most violent nature—between one's superiors. The example you had used was Etrius and Goratrix."

"Certainly, but..."

"Which actions then would be loyal? Those which promoted the interests of Etrius or those which promoted the interests of Goratrix?"

"Well, of Etrius, obviously!"

"Why obviously? At the time of that conflict, there must have been many who sided with Etrius, believing his to be the loyal course; while others rallied to Goratrix, believing his cause to be just. But by your definition, both camps would have acted loyally. Or neither, it's still hard to say."

"But Goratrix betrayed his House! He and his followers were no more loyal than…"

Sturbridge made calming motions. "No doubt, Goratrix is remembered—and justly so—as the most famous traitor in our long and bloody history. But at the time of his betrayal, choices had to be made. How could a novice of that time choose to be loyal to his superiors when his superiors themselves were divided? And there will always be such examples. The same things can be both in the interest of some of your superiors and against the interests of others. Let us look to your own case. Johanus is your superior. Is bringing a case against him promoting his best interests? I doubt he would see it that way. How can such an act be one of loyalty—much less, as you seem to be claiming, *exemplary* loyalty?"

"Ah, but Johanus is not the ultimate authority here. Where his interests are in conflict with the interests of this House or say, your person, my duty is clear. There is a structure to these things, a clearly defined structure. A hierarchy. Surely this is no great mystery. What are we if not creatures of the Pyramid?"

"Perhaps so, perhaps not. But if such is the case, then I must say that you have still not answered the question I put to you. Because I did not ask you to tell me what action is both loyal and disloyal, promoting some superior's interest but denying another's. In chastising your brother, you may find yourself doing what is agreeable to Etrius but disagreeable to Meerlinda.

Or in my best interest but not in Johanus'. And there may well be others among your superiors who have similar differences of opinion."

"But no matter what one's personal view," he objected, "all would set aside their difference and agree to the propriety of punishing a traitor. There can certainly be no difference of opinion on that score."

Sturbridge raised an eyebrow. "And have you never heard anyone arguing that a wrongdoer ought to be let off? I would say that these are precisely the questions which they are always arguing, especially in tribunals and courts of law. No one argues that an evil-doer should not be punished, but they argue endlessly about who the evil-doer is, and what he did and when. Is it not the same with affairs of loyalty?"

"Yes, certainly, but…"

"Then tell me, Jervais, for my instruction, what proof you have that—in the opinion of all of your superiors—a novice should bring charges against his brother and mentor. How could you demonstrate that the entire Pyramid backed such a claim? If you can only show me that, you will have saved me from many anxious hours while I await the findings of the Astors."

"It would be a difficult task," Jervais huffed. "But it could be done. I could make the matter very clear to you indeed, if only…" he broke off.

"I understand," she soothed. "You mean to say that I am not as quick as the judges—because to them your case will be self-evident and you will easily prove that your own part in this is just and in the best interests of the entire Pyramid."

"That is my hope, Regentia," His tone was stiff, formal, almost hurt. "If only they will listen to me."

Sturbridge gave him a long, appraising look. "I will not find fault with your argument, Jervais. Perhaps we will have the opportunity to speak of this charge at greater length later. I sincerely hope that we will. But if I am any judge of these things, the Astors will have no time to hear the details your charge tonight. The best thing you could do at this point is to return to your quarters and rest."

"Perhaps you are right," he replied. As he abandoned his effort at oratory, he seemed to deflate. "But, in this case, it seems that the best is not to be. I have other urgent errands to complete tonight. A sister of mine has asked me to look in on another of our guests. She seemed quite distraught. I could hardly refuse her."

Sturbridge's mind went immediately to Antigone, then immediately dismissed the thought. Antigone was gone now, beyond reach. Still, the novice had been responsible for that young man who claimed sanctuary at the chantry. Mr. Felton was suspected, and highly sought after, for his role in the bombing of the Empire State Building. Sturbridge realized that it would not at all do for the Astors to discover this fact. She needed to get him out of harm's way.

"Jervais, I wondered if you might do me a service as well. There is a certain guest of the house, a Mr. Felton." Jervais' head jerked up sharply, as if struck. Sturbridge ignored his reaction and pressed on. "I believe he is housed among the oblates. Please escort him down to the library. Talbott will take charge of him from there and see that he is returned to his cell by morning."

Jervais smiled a forced smile. "Of course, Regentia. Anything I can do to help you through this difficult ordeal. I am sorry to have taken up so much of your time with my own trivial worries, especially when you find yourself besieged by a thousand ships. I only wanted you to know—"

"You only wanted me to know," Sturbridge interrupted, flashing a predatory grin, "that it was not you who had betrayed my confidence to the Astors. No, please do not protest.

You played your part admirably and I think we understand each other.

"I can see no point to your flimsy pretense of bringing suit against Johanus—except, of course, to demonstrate that you clearly had not yet had the opportunity to think through such a charge—much less to formally place it before the Astors. And if you could not have accused Johanus, you could not have accused me, yes? Our discussion of your purely hypothetical case, however, did allow you to discuss certain details of the charges that await me without your actually admitting to knowing of their existence.

"And finally, you had one last gift for me. A name. You wanted me to know that you were well aware of who had spoken out against me. And you wanted to share that knowledge without having to speak that name yourself. It was very cunningly done, your drawing me into debating you in the ancient Greek dialectic form. Is that what put you in mind of the Trojan horse, or had you scripted out this entire confrontation in advance? You wanted me to understand that my role in this matter was not that of the conquering Greeks, but rather of their enemies, the Trojans. What was the phrase you used? 'Besieged by a thousand ships.' Oh yes, your ploy succeeded. I was incautious enough to take the bait, to take your double-edged gift to heart. I knowingly wheeled your Trojan horse into the city—already aware of the surprise I will find concealed there—the identity of the one who betrayed me to the Astors. A woman whose face launched a thousand ships against me. *Helena*."

Jervais smiled broadly and shook his head. "You have quite lost me in your labyrinthine chain of deductions, Regentia. But if my words have been of some comfort to you, that is all the reward I ask." With that, Jervais bowed low in formal leave-taking and retreated the length of the Hall of Daggers and Mirrors, humming contentedly to himself.

Chapter 15
As if She Were Once Beautiful

Sturbridge glided into the Hall of Audiences, drawing the imposing portal closed behind her. Summoning her resolve, she straightened to her full height and, with a swirl of her long black robes, turned to face her inquisitors.

Her footfalls made no sound on the veined marble floor. Despite its imposing name, the Hall of Audiences was more a formal sitting room than a throne room. Most of the floor was covered with a rich, hand-woven rug rendered in the indigos and argents of the night sky. It depicted the Yggdrasil, the vast world-tree whose roots brooded in the nether regions and whose exultant branches pierced the very heavens. The earth was nothing more than a luscious fruit dangling from its boughs.

The piece was one of the great treasures of the Chantry of Five Boroughs. Delicate figures peeked from behind each leaf of the great oak, locked in the intricate Dance of Days. Sturbridge could pick out the individual tools of the craftsmen—miniature hammers and awls and lathes—as they bent over their work in single-minded concentration, working directly upon the living heartwood. She saw the toys of children, chasing a ball through the tangled greenery, playing at draughts, knocking down lines of soldiers and snatching at those that tumbled from the bower out into the abyss.

The room's furnishings were ponderous, their tones, formal and languid. They clustered together in conspiratorial knots. Deep greens and cinnamons covered armchairs clearly designed to dwarf, if not utterly swallow, their occupants. A fieldstone fireplace covered most of one wall. Absently, Sturbridge noted that a low onyx end table was missing from the arrangement. And that there were the unmistakable signs of bloodstains on the priceless carpet.

At the head of the chamber seven marble steps formed a low dais. Their edges were squared, giving the feel of a ziggurat that had been pressed nearly flat. The raised platform was traditionally kept empty and unadorned, save for the regent's own seal which had been subtly and cunningly wrought into the very veins of the marble. White on white, the pattern was indistinguishable from any vantage, save that of kneeling upon the uppermost step. The sigil was that of a flaming sword quenched in a cairn of stones.

There was no sign of throne or imposing high-seat upon the dais—Sturbridge shunned such ostentatious displays of power. But tonight, the dais boasted a long, folding table, cluttered with papers. Three identical hinged metal chairs lined its far side, facing the doorway. The gleam off the institutional metal finish struck a harsh contrast to the sumptuous furnishings that dominated the lower portion of the hall.

Sturbridge immediately picked out the now-familiar form of Himes, seated at the table, on the far right. He hunched forward over an open dossier, his eyes less than a foot distant from the page. He looked up at the sound of the doors booming closed.

"Ah, Regent Sturbridge, here you are at last. We have been waiting some time, but this has given me the opportunity to review certain, erhm, perplexing details of this case…"

Sturbridge barely noted his words. Her attention was fixed on the figure angrily pacing back and forth behind the long table.

"You know my associate, Mr. Stephens?" Himes offered by way of introduction, but no one seemed to pay him any mind.

Stephens was already around the table and plunging down the marble steps towards Sturbridge. There was fire in his eyes and the promise of lightning seemed to arc between his clenching fingertips. An inarticulate, animal sound tore its way up from his throat.

No, Sturbridge thought. *This is wrong. He cannot be here. He cannot be free.*

But it was difficult to doubt the evidence bearing down upon her. The scenario she had carefully constructed for this meeting rapidly unraveled. With Stephens trapped by Antigone's *verboten* diagramma, Himes should have found himself desperately in need of Sturbridge's help in order to pinpoint his partner's location, since at that point, he could quite literally be anywhere, or even nowhere, and free him. This should have given Sturbridge a position of power from which to bargain.

Now even that prop was cut out from beneath her. In their eyes she was, once again, simply a dangerous liability—a regent who could not prevent a string of grisly murders within her own house.

These were the thoughts that raced through her mind during the moments it took Stephens to close the distance between them. She made no move to defend herself or to summon up any mystical defenses. She held her ground and then deliberately turned her attention away from him, as if he were of no account whatsoever.

She addressed Himes, her voice cool and aloof. "Your associate is clearly unwell. He has been mastered by his hungers."

Her words brought Stephens up short. Sturbridge pressed on quickly. Whatever their authority here, she could not imagine that it could be stretched to cover up physically assaulting her within her own house. "It is quite understandable. He has been through a trying ordeal. I see that I should not have left you gentlemen so long unattended. But one of the novices would have been only too glad to show you to the refectory. There is no need for any to go hungry here. You are not under some restriction—a fasting, or perhaps there is some judgment upon you?"

Stephens fumed, brandishing one sizzling fist before him. It was clear he was struggling for control. But he held the blow, instead lashing out verbally. "Judgment? You have the gall to speak to us of judgment? You have killed the legate sent from the Fatherhouse! You have assaulted me personally—by means of a dark thaumaturgic rite! You have—"

"Enough."

This third voice brought Sturbridge around sharply. It was not unfamiliar to her, but it was certainly not one she had expected to hear now, within her own hall. In fact, she had more than half-convinced herself that she would never hear that particular voice again. It was enough to shake her hastily constructed composure.

At her back, Stephens' whispered threat felt like the touch of a knife. "You will burn for this, you know," he said. "Oh, make no mistake, you will burn."

Sturbridge did her best to ignore him, fixing her attention instead upon the figure that detached itself from the fieldstone fireplace. He stood at ease, leaning with one forearm against the smooth stones in an attitude of thoughtful repose. In anyone else, the attitude would have looked posed. On him, however, it managed to look as if he were somehow vital to the scene. As if, were he to step away, the entire wall of stones would come crashing down. Although Sturbridge had welcomed guests here on dozens of occasions, she suddenly had difficulty in picturing the hall without him in it. He had somehow become integral.

She had the sudden impression that there should have been a picture of his grandfather hanging above the mantel.

He was not a daunting man. He was tall, distinguished, his hair dark and graying about the temples. His suit was expensive but a bit rumpled, as if he hadn't found a chance to change after his long trip and hadn't really been too concerned about it either. He radiated the impression of a person who was very comfortable with who he was and where he was.

Even as preoccupied as Sturbridge had been upon entering, she could not imagine how she had failed to notice him. "Your Excellency. This is an unexpected…"

He pushed himself up straight and waved aside her preamble. She was half relieved to see that the fireplace did not, in fact, tumble down around him.

"We'll waive the formalities for the moment, Aisling. This isn't part of the official inquiry. Himes, put that pencil down and Stephens…" He cast about for useful distraction. "See if you can't find somewhere to jack in that laptop and get us a head start on your breakdown of the chantry's financials."

Stephens grumbled but complied without so much as a further glance at Sturbridge. Soon she could hear the staccato tapping of the keyboard. Although Sturbridge wasn't at all certain she liked the sound of the phrase, "the breakdown of the chantry's financials." Sturbridge returned her attention to Dorfman.

"Your Excellency, I—" she began.

"I'm serious, Aisling. No formalities. The gloves are off. I need to know what the hell is going on around here and I don't want to have to go through some elaborate dance to find out. Just straight talk, understand?"

"I understand, sir. But I really — "

"Peter," he insisted.

"All right. Peter." She cringed at the familiarity, but pressed on. "It's just that I really didn't expect to see you here. They said you were...on sabbatical. In Vienna."

"Recalled to Vienna, you mean? You say what you mean and I'll return the favor. You thought I had been dragged before the Council in chains."

"No! Nothing of the sort. I only meant — "

"Damn it, Aisling! Are you going to play straight with me or not? I'm not going to pussyfoot around here. There are folks, very important folks, who are throwing around words like 'murder,' 'negligence,' and 'recall to Vienna.' And I don't like it. I also don't like being dragged away from a very delicate new assignment to find out what the hell is going on back at Five Boroughs. It's not a particularly good idea for me to be in the country at all right now. But I'm here and I'm damned well not going back until I can look Meerlinda in the eye and tell her that the situation is taken care of. Finished. Never happen again. Am I making myself clear?"

"Very clear, Your Emin...Peter." She finished awkwardly.

"Good. So you thought they had hauled me up on charges and that was the last you would see of me, is that it?"

"Come with me to my sanctum," she replied. "We can talk more openly there."

"Forget it. Whatever you've got to say to me, you can say in front of my team. I don't know what the hell passed between you and Stephens — "

"Damn it, it's not about Stephens!"

"All right," he said cautiously. "How about you tell me what it *is* about?"

"You hung me out to dry in Baltimore," she retorted, the old bitterness welling to the surface. "You ordered me to attend that farce of a Camarilla war council and then you never even bothered to show up. I didn't have a leg to stand on. Vitel chewed me up and spat me out. Do you know what he said?!"

Dorfman was quiet for a long while, which only fueled her anger. "Well, do you?!"

"My bet is that he said I sold out Washington, DC, to the Sabbat. To settle a personal score with him. Bastard. Never did like him."

"So this comes as no surprise to you? Did you think that they would listen to anything I had to say once Vitel dropped that little bomb? No. But you didn't really care, did you? You were already halfway around the world on your new assignment."

"Look, I'm sorry you had to go through that, Aisling. But you're right. I knew I couldn't be there and I had to send someone who wouldn't get flustered and blow the whole deal once Vitel turned up the pressure. And it doesn't matter now. Vitel's dead and you're—"

"Vitel's dead?! You killed him? Just like that? Geez, you guys are unbelievable! Somebody bad-mouths you a little bit and you just up and—"

"You misunderstand," Dorfman corrected. "Vitel was slain by Archon Bell. He was proven to be a traitor to the Camarilla and a Sabbat spy."

"He was the Prince of Washington, DC! He…" she broke off uncertainly, her mind racing through the webs of deception and inference that spun out from that one disturbing premise.

"And now, he is dead," Dorfman said pointedly.

"So you didn't have any role in the fall of DC to the Sabbat?"

"I was already out of the country," he said and then turned the conversation to another topic. "I don't put a lot of stock in rumors. You would not, for example, believe a fraction of the things I've been hearing about you." He studied her face intently. What he found there brought him up short. "Or then again, maybe you would. Aisling, are you all right? If you're in some sort of trouble, I can help. You know I will, whatever it takes. But I need to understand what's going on around here. And I need to know now."

"You won't believe me."

"Try me."

"Do you ever have...nightmares?" she asked.

Dorfman laughed aloud. "Nightmares? Why? What's that got to do with..."

He stopped laughing.

"The Children," he said slowly, with growing certainty.

The room had become quiet and even the now-roaring fire did little to hold back the sudden chill in the air. Sturbridge saw that both Stephens and Himes had stopped what they were doing and turned towards her apprehensively.

Sturbridge's eyes refused to focus. She gazed fixedly at some imaginary object in the middle distance. Her voice, when she spoke, was hollow and emotionless. "Who was Nina?" Sturbridge asked.

Stephens and Himes seemed puzzled by this non sequitur, but Dorfman's head snapped back as if he had been struck. Indignant, he spoke before he could stop himself. "You've got no business..."

He instantly regretted these words, but he could not very well unsay them. His outburst seemed to bring Sturbridge back to herself.

"She was very beautiful. You must have loved her dearly."

Dorfman snorted, choking off a retort. He turned his back on her. "I don't have time for this bullshit. Stephens, Himes, you guys look in on the interrogation of the novices in the Grand Foyer. We're going to need at least eight or so strong candidates for relocation. And if you come across any likely 451s, I need to see them before I turn in. And Stephens, you stop off at the refectory. You look like hell."

As Stephens put up a half-hearted objection, Himes sighed and patiently restacked his daunting pile of scattered manila folders. He scooped up the top dozen or so as he joined his partner en route to the door. It was really only the topmost dossier that concerned him, but there was no sense in drawing attention to that particular one if Dorfman should think to peruse the files in Himes' absence. Not that that was likely. But Himes had not gotten where he was by being careless.

The file belonged to one of the latest victims of the mayhem that plagued this godforsaken chantry-tomb. The name typed on the tab of that folder was Francesca Lyon and Himes found the contents of that dossier rather suspicious. The subtext of the briefing spoke of disturbing entanglements between the victim and both Regent Sturbridge and Dorfman himself. Very curious indeed.

Only reluctantly did he withdraw. The interaction between Sturbridge and Dorfman merited further scrutiny. Himes had a healthy distrust of games where he could not see where all the cards were.

No sooner had the door clicked closed behind the two inquisitors than Dorfman wheeled upon Sturbridge.

"Look, Aisling, I don't know what you were trying to pull just now, but let's get one thing clear: I don't like it. Things are going to be difficult enough for you as they now stand. I'm trying to help you, damn it. And you pull this kind of shit with me?"

But Sturbridge would not leave off. Without ever raising her eyes, she said, "She still misses you terribly."

Dorfman snorted and threw up his hands in disgust. "Jeezus, I don't know why I bother going out on a limb for you! I didn't have to be here, you know. I could have just let Himes and Stephens carry out this operation. But I thought, no, there's just no way Sturbridge would have let things get as fucked up as what I'm hearing. There's got to be some good explanation— she's hurt or...hell, I even thought you might be dead for a while there. So I take this one myself, drop everything, take the first flight out of Vienna. And this is what I find. The sharpest young regent I've seen in a dozen generations mumbling some half-baked fortune BS. So how about we cut the crap and you just tell me what the hell is going on around here, okay?"

"It's not BS, Peter. She is here now. Inside me. I can't explain it; it was something that was done to me. I'm the victim here." Sturbridge laughed nervously. "Hell, I guess we're all victims here. They're within me, all of them. All of our casual brutalities, our humiliating failures, or slumbering reproaches. And she's there too, Nina. I don't want to hurt you, Peter. But I need for you to believe me. Even Helena thinks I've lost it."

"We've got her statement," Dorfman muttered. "Helena's been signing her own death warrant, trying to protect you. You know what she's been doing? She's been—"

"Falsifying the reports to Vienna," Sturbridge finished for him. "She's a good second-in-command. She'll make a damned good regent one day. Don't screw things up for her."

"What am I supposed to do, Aisling? I've got to get to the bottom of whatever the hell is wrong around here and right now, you seem to be the prime suspect. And all you can give me is some mumbo-jumbo about nightmares and victims and reproaches. Well, guess what, somebody's going to come in for a big old funeral pyre of reproaches over this. And it's not going to be me."

"So do it. Go ahead and burn me at the stake if that's what you want. No more uncomfortable disturbances from the

Chantry of Five Boroughs. You go home a hero. Everybody's happy. You just leave my girls alone."

"Well, that's Plan B," Dorfman said, his voice icy. "I'm trying to cobble together a decent Plan A on short notice and, to be really frank, you're not helping. Damn, but you are infuriating. It's a wonder you've managed to live out a decade with your uncanny talent for failing to see who's actually on your side. I'm trying to give you an even break here, so how about you throw me a bone?"

Sturbridge was silent for a long while. When at last she spoke, her voice had an eerie, distant tone to it.

"There is a young woman crying," Sturbridge continued as if she had not heard him. "Her eyes are almond, peerless almonds. Her skin... I can no longer tell the complexion of her skin. She has been too long beneath the waters. But she must have been beautiful. She carries herself as if she were once beautiful."

"Shut up!" Dorfman yelled, his face mere inches from her own. "I don't know what you are playing at, but if you thought for one minute that you could use the name of my...that you could hold this over me—that you could threaten me!—you were sorely mistaken. And you will pay for your presumption."

Sturbridge droned on as if she did not hear him, as if she could not actually feel the heat of his breath against her face. "In her hand she is clutching a scarf. It may have been silk. And red! As red as tears. There is a knot at its center. And something bright. Something gleaming, knotted in the silk..."

Dorfman took her by both shoulders and shook her. "Enough!" His nails bore down cruelly into the hollow between the bones.

"It's a ring!" Sturbridge whispered in surprise and wonder. "But why does she press me so intently? She forces the scarf into my hand. She closes my fingers around it and turns away."

"No. Nina, please. Come back!" Dorfman felt a chill of horror at hearing his own words of years gone by parroted back to him in Sturbridge's voice. They were uttered with precisely the same inflection, the same desperation.

"She is running, now," Sturbridge continued. "Sobbing. There is another flash of metal." Her voice pitched louder as if her words were fighting their way across a vast chasm of years and distance.

There was a resounding crack. Dorfman stared stupidly at the back of his left hand. There was a spot of blood there, at the knuckle. Just above the band of pale flesh around the base of his ring finger—a mark that not even the passage of decades had managed to erase.

Sturbridge's own hand went to her mouth and came away red. She shuddered as the warm trickle of seeping life brought her back to herself. Absently, a tip of pink tongue peeked out to reclaim the lost vitae.

Dorfman would not look at her. "I'm sorry," he said, choking back a sob. "I am so sorry."

Sturbridge could not say with any certainty that it was she whom he addressed.

Chapter 16
Picking up the Redress

"This is silly," Johanus said, pushing through the crowd. "If you're coming all the way back to the chantry with me, you can just as well go in and get your friend yourself."

"Pardon me," Antigone said as she bumped into a small dark woman who was gesturing energetically. She caught the woman's arm to steady her and gave a brief, reassuring squeeze. Then she broke away to hurry after the retreating adept.

The woman started at the uninvited contact. The look she threw Antigone was one of undisguised hostility and suspicion. She muttered a curse under her breath before turning back to the tight knot of listeners clustered about her. She gathered them in again like a mother hen, with soothing cluckings and flappings. Antigone was preoccupied with trying to stay near enough to the adept to follow what he was saying over the surgings of the crowd. The woman's words did not really sink in until Antigone was almost to the door.

"And you believe them?" the woman had demanded incredulously. "If that is what they told you, then they are worse than liars. All this," she waved her arms broadly, encompassing the entire proceedings, "this cannot keep you safe. Mark my words, before another night has passed, we shall see how this prince and his paperwork keep us safe."

It was not so much the words that brought Antigone up short as the voice. Antigone was good at remembering voices — a legacy of her service with the Army Signal Corps during the war, which she had parlayed into a job on the telephone exchange after she returned stateside. And this voice was familiar.

"Are you coming?" Johanus called, breaking in upon her musings. He held the fire door open for her. The klaxon alarm that the door threatened to blare out if it were so much as bumped, utterly failed to materialize.

"Thank you," she whispered, sweeping past him. The cool night air had the effect of drawing her even farther out of herself — of snaring the senses and forcing them to focus upon things on a grander scale. It drew the eyes upward to the city's crown of skyscrapers and the smudge of distant stars. It filled the head with the aroma of human prey grazing in the immense concrete pasture — the smells of coffee and alcohol and cigarettes and cologne.

But that voice kept nagging at the back of Antigone's mind as they struck out towards the chantry. She knew that voice, but she couldn't immediately place it. In the back of her mind, she had this image of a bird. Not the fluttering hen that she had first imagined, but a black bird, a crow. The broken body of a crow.

Oh no.

With searing clarity, Antigone realized where she had heard that voice before. At the Conventicle. During the Gathering of Crows.

Again Antigone saw the shadowy figure stride boldly into the center of the circle of conspirators and pick up the Redress — symbolized by the inert bundle of black feathers. The broken body of the crow, its neck neatly wrung.

At the time, Antigone could recall being struck by the woman's voice. It was a rare enough thing for there to be a woman among their number at all. The Conventicle, and the dangerous game of resistance they played, had always struck her as something of an old boys' network. And that had always rankled.

Antigone could vividly recall the woman striding to the center of the ring and, ignoring the commotion, taking up the small, broken bird. She held it high for all to see and the room gradually quieted.

"We don't have to kill him to stop him."

A chill ran up Antigone's spine. The woman had been talking about Johanus. Complaint had been brought against the Tremere for what was seen as his meddling in the formal presentation of the new arrivals to the prince.

What else had she said? Antigone struggled to recall the exact words.

"We can divert the flow of refugees and immigrants. They are already fearful, uncertain, fleeing from the worst excesses of the Sabbat. We can use that, feed their fear and uncertainty. When we're done, they won't dare show themselves, to him or anyone else claiming to be in authority."

Oh God, no. Not here, not tonight, not…

Antigone grabbed Johanus' arm and the words tumbled out of her. She was hardly aware of what she was saying. Before her eyes, she could still see the broken body of the crow dangling, almost forgotten, from the woman's fist.

"Calm down," the adept was saying, trying to extricate his arm from her viselike grip. "Who's going to what?"

"You don't understand. We've got to get them out of there. All of them. She's going to…"

Her answer was engulfed in the roar of erupting flames and cascading glass. The ground leapt beneath them at the force of the explosion. Johanus was yelling something at her, but she couldn't hear anything. He turned and ran back towards the school. She tried to yell after him, to tell him it was already too late, but even her own shouts failed to produce anything but the faintest rumblings in the bones of her skull.

She raised one hand to her ear and it came away wet with blood. *Burst eardrum,* she thought. She should go after him. She knew she should. But she just stood there, unmoving. Staring at the blood on her fingertips.

Chapter 17
A Preposterous Red Scarf

Sturbridge lay in bed, staring blankly at the ceiling, when the knock came at the door of her sanctum.

The sound was soft and hesitant, as if whoever it was were hoping that she were not at home. "Who is it?" she called, irritably.

It was not the person on the far side of the door, but rather the voice of the security-systems daemon that answered her. "Dorfman, Peter. Pontifex."

Sturbridge groaned. One distant mechanical part of her mind noted that they needed to update his profile in the chantry security system. Whatever Dorfman might now be, he was no longer Pontifex of the Washington, DC chantry. Her next thought was how utterly beside the point such concerns as updating the security database had now become.

"Go away," she shouted.

"Opening communications node," the system replied.

"Don't bother," Sturbridge said.

"I beg your pardon?" It was Dorfman's voice being piped through the com port.

"Not you," Sturbridge replied irritably. "Open the door."

"It seems to be locked. May I come in?"

His final words were drowned beneath the hydraulic hiss of the bolts being thrown back as the security daemon processed Sturbridge's command. A moment later, the massive steel portal swung inward.

The steamer trunk still stood open in the center of the room, its contents trailing out across the floor. It appeared he had caught her in the midst of her packing. The once carefully arranged shelves of books looked as if they had been picked over. The remaining volumes leaned dejectedly together for solace. The only sound in the room was the hum of the monitor on the bedside computer desk. Dorfman recognized the form of the official chantry dispatch that was still open on the screen. The subject line read, "Status change—Resignation."

Dorfman stepped across the threshold. Sturbridge lay stretched out on the bed, ignoring him. The bed curtains had been torn down violently. A few scattered rings, boasting scraps of fabric, still dangled from their post.

"I like what you've done with the place," he offered.

Sturbridge did not so much as sit up to welcome him. She remained staring fixedly at the ceiling. "An opinion, it seems, that is not shared by your superiors," she said.

There was an uncomfortable silence. Dorfman hovered just inside the doorway as if he were reluctant to intrude further. Finally he broke the silence. "Look, Aisling, I just want to say that I am…"

"You make a lousy consultant," Sturbridge interrupted him. "Here, let me clue you in to how this is supposed to work. The trick is to find out which people your client most wants terminated and then, after a few weeks of 'investigation', you recommend that things be restructured so that those people become redundant. You have to tell the client what he wants to hear."

"I'll bite," he said. Having committed himself, he advanced more confidently into the room. He righted an overturned chair and dragged it towards the bedside. "What do they want to hear?"

"They want to hear that I am responsible for the deaths of all of those novices and that I should be dragged back before some formal tribunal in Vienna. They want to hear that Helena and Johanus conspired to falsify official chantry documents — to conceal the full extent of what was happening here — and that they should be busted down a rank and transferred off to separate backwater chantries. They want to hear that C5B is no longer a front-line war chantry and that this change calls for the transfer of a proven leader from the outside, probably one drawn from Vienna itself, to cement the ties to the Fatherhouse. How am I doing?"

"I'm not going to lie to you, Aisling. You were already in way over your head when they sent that legate here. At that point, you needed to start scrambling on the damage control. Instead, the ambassador turns up dead. Now, how's that supposed to look? Frankly, at this point, there are those back in Vienna who — perhaps justifiably — are demanding somebody's head on a pike. I'm not sure they much care whose, but yours is pretty high up on the short list of contenders. But I didn't come here to talk about the inquiry—"

"So they send you down here to be the tough guy," Sturbridge said. "To turn everything upside down. To mark the victims. To rough everybody up a little."

Dorfman sank into the chair, seeming to deflate. "Aisling, I am sorry. I should never have hit you. It was inexcusable. It's just, all those things you were saying. About Nina. How could you have… No, you could not have known. You could not have been saying them. I thought that you were hysterical. Or maybe I was. And I had to make it stop. I'm sorry."

Sturbridge sat up and glared at him. He was close enough now that she could have hit him back if she chose. "She was your wife," Sturbridge accused, unable to keep the note of censure from her voice. Again she could see the face of the fiery, dark-maned beauty rising up from the silent waters.

Dorfman hunched forward, elbows on knees, head bent. "Yes." His voice was a rasping whisper. "She was the one great love of my life. Have you ever been in love, Aisling?"

Sturbridge ignored his question. "She tried to give the ring back to you. She came to tell you she was leaving." Sturbridge's hands, seemingly of their own volition, fidgeted with a torn scrap of the bed curtains. They retraced the motions of threading the ring through the red silk scarf and carefully tying it in the middle.

"She was so young. So full of passions and convictions." On his lips, the words sounded like a condemnation. "She said she could not live with…with what I had become. She said it was better that I should have died." Dorfman broke off, mastered by some emotion from across the span of years.

Sturbridge leaned closer. Her gaze was hard and predatory. "She put the scarf into your hand, folded your fingers around it."

"No! I didn't want to take it. Damn it, I didn't want the ring. She could keep the stupid ring. What the hell did the ring matter to me if she was gone? But she didn't hear me. Wouldn't listen. She broke away, sobbing. Nina! I went after her. What else could I do?"

Sturbridge could almost feel the warm rush of tears, the gasping, broken sorrow turning, becoming something more sinister. "And then she turned. Looked back over her shoulder. And for the briefest moment you allowed yourself to hope. In that instant you thought that everything just might be all right again. That she would come back. That you would be given your old life back. And then, seeing you coming after her, she screamed."

"She was afraid for her life. Terrified. Of me! And I knew then that there was no going back. No denying what I had become. No clinging to the comforting trappings of my former life. A month before she had looked at me as if I were the center of her world. Now she looked at me like I was something less than human. A monster, nothing more. Faced with that loathing, I found myself doubting all those other longing gazes—the devotion, the desire. The past years felt like ashes in my mouth. As if I had swallowed a lie. I reached out desperately. For her, for something to cling to. I was a drowning man. I found I was still clutching that preposterous red scarf, clinging to it as if it were the last link to my old life. All I had left now was the scarf and that screaming. That damned screaming. I couldn't make it stop. Why wouldn't it stop?! My fists knotted in the silk. I think my first thought was to rip it in two. As if maybe just the sound of fabric tearing would blot out those mind-rending screams. I pulled it taut. There was something unreal in the very air. As if all this were some nightmare. I felt as if I were moving in slow motion, as if the air were as thick as syrup. As if from over my own shoulder I watched as those hands snaked forward, over her head and then down. They crossed and again pulled taut. The screams fell silent then. It was all over in a moment. I really never even had a chance to steel myself for the task. It was over almost before I realized what had happened."

Sturbridge felt a knot in her throat. She could see the bloated, almond-eyed face floating mere inches from her own. She could see the faded red scarf wrapped tightly around the delicate line of throat. Its frayed ends drifted lazily atop the dark waters. She could see the gleam of light from the band of gold where it gouged deeply, agonizingly, into the soft bluish flesh of her throat.

They were silent a long time, Dorfman's final rationalizations hanging heavily between them.

"She was right to fear you," Sturbridge said at last. "You could not hold her. You could not bring her back. All you could do was prove that she was right to fear you."

Dorfman's head sank within his hands. He spoke through his fingers, his voice muffled. "How can you know these things?"

"Peter, look at me," she said.

When he raised his face it was flushed red. She had a sudden flash of how he must have looked all those years ago, when there was yet life within him.

"I didn't tell you those things to hurt you, Peter. Although you certainly deserve that and worse for what you've done. I'm telling you this so that you will believe me when I tell you certain other things. Some very disturbing things. About the ambassador, and about Eva and about what's been going on here lately. Do you understand?"

He nodded, but seemed distracted.

"Is she—?" he began haltingly. "Is she all right, Aisling? Where she is now, I mean. She's not…"

She had no reassurances to give him. "I don't know Peter. I don't know if any of them are all right. I don't think the Children are like ghosts, if that's what you mean. I can't summon them up and ask them about what things are like for them now, or if there's a life after death, or if they're happy where they are now. It's all kind of hard to explain and I'm still finding my way. I think the Children are more like the dark dream of the Father, the recriminations and reproaches that haunt him when he closes his eyes. I think just as we inherit the dark power of his blood, he becomes party to all the sins of our blood. He becomes responsible for all of our victims. But the nightmares are too much for one man—even one such as he— to contain. They bleed out into the world through his heirs. Through us! Just like thaumaturgy—the power and majesty of the blood—it proceeds from the Father."

"But why would...why would the Father's rest be troubled by my sins? By the things that reproach me in dreams?"

"I don't know," Sturbridge said. "And *that* has been what keeps me sleepless."

Chapter 18
The Daemon of the Well

Antigone tried to block out the screams of the dying. She deliberately turned her back upon them and set her steps back towards the chantry house.

She thought of Marcus, Clarissa and Livonia—the three novices she had condemned to a fiery death in the novice domicilium. At the time she'd given that fateful order, she had not even known the names of the three trapped novices. But Jervais knew. And he had threatened to avenge their deaths upon Felton. And that she could not allow.

Johanus could use every last hand right now—in rescuing as many as he could from the burning wreckage of the high school, and in covering up the full extent of what had been going on there when the police and media arrived. The cost of such disasters was not tallied solely in body count and tens of thousands of dollars worth of damage. It was measured in risk, the threat of a breach of the Masquerade. She did not envy Johanus the task ahead of him. Already she could hear the sirens. The howl of the human scavengers gathering.

But Antigone knew she must get back to the chantry now at all costs. To prevent Jervais from making good on his threat. If left to his own devices, Jervais would ensure that Mr. Felton would be the next victim of this ongoing fiery holocaust.

It was barely an hour before dawn. The campus of Barnard College was silent and deserted as she hurried across the quad towards Millbank Hall and the Exeunt Tertius. She was worried that the Astors might have already gotten to Helena or Sturbridge. If the Astors had managed to lock down the security grid, Antigone's own codes might already have been canceled. Worse, they might have been able to reprogram the clearance hierarchy to recognize Antigone as a renegade and intruder. If so, her attempt to rescue Mr. Felton would be a short-lived one.

Antigone slipped through a side door of the campus administration building and down a long, silent hallway until she came to a door whose frosted glass pane ominously proclaimed *Associate Dean of Interdepartmental Academic Disciplinary Review* in neat black letters. The writing itself looked bureaucratic and daunting. The effect was calculated, no doubt, to turn away the merely curious—an epithet that encompassed the vast majority of those who haunted these modern universities.

Antigone was not put off by the inscription. Her fingers brushed lightly across the raised lettering. Only a very shrewd observer would have seen her fingers gently tapping out the letters of the word 'eidetic' as they glided across the glass. The door swung inward at her touch.

It opened upon a compact office dominated by an imposing desk. Two chairs faced each other confrontationally across the formidable barrier. A bank of filing cabinets rose up behind the nearest chair, looming over it. A plain wooden door on the far wall promised access to a storage closet.

That door was her destination, the Exeunt Tertius—a disused side entrance into the chantry. It had acquired something of a sinister reputation of late—stemming from the fact that one of the senior novices, Aaron, was found murdered just outside it.

Antigone knew that she would be sure to be challenged if she were to come by way of the main entrance. She hoped that this less direct route would let her avoid detection until she was actually within the chantry. Of course, detection within the chantry would be little better.

Beyond this office, she would be within the domain of the chantry security system. This was her last place of refuge before beginning her descent. Taking a deep breath, Antigone placed her hand upon the knob of the closet door. She muttered a few syllables under her breath and slowly turned the knob. Instead of a closet interior, the open doorway revealed plain concrete walls and a narrow metal stairway leading downward. The confined space was cool, damp. Something about the view put Antigone in mind of gazing down a well. She realized she had been holding her breath and forced herself to exhale. No wardings, no klaxons, no sign of arousing the security systems daemon thus far.

She could not have known that she was precisely retracing the route that the assassin had taken just weeks before when he had infiltrated the chantry to kill Johnston Foley—the first in the string of grisly murders that had brought them to the present impasse.

Antigone winced at the sound of each reverberating footfall upon the metal steps. The noise echoed down the central well. She found herself counting off the precise number of steps to each turning (seven); the total number of landings (fifty-two); the number of doors she passed on the downward spiral (four); the number of times she stopped completely to engage the wardings (twelve).

She knew the numerology by heart already, of course. Her mechanical tally merely served to occupy some part of her mind that found number, sequence and closure satisfying. The descent was like turning back pages of a calendar for her. Seven days to a week. Fifty-two weeks to a year. Four seasons and twelve months to mark out the steady passing of time. Walking the endless spiral back to her past.

At each turning, she paused, listening for the distant plish of falling water. She timed the return of the echoes of her footfalls clanging back up to her from the depths. She tried her best to ignore the sound of faint voices rising up to her from the depths of the central well. Antigone was well aware that the voices were merely a trick of the acoustics that rendered the lull of trickling water into pleas and entreaties. Children's voices.

Absorbed in her musings upon lost nightmares, Antigone jumped when confronted by a voice that was not summoned up by her imaginings.

"Antigone, Novicia," purred the security systems daemon. "You are required in the Hall of Audiences. Message completed. Confirmation requested. Sending confirmation...."

"Abort confirmation!" Antigone barked, breaking free of her musings. And none too soon. The last thing she needed now was for the system to go announcing her return in the Hall of Audiences.

There was a pause. "Aborted. Do you wish to send confirmation at a later time or delete confirmation message?"

"Hold confirmation, pending recipient's *next* return to chantry," Antigone ordered. If someone were to check on the status of that summons, it would not do for him to find out that the confirmation had been deleted. That would imply that someone had received that message—that Antigone had been back to the chantry. The next logical course of action would be to find out whether or not she were still within the chantry—within easy reach.

"Acknowledged," the daemon replied sweetly. Its lilting feminine singsong was faintly reminiscent of the south of Ireland. "User Baines, Antigone. Security clearance: expired. Please hold your position and await arrival of security team."

Antigone cursed and slowed her pace. She had been close. She knew she was within four turnings of the base of the well and the portal that would give access to the rest of the chantry. Peering over the railing, she could see the smooth stone floor below. She deliberately counted off the pacings. Four, five, six, seven, turn. One, two, three, four, five...

"Baines, Antigone. Please hold your position and await arrival of security team. This is a second request."

Six, seven, turn. One, two, three, four, five, six...

"Baines, Antigone. Please hold your position and await arrival of security team. This is a third and final request. Further disregard of security instructions will result in immediate reclassification of user as an intruder."

Seven, turn... Something was wrong. That last turning should have brought Antigone to the final flight of steps. She should, even now, be gazing down at the bottom of the staircase and the portal. What she saw before her, however, was only another turning.

She hastily retraced her calculations, hearing once again the internal voice mechanically ticking off each step, each turning. No, she could not have been mistaken. With growing desperation, she glanced over the railing and down. There was the slick stone floor below, just as it had been a few moments before.

Exactly as it had been, she realized. Three turnings still separated her from her objective. She was no nearer to the bottom than when she had first attracted the attention of the daemon.

"User status change: Baines, Antigone. User reclassified as—"

Antigone froze. "Acknowledged," she called. "Awaiting rendezvous with security team."

There was a long pause. "Security team en route," the daemon replied at last. Antigone had the briefest impression that the voice was dripping with self-satisfaction, but she quickly dismissed the thought as both improbable and unworthy of her. Instead she turned her thoughts to more practical matters, like saving her own skin.

"Location of security team," she called.

"Insufficient access," the daemon replied pleasantly. "Estimated waiting time until rendezvous, three minutes."

"Thanks ever so," Antigone said. "Systems status?"

"Insufficient access."

"Suspected systems integrity failure," Antigone countered. "Run diagnostic."

"Insufficient access."

"Access local security daemon, Exeunt Tertius. System reconfiguration code, *Visita Interiora Terrae.*"

There was a shrieking of winds, racing up the central well. The force of it hurled Antigone backward into the outer wall. It held her there, pinned and wriggling. While she struggled to free herself, one cynical part of her mind noted that it seemed that Sturbridge's personal system-reconfiguration codes were still working. That was promising. It meant that there was still hope. The Astors might have gotten to the security hierarchy already—and written Antigone out of the picture—but they had not managed to cut Sturbridge off entirely. Yet.

That information should even be useful, assuming that Antigone could get a word in edgewise with the local security daemon. She struggled fiercely to free herself, or even to move. She managed little more than stretching one foot far enough to again contact the surface of the stairs. The rushing of winds showed no signs of abating or even slowing.

Antigone tried shouting above the maelstrom, but her words were snatched away and shredded instantly. She could not even hear them herself over the tumult. Her head ached and she felt the first hot trickle of blood seeping from her ear. Her eardrum, ruptured in the explosion earlier this evening, bled anew under the pressure of the howling winds.

Then Antigone felt the subtle shift. The winds seemed to press her even more closely, more ravenously. There was no other way to describe it. It was as if she were being held under a magnifying glass. Scrutinized, dissected.

The wind's furor seemed to change emphasis, to recede slightly. She slumped to the stairs in a heap. She was still aware of the fury of the gale spiraling up the central well, but she felt removed from it now, sheltered from the brunt of its rage. Things around her had grown suddenly still.

Antigone was aware of a tentative stirring of air directly before her face. She felt it like the gentle brush of a breeze, faintly stirring the hair at her ear. Then it grew more certain, brushing back the hair like a caress, smoothing it back, exposing the delicate line of jaw and the trickle of blood winding its way down it.

She felt the ethereal fingertips trail across her cheek and pause at her earlobe. She felt the warm drop of blood smear and, as she watched, a faint spiral of wind, tinged red, pulled slowly away from her.

The reddened wisp continued to withdraw, spiraling away from her and out into the maelstrom.

The howling winds took on a different tenor now. A single note, she almost fancied it a word. *"Who?"*

"I am Antigone, sometimes called Jackal. I am no stranger to this chantry. Like you, I have kept careful watch over this house of the undying."

The roaring winds seemed to pulsate. There were words carried in those winds. Words uttered here, long ago. Lost and forgotten. But the wind remembered. The words were all that was left to it now.

Antigone could not so much hear the words spoken aloud as much as they were transmitted to the bones of her ear

directly by the sanguine link she shared with the wind spirit—
the wispy umbilical of her own spilled blood.

"I know you. You have called me. Speak."

The words were a collage of many different voices—some
male, some female, some young, some old—all gathered and
guarded painstakingly throughout the ages of the spirit's
service to this house.

"The other," she began uncertainly, "it would not let me
pass. It tried to keep me here. Against my will. I have appealed
to you, for help."

"If the One says you shall not pass, you shall not pass."

"But you have already accepted the price of my passage, my
blood. These things are beyond either of us. The pact was fixed
at the time of the Binding. Is it not said, *'You will know them by
their blood'?"*

"I know you," the wind chorused.

"If ye had known me," Antigone recited the words of the
ancient pact, *"ye should have known my Father also."*

The wind became still.

*"It is enough. You will not invoke that name here. Go in peace,
Antigone Jackal."*

Antigone picked herself up and smoothed her skirts back
into some semblance of order, mustering what dignity she
could. "Thank you. There is one thing further. The One is
malfunctioning. It needs to go into diagnostic mode..."

*"I do not understand your words. Yours is not my first tongue
and few are my chances to practice it of late."*

"The One is unwell. It needs time to rest and to heal. It must
examine itself. *Visita Interiora Terrae.*"

"Rectificando Invenies Occultum Lapidem," the voices replied,
giving the correct response. *"Visit the center of the earth and by
purifying, you will find the secret stone. It will be done."*

The wind died away suddenly and Antigone stumbled, not having realized until that moment that she had been unconsciously leaning into it for balance. The lights along the stairwell flickered and died. A moment later, the chantry's emergency backup kicked in, bathing the scene in a sickly yellow hue.

"System status?" Antigone called experimentally.

There was no response.

With a smile she again set off down the stairs, descending the last remaining flights to the bottom of the well.

Chapter 19
The Domicilium

"This way, if you please, Mr. Felton. Oh, do not look so surprised. Ms. Baines told me all about you and why you have come to us. She is waiting. It will not do to keep her waiting." Jervais leaned around the door which, until a moment ago, had been securely latched. He peered into the tiny cell.

Felton looked openly skeptical. He stood up from the reading desk and stretched, trying to work the kinks out of his joints. How long had he been crouched over that volume of Aquinas? Hours, certainly. It must be nearing dawn.

He tugged at the ill-fitting oblate's robes. The unbleached wool would not hang right and worse, it itched. "She said to stay put. Here. I intend to do just that."

"The timetable has been stepped up," Jervais said. "Antigone said it must be now if it is to be at all. The regent has instructed that I escort you to the main entrance, where you will be handed over to the prince's men. If you come with me now, I will take you to Antigone instead."

"I'm not buying it."

"Security systems daemon," Jervais called. "Confirm orders for Felton, oblate."

"Felton, oblate, to report to Gatekeeper at chantry main entrance to receive new assignment. Ordered by Sturbridge, Regentia."

"But Antigone promised me…"

"And she is trying to make good on that promise. However, you are not making things any easier. If you hurry, there may still be time."

Felton snatched up a battered manila envelope from the desk and stuffed it into an inside pocket. It contained the evidence that he still hoped would help clear his name. He pulled the robe's cowl down over his face. "All right. Change of plans. Let's go. I didn't catch your name."

"Jervais. This way and stay close to me. Don't say a word until we reach the rendezvous point, you understand?"

Felton nodded and the two slipped from the cell and down the corridor.

The lower halls were deserted. Antigone imagined that there would be a bit more activity centered on the security control room right about now. She hurried on towards the oblate cells.

At one point, she thought she saw the sweep of black robes coming towards her and she hastily pressed back into the shadow of the nearest doorway. A novice hurried past, obviously agitated and heading in the direction of the new domicilium. Antigone had a jolt as she recognized the novice as Clarissa. But that could not be right. Clarissa had been among the three who perished in the fire that destroyed the old novice domicilium.

Antigone berated herself and dismissed the occurrence.

She was just congratulating herself at having made it all the way to the cells without arousing any suspicions, when she saw that the door to Felton's room stood open.

Antigone knew that there was no circumstance in which the door to that cell should have stood open. Most often, Felton stuck to his chamber, giving the regular novices a wide berth.

As a group, they were twice as dangerous as a clutch of serpents and not half as good natured. He was under strict orders to keep that door bolted at all times. Nothing aroused the novices' suspicions quite so much as an unlocked door. It was paramount to throwing down the gauntlet.

With the Astors' arrival, Felton's position had become even more precarious. With strangers abroad in the halls, he would surely be keeping well out of sight, laying low. Unless, of course, he had already been discovered—in which case, he would most likely be under arrest and confined to his cell until the Astors could arrange to hand him over to the prince's men.

No, Antigone could think of only one reason for Felton to be out of his room tonight and it was not a comforting one. Jervais had made good on his threat. He had gotten to Felton first.

A quick peek inside confirmed Antigone's worst fears. Felton was gone, the room deserted. But where would Jervais take Felton to enact his vengeance?

Her feet were already pounding down the corridor to where she knew she would find them, even before her mind had formed the answer to that question.

Jervais sealed the doorway behind him and turned back to Felton. "Here we are. Antigone will join us directly. Make yourself comfortable."

Felton surveyed his surroundings. The room had once been a barracks of some sort. He could still make out the blackened iron bedframes dotting the wreckage. Like the rest of the room, the metal supports bore the telltale signs of some great conflagration that must have raged here. "Comfortable?" Felton laughed, searching his escort's face for some hint of a smile and finding none.

"You must pardon the mess," Jervais said. "You may find this hard to believe but this is actually quite an improvement. You should have seen the place a week ago."

Felton shook his head and began to pace. His trained eye took in the strategic details at a glance. He was not entirely pleased with what he saw. There were no other doors or windows. No way out of here if trouble should arise, except back through Jervais. He stepped carefully over a strange construct of ash and melted plastic puddled on the floor. "What the hell is this place?" he asked.

"This is the old novice domicilium," Jervais replied with evident satisfaction. "I myself resided here when I was first assigned to this house."

Felton shivered involuntarily. There was a note in Jervais' voice that he did not like. He sounded just a bit too pleased with himself, or maybe too pleased with the destruction that had been wrought here.

"Did you…how did this happen? I mean, there was a fire, obviously."

"Tragic, really," Jervais sighed. "Would you believe that three novices lost their lives here? Three. Such needless waste." He walked over to the nearest tangle of wiring peeking from the wall near the doorway. "It will be another week before the damage-control crews even have the electronics back online," he continued matter-of-factly, as if the loss of time were on a par with the loss of life. "Com port's down. And the security-systems link. That means we can speak freely here. Without any fear of being overheard."

"So that's why Antigone picked this place to meet. For the privacy?" Felton caught the glint of metal peeking from under the edge of a slagged mattress. He stooped to extract it from the sticky mess. It might once have been a wedding ring. It was now little more than a streak of gold fused around a charred stump of knucklebone.

Jervais looked up, distracted. "Yes, no doubt Antigone wanted to ensure that we would be undisturbed."

Felton was barely listening to him. He turned the blackened knot of bone over and over in his hand. What a strange memento to find here of all places.

His thoughts went instinctively back to the long nights during the lean years of the Sabbat war. Nights spent laying low in cemeteries, sifting handfuls of grave dirt through an old window screen. Panning for wedding bands and gold fillings.

Even as this memory flashed through his mind, Felton felt the scene around him shift dramatically. In that instant, he had a searing glimpse of what this place really was. This was no military barracks, it was a graveyard. A place where the dead snatched what fitful slumber their conscience allowed them.

"How did they manage to sleep here?" he wondered aloud.

"Do not make the mistake of thinking that the dead rest peacefully here," Jervais said. Felton turned at the strange note in the novice's voice. Jervais' eyes were fixed, not on Felton, but on the rubble in the room's far corner, where the destruction had been most complete.

"You can hear them still, if you listen just right," Jervais continued in his hollow, maddening voice. He cocked his head to one side.

Felton knew something was very wrong here. He slid the charred fingerbone into his pocket and began edging slowly and carefully around towards the doorway.

"How long," he ventured, "did Antigone say she would be?"

Jervais looked up, distracted and annoyed. "What's that? Antigone? Ah, yes. It will not be long now. We will all be together again soon." He eyes lost something of their fanatical look and his voice resumed a normal conversational tone. "Do relax, please, Mr. Felton. Your pacing is starting to put me on edge. Here, you can give me a hand with this. It will help to pass the time."

Jervais bent to the nearest twisted metal strut. It jutted up sharply from a pile of debris. He began working it back and forth to free it.

Felton edged closer.

"If we stack the metal bits here, it will save the cleanup crews some work. And it might keep your mind off less pleasant matters." He succeeded in freeing the strut and used it to clear a roughly circular patch at the room's center. Something about this operation reminded Felton of his own efforts to clear a similar circle atop the observation deck of the Empire State Building earlier this evening. He watched Jervais warily out of the corner of his eye, but did as he suggested.

Felton crossed to the circle and laid a blackened strut deliberately across the center of the space Jervais had cleared. When the novice returned to the growing nest of cast-iron struts, he took the time to reposition Felton's piece—again clearing an open space at the center.

"Sorry," Felton murmured. "I didn't know you were stacking them a particular way. Where do you want this one?"

"Anywhere's fine," Jervais replied vaguely. "Just pile them up here."

Felton let one edge of the frame fall loudly to the floor and regarded Jervais with open skepticism. "All right, I'll bite. What's this all about?"

Jervais took the bar from Felton's hand. The latter did not resist him. The novice nodded his thanks and positioned it with studied nonchalance.

"She's not coming, is she?" Felton asked.

"Who's not... Oh, yes, Antigone. She will be here, Mr. Felton. Have no fear on that account. Would not miss it for the world." He busied himself fussing about his ad hoc protective circle. It was nearly completed.

"Is this another one of those 'apportings'? Is that it? That how you folks plan to get me past the prince's goons at the gate?"

"That will have to do," Jervais said, stepping back to study his efforts. He ignored Felton's question. He found the speculations of the uninitiated were always painfully underinformed. Felton was proving no exception. "I do hope she hurries," Jervais said. "I do not know how long the prince's men will be put off by Talbott's rambling excuses. It might be best if you were to take up a position within the circle, Mr. Felton."

Felton regarded him warily. "Okay, give me the knife." He held out one hand towards Jervais.

The novice rolled his eyes heavenward. He spoke very slowly. "I am not going to cut you, Mr. Felton. I don't know what you have heard about the blood magics, or what you think you know. But your best chance of getting out of here in one piece is to follow my instructions precisely. Do you understand?"

"I'm not afraid," Felton said. "I'm a big boy. I've been under the knife before and I think I can handle it." He rolled back one sleeve, revealing an arm that was crisscrossed with old battle scars. A fresh red weal ran the entire length of his forearm from elbow to wrist. The flesh was still pink and puckered around the edges.

Jervais raised an eyebrow. "I see our sister has taken a personal interest in your studies. Very good. But if there is a blood price to be paid for what we do here this night, it is I who will bear it. Now, if you will take your position…" He gestured towards the circle.

"I'm not going near that thing until Antigone gets here," Felton replied flatly. "Or until the prince's goons bust in that door."

"Ungrateful wretch," Jervais muttered darkly. "Suit yourself then, but do not think that I will sacrifice my own life for the sake of your stubbornness."

He stepped over the threshold and into the confines of the circle.

Felton watched apprehensively, expecting Jervais to vanish from sight, abandoning Felton to his fate. When it became clear that the novice was not, after all, about to disappear in a puff of smoke, Felton was a bit disappointed. He was finding that Jervais' continued presence was not much comfort.

The novice, meanwhile, was muttering to himself in the tones of some unknown guttural tongue. One arm shot out in front of him. From it rained a gentle patter of blood. As the falling lifesblood struck the twisted metal bars below, it hissed and sputtered. Soon the metal began to glow, white hot.

Felton took a step backwards, wiping sweat from his forehead with the back of one sleeve. It came away smudged red. The room was sweltering and he felt lightheaded. As he watched, Jervais' outline rippled in the waves of heat that rose between the two. Felton cast about for a way out, but could only barely pick out the outline of the door.

He experienced a brief moment of dislocation. He could have sworn that, when he had backed away from Jervais' circle, he had backed towards the door, not away from it. But now the ring of white-hot metal definitely stood squarely between Felton and any hope of exit. The shimmering doorway seemed impossibly far away.

With a jolt, Felton came to a stop, realizing he had backed all the way into the corner of the room. There was just no escaping the rising swell of the heat. The walls themselves seemed to moan under its intensity.

Only then did Felton realize that Jervais was no longer reciting in some unknown tongue, but had returned to Felton's native English and was addressing him.

"There," he said, gesturing towards Felton. "Marcus stood right about there, were you are now. The flames pressing all around him. But I couldn't break through to him. I tried three times and each time the emergency-response team dragged me bodily back from the flames. What could I do? I watched him die."

"What the hell are you talking about?" Felton shouted above the roaring wall of heat. The other two novices pressed themselves farther back into the corner, edging him outward towards the center of the blaze and the rogue salamander spirit that raged there.

The other two novices?

Felton wheeled upon them, but they only shrank back farther. One had ripped the mattress off the nearest bunk. He crouched down behind it, trying to interpose it between himself and the rapacious flames.

It was a mistake. Felton knew that the mattress would transform into a deadly searing slag under the intensity of this heat. Although only a few feet separated them, Felton had to shout his warning to have any chance of it winning through. If the young novice heard him though, he gave no sign of it. He ducked down behind the makeshift firebreak, lost from sight entirely save for the flash of gold from where his right hand held up the corner of the mattress.

Felton's hand went instinctively to his pocket, to the prize he had earlier salvaged from the wreckage of the domicilium — the gold wedding band melted around a charred fingerbone — but he found the pocket empty. His hand came out covered in a pulp of blood and soot.

Shaking the grisly muck from his hand, Felton wheeled toward the crashing noise behind him—the sound of the door bursting open and rebounding off the wall. He could make out a familiar figure charging unheedingly into the blaze. For a moment, his hopes rose at the thought of rescue from the inferno. But it was a short-lived hope. The headlong charge into the cataclysm of flame was suicidal; Felton's trained eye saw that in an instant. He could only watch helplessly as a wave of fire rose up to meet the newcomer and broke over him. Flames danced across the figure's black robes and a howl of agony rose above the din. The sound was barely human, but that small shattered part of it that was human was unmistakably Jervais' voice.

But how could that be? Jervais still stood at the center of the holocaust of flames, in the midst of his ring of molten iron bedframes. Felton double-checked to make sure. He did not understand any of this. But he did not really have the time to puzzle it all through right now. He knew that the firebreaks hastily erected by the emergency crews could not hold. The flames would soon spread, spilling out into the corridor and engulfing those who tried to win through to their three trapped comrades.

Felton was pinned between two walls, the pathetic barrier of the mattress at his back and the wall of flames before him. There was another scream and he saw the mattress-shield in the corner collapse into a bubbling black slag. The hand that clutched at one corner contorted into a gnarled mass, dripping liquid flesh and burned plastic.

Felton knew he was going to die.

He resigned himself to a last futile dash for the doorway and freedom. He knew he wouldn't get three steps through this conflagration, but it was something. An act of defiance. Or maybe just an act. Something to do, rather than stand here and wait for his fate to overtake him.

Now.

He broke into a run, launching himself into the very heart of the blaze. One step...two...

As his second foot hit the ground, he heard a longed-for voice above the roar of the flames and he knew another brief surge of hope. It was Antigone. She had come at last.

But her voice was strained, weary, crackling with static.

"Emergency-response team, report!"

Three steps. A blinding wall of fire reared suddenly before him. He tried to check his charge, to change direction, but it was already too late. He might have screamed.

From somewhere on the far side of that wall—three feet and an entire lifetime away—another voice bellowed back to Antigone. "We can't hold it. And it sounds as if the defensive grid has finally burned itself out. We're going to have to implement that evacuation plan and fast."

Felton crashed through the wall only to find himself staggering, struggling to catch his balance as the resistance suddenly gave way before him. He was through. He could hear the laughing cackle of the flames racing along his robes and hair. He blazed like a star.

"Like hell we are," Antigone's voice retorted. He could barely make it out now above the mocking laughter—coming from Jervais? The salamander spirit? The flames themselves?—and the crackle of the com port shorting out.

"We're cutting our losses," Antigone ordered. "You've got exactly thirty seconds to get everyone out of that room and the adjoining corridor. Do you understand?"

Felton stopped dead in his tracks. Cutting our losses? Leaving him here to die? He could feel the flesh of his arms and back bubble and run. Hope hissed like steam from his body. He could hear the cries of "Go. Go. Go." coming from the corridor outside, beyond the black chasm of the still-open doorway. He didn't bother to count off those thirty seconds. He slumped to his knees, defeated.

He didn't think he could go any lower, and then he heard Antigone's voice one more time, sounding like a death knell. "Seal access corridor to the novice domicilium and depressurize."

There was a sudden whoosh of air and the flames flared one last time, towering higher than ever before. Then the unmistakable sound of screaming carried him into darkness.

Chapter 20
The Leering Face of the Jackal

Antigone careened around the corner and past the refectory at a dead run, no longer making any pretense of stealth or even basic caution. Any late-night wanderers would not fail to note the apparition, the fleeting image of the pallid, distraught woman swooping through the empty corridors. The skirts of her long black mourning dress—her Widow's Weeds—streaking out behind the banshee as she passed.

Just ahead of her, the door to the novice domicilium leaned drunkenly on its hinges. Someone had obviously gone to some effort to prop it up into place and wedge it shut, but the effort had not been entirely successful. An angry red light pulsed through the crack between door and jamb, beating time to a fugue of roaring flames.

Antigone felt the first notes of the familiar nightmare wash over her, bringing with it the prickling caress of dread.

No! Not here. Not again.

She had relived the conflagration in the novice domicilium and the screams of the dying each night since she had condemned those three novices to the final death.

But I did the right thing! The only thing I could do. I stopped the fire from spreading. I saved the rest of the chantry.

But three of her brothers and sisters were dead, and upon her order. And now Jervais was going to avenge their deaths upon her. By committing Felton to the pyre.

Antigone didn't even slow. She hit the door at full speed, heard metal squeal, ignored the crunch and searing rush of pain in her shoulder. With agonizing patience, the door scraped through the debris blocking it and the crack widened.

Before her, Antigone saw a scene conjured straight from the realm of nightmare. In the center of the domicilium stood Jervais, surrounded by a tangled nest of bent and scorched metal struts. His face was lit with the same pulsing red light she had seen from the hall, but she could not discern its source. One arm was raised on high and a steady patter of blood fell from his wrist and sputtered and danced as it struck the blackened metal.

Antigone followed the line of his arm out to where the broken figure of a man knelt amid the wreckage. Felton! He writhed and tore at his oblate's robes as if they were devouring him alive. By some supreme effort of will, he managed to crawl his way to within six feet of the doorway.

"What the hell is going on here?" Antigone's voice rang overloud in the stillness of the room, for the entire pantomime within was being played out amid an eerie silence.

Jervais' head pivoted sharply and, seeing her framed in the doorway, he smiled. It was not at all a pleasant sort of smile.

"Ah, here you are at last. And none too soon, I might add. You had us quite worried, didn't she, Mr. Felton?"

Felton, whose head had snapped up at the sound of Antigone's voice, his eyes burning with a fierce, last-ditch hope, could not seem to make out her words. He could hear the demand in her voice, could hear Jervais' smug satisfaction as he answered her.

A low animal sound escaped Felton's throat. A whimper. He slumped to the floor.

He could still hear Jervais' words, pattering on with a maddening patience. Felton could not seem to block out the sound. The same damning dialog, playing itself out over and over again. He curled in upon himself, but could not wall it out, could not make it stop.

"We can't hold it," Jervais said, parroting back the words of that fateful night a week before. "And it sounds as if the defensive grid has finally burned itself out. We're going to have to implement that evacuation plan and fast."

Antigone recoiled as if she had been struck. "Stop it!" she shouted. "This isn't funny, Jervais. I did what I had to do, damn it. I am sorry I couldn't save Marcus and the others. I can't tell you how sorry. If I could bring him back I would. But you've got to stop this, here and now. Look at him! You're killing him!"

Felton looked up with a desperate hope at the sound of Antigone's voice. But her words fell very differently upon his ears. What he heard was: "We're cutting our losses. You've got exactly thirty seconds to get everyone out of that room and the adjoining corridor. Do you understand?"

Jervais only shrugged. "And what is that to me?" he asked. "Are you saying that he doesn't deserve to die? Do you think I don't know who he is, Antigone? That I don't know what he has done? He's a murderer, an arsonist, a common street-brawler and an erstwhile assassin. There are some that would thank me for executing judgment upon him." He ticked the offended parties off on the fingers of one hand. "The prince, for one. And the police, of course. The FBI, his own colleagues and co-conspirators and yes, even some luminaries of this house. I had thought that you would be among the first to congratulate me—for relieving you of the burden of carrying out his sentence yourself. After all, you made all this possible—"

"What are you talking about? I don't want him dead! You know that. You're just hurting him to try to get to me. This isn't about justice, it's about revenge. Your little paramour is dead and you blame me. Well, I'm not going to stand by and let you — or anybody else — kill him. You think you have a personal score to settle with me? Okay, then let's settle it."

Antigone felt white-hot rage rising up within her. She reached the edge of Jervais' protective circle. Without so much as slowing, she stooped and snatched up a twisted bar of blackened iron.

She howled in pain and surprise as the metal seared itself into her flesh.

Somewhere close at hand, trapped in his own personal torment, Felton heard that howl. In his mind, he could pick out the individual syllables that made it up, the voices shouting "Go. Go. Go!" as the damage-control teams turned their backs on him and fled the inferno.

"That was very foolish, Antigone," Jervais said as Antigone staggered backwards. "You'll likely have a nasty scar. But we have indulged ourselves in these reminiscences too long. You are here with us at last and that is what is important. Mr. Felton dies now." He raised a hand in parting salute.

Antigone gritted her teeth and forced her fingers to fold around the white-hot metal. Her entire arm trembled with the effort. The rod flashed in the ruddy glow as Antigone's fist arced high. It crashed down upon the crown of Jervais' head with all the strength Antigone could put behind that blow.

There was a resounding crack and then silence.

Antigone took one staggering step back from him. Jervais' eyes were wide with surprise, almost outrage. His hand came up, fluttering, questing for the gaping wound in his forehead. He found it, one finger vanishing from sight altogether as it probed the blood-matted wreckage.

Then he was falling. His heel caught in the tangled rat's nest of metal struts and he went over backward. He landed heavily and lay still.

Antigone stared dumbly at the body crumpled amidst the tangle of twisted bedframes. She wanted to turn away and retch, to let the darkness close over her as well. But the smoldering fire in the metal bar in her hand brought everything back into sharp focus. Bracing herself, she tore her hand free. Now blood glistened on both ends of the deadly implement. It was done.

She turned towards Felton, but the sight of the foreboding figure standing in the doorway brought her up short.

The adept stood with her arms folded before her, blocking the exit. Her face was impassive, hard to read. A pillar of smoke.

"Helena, I…" Antigone took a hesitant step forward.

"A messy business," the adept interrupted. "You all right?"

"Look, I'm fine. I'm just…" She stooped over the crumpled body of Felton on the floor, swiping distractedly at the hair that fell over her eyes. Her efforts left an angry streak of red across her forehead. Then she got her first good look at him. "Jeezus."

Antigone started peeling away the tattered strips of unbleached linen that had once been the oblate robes. If she were still aware of the presence of Helena, now hovering at her shoulder, she gave no sign of it. Antigone knew that Helena's presence here meant that it was all over. She was under no illusions as to what it meant for her to be discovered here within the chantry. She knew what fate awaited her at the hands of the Astors.

But maybe it was not yet too late for Felton. It couldn't be too late. But each scrap of cloth that she painstakingly peeled back, came away covered in blood and blackened flesh.

"He's not going to thank you for doing that," Helena pointed out. Antigone doubted whether anyone less familiar with the adept would have detected the faint note of concern in Helena's voice. "He alive?"

"Yes," Antigone said. "Although I doubt he's going to thank me for that either."

As she said this, a low moan escaped the shattered husk that was Felton.

"I'm here," Antigone said. "You're going to be all right, do you understand me? You're going to be all right."

"Got to get out," came the broken rasp. "Thirty seconds…"

"It's all over now," Antigone said. "You made it out. You're going to be fine."

"He's going to need blood," Helena said matter-of-factly. "And a lot of it, by the look of him."

Antigone nodded, but knew that to leave him now would be to condemn him to certain death.

Helena shook her head and sighed, rising to her feet in one fluid motion. "You know it's as much as your life is worth to be caught here, right?" She crossed back toward Jervais' body.

Antigone nodded. "Look, Helena. I need to get him out of here. Sturbridge said I've got to take him to—"

"No, no, no. Wherever you're going, I really don't think you want me to hear that. So how about you settle for telling me what's so important that you think I'm just going to look the other way here. You're a fugitive now, you know that, right? They say you attacked one of the Astors. And that you invoked some sort of forbidden rite. Now you come showing your face back here. You purposefully sabotage the security system. No, don't even pretend you don't know anything about that. I'm not yet sure what you hit it with, but the crew still hasn't managed to get the damned thing back on line."

"Transferred control to the local daemon at the Exeunt Tertius," Antigone admitted miserably. "Convinced it the over-daemon was malfunctioning. Threw the whole system into diagnostic mode."

"No…" Helena said. She spoke very slowly, as if explaining things to a particularly slow student. "What you did was convince the local daemon the controller was unfit for duty. It then initiated something of a coup."

"Oh," Antigone said. "I didn't intend..."

Helena only glared at her. "So how about you come clean with me and tell me why you are going out of your way to perpetuate the impression that this chantry is dangerously out of control, and that novices are dying here by the dozen? This is not exactly the kind of PR that is going to get us through this present crisis. Or do I need to remind you that some of us—the ones who are not murdering our brothers and sisters—have to stay here and face the Astors?"

"Helena, I'm so sorry. He was going to kill Felton. Another moment or two and he might very well have succeeded. I had to stop him. I just grabbed the first thing that came to hand...."

Helena was still bent over Jervais' corpse. Fussing over it. "Well, in that case, I'm sure you'll be pleased to know that you did not, in fact, manage to kill him." She busied herself with tearing long, makeshift bandages from the hem of his robes. "He's lost a hellish amount of blood, but I guess not all of that is your fault. You want to tell me what dark thaumaturgic rite you two were enacting this time?"

"That's not funny. You know that I'm hopeless with this blood-magic stuff. Jervais was going to kill, Mr. Fel...er, this oblate. I don't know how he did it, but somehow he took him back to the fire. Jervais was really bitter about that, obsessing on it. He lost someone very close to him in that fire and I gave the order that killed him."

Helena rechecked the bandaged and grunted, satisfied with her handiwork. She picked up the bludgeon that Antigone had discarded nearby and examined it curiously.

"And what's the significance behind this little number?" Helena asked. "You expect me to believe that you just happened to be carrying this around when you came upon the two of them? Level with me. You came here expecting to find Jervais and expecting to kill him."

"What are you talking about? What little number?" Antigone craned around to see the adept. "That? That's not mine. It's just some old twisted piece of bedframe I pulled from the rubble."

"Is that right?" Helena rose and came closer until she loomed directly over Antigone. "You're saying you've never seen this before?"

"I told you I just found it. It was part of that protective circle that Jervais had constructed."

"Hmm. I suppose one of these guys will confirm your story? Assuming either of them regains consciousness. But you have to admit, it is an interesting little piece, isn't it?" Helena regarded the smooth metal rod. She snapped her wrist sharply, sending a spatter of gore across the nearest wall. "You say you just found this, lying around?"

Helena extended the rod towards her. Its tip hovered just inches from the novice's nose. With growing horror, Antigone saw that its head was carved into a fierce animal visage. The leering canine face of a jackal.

"A bit of old bedframe," Helena repeated. "Just lying about."

"Helena, I...I don't understand. I've really never seen that before—"

"Get out. Just take him and get the hell out of here before I change my mind."

"Helena. I'm sorry," Antigone muttered. "I wish there were some way I could make you believe me. I didn't do anything wrong."

She stood and hauled Felton to his feet. He was as light as a bag of autumn leaves. And he crackled as he moved. There was no hint of the earlier resistance left in him. She draped him over her shoulder and threw her own arm around him to steady him.

Under her urging, his feet resumed their ingrained habit, lifted and fell, lifted and fell. Together, they shuffled towards the open doorway.

"Antigone," Helena called after the retreating pair.

Antigone half turned and braced herself for some new reproach. "Yes, Adepta?"

"Do not go back by way of the Exeunt Tertius. They will have isolated the system failure by now. The security team…"

"Thank you, Helena." Antigone searched for some parting words, something to express her gratitude for not just this final unexpected favor but for all that the adept had done for an awkward and unpromising novice over the years. All she could come up with was one last exhortation: "Keep her safe."

Helena nodded grimly. She did not need to ask whom Antigone was referring to. "Go," she said gruffly. The adept turned her back on Antigone to preempt any further discussion. Shaking her head, she tossed the murder weapon back onto the heap of scrap metal in the room's center.

In Antigone's ears, that single word echoed and reverberated—mirroring back upon itself, redoubling at each turning. "*Go. Go. Go!*"

She hardened herself to the mocking whispers of the past and hurried from the access corridor as if that last means of escape might suddenly evaporate before her eyes. Another mirage, a dim after-image of past reproaches refracted through smoke and swirling heat.

Chapter 21
Eyes of Royal Blue

"I didn't tell you those things to hurt you, Peter," Sturbridge said. She pressed closer and laid a hand on his shoulder. "I'm telling you this so that you will believe me when I tell you certain other things. Some very disturbing things. About the ambassador, and about Eva and about what's been going on here lately. Do you understand?"

"I don't understand any of this, Aisling," Dorfman said. "You're trying to tell me that these murders at the chantry— these assassinations—that they were all engineered from the Fatherhouse in Vienna? You must admit that this is all somewhat...hard to credit."

"I know. But you must realize that there are some powerful people behind this, Peter. Some very powerful people. If you take me back to Vienna now, if you put me in front of some tribunal, I'll be dead before I can give a single word of testimony."

"Aisling, you're being dramatic. Why should anyone at the Fatherhouse want to see you dead? Or, for that matter, why would they want to arrange a string of murders at a chantry half a world away? It doesn't make any sense. What possible proof could you have to support these claims?"

"I've talked with the victims," she said flatly. "Not the murder victims, although they're all there too. But the victims of the grander plot—its pawns. Eva, Aaron, the ambassador, they are all within me now. Their secrets are my secrets."

"Enough! You would have me believe that you are somehow…cross-examining the dead?"

"Not the dead, exactly," she said. "More like the things that reproached the dead in their sleepless hours. Like your—"

"No! Not like my anything. Look, I don't know what you did to me. That was all very impressive, but for all I know it's just some improved mind-reading variation you've developed. I can't very well go back to the Council and say that it's all been some big misunderstanding. Just because you said some things. Just because you found out some things about me. No one's going to be satisfied with that, Aisling. Nobody."

"I'm not saying they'll be content, Peter. All I'm saying is that, if you drag me back there now, they'll kill me. To keep me from telling what I know before a tribunal. And my death will be on your hands."

"Be reasonable, Aisling. What choice do I have? Believe me, it will go easier on you if you return to Vienna with me. The only other way out of this is to produce a body. It's either the ambassador's body—up and moving—or it's yours, not so moving."

"And what will happen to them, I wonder? Once I am gone."

"They're going to be fine, Aisling. I do have a little bit of pull here. I can see to it that the other novices are spared the brunt of this."

"I'll hold you to that," Sturbridge said. "But I didn't mean the novices. I meant the Children."

Dorfman sighed and rubbed the bridge of his nose. "Look, Aisling, I know you've seen some things. Some very disturbing things. But even I'm having trouble believing all this about the nightmares, about your having 'eaten our dead.' There's just no way I can report something like this back to the Council and not have them yank the both of us back to Vienna before the ink is even dry on the paper."

"I know that, Peter."

"So what exactly is it that you want me to do?"

"I want you to believe me," she replied.

"I do believe you."

"No, you don't. If you believed what I have been telling you, you'd be scared by now. Because there's some conspiracy afoot and it's a big one. And you're caught up in it and know absolutely nothing about it. And that shortcoming, incidentally, is going to get us both killed."

"All right, I'm listening. How about you tell me what exactly it is we're supposedly going to die for, here. Stumbling into the middle of some conspiracy? Because of some bad dreams? What?"

His tone was mocking, but his eyes bore into hers intently. Searching, compelling, trying to wrest from her her secrets.

But she was prepared for him. In her eyes, he found only his own face, mirrored, inverted. He broke away and resumed a restless pacing.

"How am I supposed to help you if you won't even let me inside? I need the truth, Aisling. Hard facts and harder evidence."

She shook her head. "You're looking in the wrong place. I don't have the truth anymore. All that's left to me now are recriminations and failings, my own and those of others who are now lost to us. If you want answers—if you want to help—you've got to go back. To Vienna. To the Fatherhouse."

"And what's that supposed to accomplish? Let's say I just go back and tell them the ambassador's dead, case closed. You don't think they're going to want to know how he died? And why?"

"He died because he had become a liability. He was asking too many of the right questions. He was doing exactly what you're doing."

"Are you threatening me?!"

"I was not the one who killed the ambassador. But if I stood up in the Fatherhouse and spoke the name of the one who did kill him… But I would not be allowed to go so far."

"Who killed the ambassador?" he asked in a more level tone of voice.

"She called herself Eva. Eva Fitzgerald. She was a novice of this house. I had come to look upon her as my protégée." Sturbridge laughed. It was a coarse, grating sound, like something tearing inside. "My most promising student, and no wonder."

"And you're telling me that she was some kind of plant, that she was sent from Vienna?"

"A plant?" Sturbridge laughed. "A curious little flower, one both beautiful and deadly. I am not certain that 'sent' is the right word. But she certainly came from the Fatherhouse all the same."

A look of concern flitted across Dorfman's face. "Aisling, I—"

"The name she chose is suggestive, don't you think? I think she may have chosen 'Eva' because it was so close to that of my own dear daughter. Maeve. Certainly she chose her physical appearance for that reason, to play upon my sentiments—upon my loss, my regrets."

He took her by both shoulders. "Aisling, stop it. You're not well—"

"But the 'Fitzgerald' was suggestive as well. Did you ever know any Fitzgeralds, I wonder, my little one? In London, perhaps. It is traditional there, I believe, for scions of the royal line to take that name. Or would that have been before your time?"

"Aisling!"

Her head came up sharply, but cocked to one side like that of a curious bird. She met his eyes. Within those depths Dorfman saw, not the familiar mirrored surface of her carefully constructed defenses, but infinite depths of chill, murky waters.

There was a face there, a child's face. Bobbing silently in time to some mysterious current. It was as radiant as a moon and framed in tangled strands of what must once have been golden hair. A bedraggled crown. But it was the eyes that drew his attention, would give him no peace. They were blue, a royal blue, but vacant, glazed over, lifeless.

Then, as Dorfman watched in growing horror, the face smiled up at him contentedly. The mocking bluish lips parted and contracted, mouthing silent words. Against his better judgment, Dorfman leaned in closer.

The thin, whispered exhalation was stagnant and stank of a watery grave. He did his best to ignore the foul reek and bent even closer.

"Tell him," Eva whispered, exultant. "Tell Father that it is done."

Nothing more but a trickle of blackish waters passed her lips.

Dorfman wrenched away from her and found himself, once again, standing over Sturbridge, staring down at the trickle of blackish blood from her cracked lips.

Sturbridge's lips parted, but it was not her voice that came out. "Ask him if he's proud of me, Peter. Promise me that you'll ask him."

"Stop it!" he roared. He jerked to his feet, overturning his chair, and propelled himself towards the door.

"Where are you going, Peter?" It was Sturbridge's voice this time, groggy, disoriented.

"To Vienna. I need some answers. Some real answers. Not more of these ravings and insinuations. It seems someone has not been entirely forthright about this little investigation. I don't like it when people keep things from me. Especially things that might get me killed."

"But how will you know the people you are looking for once you've found them?"

He turned. "That, Aisling, is the easiest puzzle of them all. I will know because they will try to kill me. But don't worry yourself. I am quite accomplished at finding people who are trying to kill me. In the meantime you will remain here. And by 'here' I mean in your quarters. I will put you officially under house arrest if I have to."

He was prepared for an argument on this point. When she made no protest, he regarded her with open suspicion.

"I mean it. Don't fight me on this, Aisling. I've got to know that you're going to be safe until I can return. And I can't have you running around scaring the novices and riding roughshod over my men. I'll be back as soon as I can. In the meanwhile, you're confined to quarters. Doctor's orders. And I want you to stay the hell away from my people. I'm sure I don't need to tell you what a royal pain in the ass it was for me just to locate Stephens—never mind actually prying him out of that damned diagram of yours down in the crypts."

"It wasn't my diagram," Sturbridge muttered.

"I don't care whose diagram it was—yours, that renegade novice's—the point is—"

"It was Eva's diagram."

Dorfman bit off a profanity. It seemed the things he did not know were determined to get him killed, one way or the other.

"Anything else you're not telling me?" He could not keep the tone of exasperation from his voice.

"Yes," she said. "I'm coming with you to Vienna."

"Like hell you are! You're staying right here, out of harm's way."

Sturbridge ignored his outburst. "But I'm not going to the Fatherhouse as your prisoner," she mused. "No, the only way out of this that I can see is that you have to take me into your confidences as an equal partner in your investigation. If you stick close, I might be able to keep you from asking the wrong question of the wrong person."

He laughed aloud at this latest presumption. "You're crazy. You know that, right? I can't just take you on as a partner. I'm here to investigate you, remember?"

"Then you file a report officially clearing me of any wrongdoing and another formally asking my assistance in your investigation. That should light a fire under them. And then when we show up in Vienna—"

"Out of the question," he declared. "I would remind you that just a minute ago, you were assuring me that they would kill you sooner than let you speak out against them at the Fatherhouse. Whoever 'they' are."

"That's why we're partners in this. I keep you from saying something foolish and getting yourself killed. You keep me from getting killed until I can say something foolish. Deal?"

He turned his back on her and strode out of the chamber.

Chapter 22
The Blade of Damocles

Dorfman stormed into the Hall of Audiences through the regent's private entrance, behind the dais. Himes and Stephens were engaged in interviewing an increasingly haggard-looking Helena. Even her stance made it clear that she had pressing business elsewhere and very much resented being interrupted and hauled back in here yet again.

"This is quite remarkable." Stephens was bent over the elaborate Table of Correspondences spread out between them. The parchment draped over the sides of the long folding banquet table. It must have measured a meter across and twice that in length. The sheet was bursting with finely detailed illuminations and intricate scrollwork. "May I?"

Helena rolled her eyes. "Really, gentlemen. I'd love to help you go through each and every curiosity from the novice domicilium, but right now I'm in the middle of a ticklish security-system outage, not to mention a medical emergency, and if it is at all possible that you could spare me…"

Helena looked up as Dorfman entered. Seeing Sturbridge follow closely at his heels, the adept fell silent. She looked decidedly uncomfortable and would not meet her regent's gaze.

Taking Helena's silence for a concession, Stephens' hand traced down the convoluted route of occult symbols with one finger, taking care not to touch the work itself. A bold red line grabbed his attention. Words adorned the line like fruit swelling upon a vine. He puzzled over the enigmatic inscriptions which meandered from the Greek to the Latin, Hebrew to Aramaic, Sanskrit to Norse runes to Egyptian hieroglyphs.

He was no great linguist. He leaned heavily on the marginal illuminations for most of his interpretations. "I can make out Mars—the planet and the god, they are both here. Fire, Ares, the color red. War, a red horse, strife, anger, swords. The double-edged sword, the blade of Damocles, the Tarot suit of Swords, Excalibur. Agni, south, the desert wastes. Exile, temptation. Something in Hebrew, 'Gevurah'? Passion, Brigid, poetry, the crux. The generative element, power, the fifth chakra. Din, Micha-el, the guardian..."

He seemed to lose himself among the labyrinth of images, concepts, conjectures that rose up at him from the page. Stephens shook his head as if to break free of its spell.

"Stunning. The closer I look, the more I find myself at a loss. This is not only a work of art, it is a riddle, a puzzlebox. At times I think I have caught a glimpse of some hint of reason darting like a frightened woodland creature among the disparate elements. And then it is gone again."

"You must be wary of that creature," Sturbridge said cryptically. "It is not, as you imagine, a glimpse of reason. Quite the contrary, it is a wild thing. A beast that preys upon logical connections, upon reason, upon discipline. These are its victims. It lures them, traps them, rends them, bleeds them."

Stephens started at the sound of her voice, becoming aware for the first time of Sturbridge's and his superior's presence. He glared at her.

"Is that a threat, Ms. Sturbridge?" Stephens straightened to his full height, bristling. He purposefully refrained from giving the regent her proper title. He was not likely to forget or forgive the fact that Sturbridge had been party to his all-too-recent imprisonment.

"Those who would delve into our secrets," Sturbridge replied levelly, "must first learn to be wary of the beast in all its guises. It appears to you as a riddle, an enigma. But you are, perhaps, overly enamored of mysteries."

"We each serve according to our abilities," Himes interrupted, trying to defuse the rising tension. "My associate here is, as you say, quite adept at ferreting out what is hidden. Others have different talents. This piece here, for example, is quite remarkable. The adept was telling us that it is the work of a mere novice, although I must admit that I am having trouble crediting it. Look at the detail, the spatial relations between the complementary elements. It is a work of genius, both from an arcane and an artistic point of view. I must say, I am quite impressed. I would very much like to meet this novice."

Helena shifted uncomfortably at Himes having again drawn attention to her presence, but it was Sturbridge who answered him. "That's not going to be possible, I'm afraid. Miss Fitzgerald is no longer among our number."

"Miss Fitzgerald?" Himes asked.

"Eva," Helena supplied. "Now if you gentlemen will excuse me…"

"Ah yes, Eva!" recognition lit Himes' eyes. "The regent's protégée! My condolences, Regent Sturbridge. It is never easy to lose such a promising apprentice. Especially under such…unpleasant circumstances." He watched her face shrewdly, but Sturbridge gave no sign of rising to the bait.

"We don't have time for this," Dorfman snapped. "As soon as you two have finished with the adept, you will see that she is escorted back to her quarters."

Helena began to protest about the amount of work she still had to do this morning.

"Get some rest," Sturbridge said. "I will be relying upon you to look after the novices in my absence. You will also give the investigators every assistance in my absence. It is imperative that they be allowed to conclude this inquiry as quickly and painlessly as possible. I trust I am understood?"

"Yes, Regentia, but there's something I have to tell you. Something that I have done that—" Then her words seemed to sink in. "In your absence?! Surely you do not mean that...?"

Sturbridge came around the table and laid a hand on Helena's shoulder. "It's all right, Helena. Have no fear on my account. I am returning with the Pontifex to Vienna. This morning."

Helena stared at her uncomprehendingly. Her voice was little more than a whisper. "To Vienna? You are being recalled to Vienna?"

Sturbridge smiled. "Nothing so romantic, I'm afraid. Peter agrees that there are some answers that the Council simply will not be able to accept, unless they come from me personally. How will they believe what has happened here—with the ambassador, with Eva, with the Children—unless I am there to show them? Even you didn't believe me, at first." She gave Helena's arm a reassuring squeeze. "It will be all right, Helena. But I need you to carry on here, to be strong. For the novices."

Helena could only shake her head. "So that's what this is. Just another something to keep me busy, to keep me quiet. Well, I'm not biting. And I'm not leaving you. If they drag you off to stand before some tribunal at the Fatherhouse, they're going to have to drag me off too. After all, it was I who...I've got to starting putting things right."

"Helena. Think a minute." Sturbridge drew her aside by the arm. She pitched her voice low so as not to be overheard. "I'll order you to stay if I have to, but I don't want to. Dorfman's willing to give you another shot. You don't often get second chances in this game, trust me on this. You'd be an idiot not to

196 / Eric Griffin

take it. Just hold things together here, just for a little while longer. You play along, you bend over backward to help the investigation. And then, when this is over, you're the person that they know they can count on here. You keep your head and there's a junior regency for you here. When I think back to what I had to give up to become the junior regent here… Anyway, I'm not going to let you blow this. You're staying here. You're going to see that the things we worked so hard for—during all the years of the Sabbat siege—are brought to fruition. I'm relying upon you."

Helena hung her head and would not meet the regent's eyes. "But Regentia, you don't understand. What I've been trying to tell you is that *I'm* the one who—"

"Enough. None of that matters now. We've all done some stupid things these last few weeks. Be grateful that your mistakes haven't gotten anyone killed. I can't make the same claim. But that's over now. What matters is that you do the right thing now. I know it hasn't been easy for you, Helena, but I'm proud of what you have done. Don't screw it up now."

Helena still would not meet her eye. She was hurt and angry and didn't have anyone to hit back at. "You're not coming back, are you?" she demanded.

"No, Helena. I can't promise you that I'm coming back."

"Then what the hell's going to happen to us? Not the chantry, I mean. I know what you're asking me to do about the chantry. But when you're gone, what will happen to us? I thought I had it all figured out until that damned day the nightmares stopped. And nothing's been right since. Nothing! These Astors, they don't know what happened that night. And there's no way some stupid investigation is going to make it all just go away again. What do they know about the Children? About the nightmares? About the hurt that was inflicted on us?

They can't fight this thing—they can't even see what's going on. There's nothing for them to hit."

Sturbridge could feel the adept's hurt, could smell the blood upon her. From the bleeding that would not stop. From the wound that was no wound.

"I'm not giving up yet," Sturbridge said. "So I'm not going to have you give up on me. If they return—the nightmares, I mean—then you'll know that I'm... Well, you will know that I've failed. That I could not convince them. But until that happens, you will know that I am well. That I'm still out there fighting. And I can see what we're fighting against."

She smiled and, taking Helena's chin in her hand, raised the adept's face until their eyes met. "Take care of my novices," she said.

Helena tried to pull away, but Sturbridge held her firm. At last, the adept relented. "As you will, Regentia."

Sturbridge embraced her.

"We've gotta go," Dorfman said at Sturbridge's shoulder. He turned and called to Himes and Stephens, "I will be expecting nightly reports of your progress until I return. On my desk, in Vienna, by the time I get up. I would like this matter wrapped up without further delays. You will interview Master Ynnis immediately after he has assisted us in our travel arrangements. Tomorrow night you will seek out the adept, Johanus, if he has not returned to the chantry. That will leave you one additional night to conclude your inquiries. Three nights, no more. Do I make myself clear?"

"Perfectly so, my lord," Himes said. "We wish you every success on your journey."

"Thank you. And good hunting. If you haven't heard from me in three days' time, you will proceed to the contact point and await further instructions. Regentia, after you."

Sturbridge bowed slightly and preceded him from the Hall.

Chapter 23
A Blackened and Desiccated Corpse

They must have cut an odd spectacle as they hobbled into the Grand Foyer, arm in arm. The blackened corpse that was Felton could not even hope to stay upright without Antigone's assistance. With the dawn fast approaching, the hall was deserted. And that was some small comfort. The room still bore the signs, however, of the Astors' investigations abandoned mid-course.

Even Antigone, long familiar with the room's unsettling habit of picking up cues from its visitors, was not prepared for the scene before her. In places, the hall had taken on a positively medieval appearance. The trappings of Inquisition lining the dank dungeon-like walls must have come as an unwelcome surprise to the Astors. Stray apprehensions picked from the minds of the novices they interviewed here, given life.

But none of the instruments of torture had as pronounced an effect upon Felton as the sight of the Great Portal itself. When the exit first came into view, he became agitated, increasingly so as they crossed the foyer. He did his best to dig in his heels, rasping something around a dry and shredded tongue. After a few moments of puzzling it out, Antigone thought it might have been, "Must go back."

"We can't go back now," she explained in hushed tones. She wasn't taking any chances on encountering any of their "guests" finishing up some last-minute business. Despite her caution, however, her words echoed in the vast open space. She shrank back from the sound of her own voice, as if it were something monstrous. "We're almost there, almost out. It's just a little bit farther."

"No! Can't go without it. No other way."

This is ridiculous, Antigone thought. For a moment, she considered just throwing Felton over one shoulder and carrying him out bodily. Then what he was saying struck her.

"Can't go without what?" she demanded.

"Papers. My briefing. Innocent! Can't prove it without them."

"Oh, for God's sake, forget the damned papers. We don't need them anymore. We know who blew up that building, who set you up. But we've got to hurry. If we're caught here…"

He shook his head stubbornly. The movement was slow and excruciating. She could see the exposed flesh of his throat cracking and peeling. There was a trickle of blood and the vast hall seemed to drink in the heady scent of it. Antigone nearly tripped over a branch jutting from a tangle of kindling piled high and encircling a tall pole. She could have sworn the waiting stake and pyre had not been in their path a moment before. Antigone growled something inaudible and turned him to face her. "You've got to knock that off. The room picks up on unguarded fears and desires. Gives them flesh. You've got to—" She broke off as a tongue of flame leapt to life and ran the length of the nearest stick. She realized it was futile. His hurt was too near the surface, his fear to raw. Her best bet was just to get the two of them out of here and fast.

She tried another tack. "Okay, where did you leave the damned papers?"

"I had them. In the fire. With Jervais, I…" he broke off uncertainly, his hands absently patting the smoldering tatter of robes that still clung tightly about him.

"Hold still," Antigone ordered. Slowly, she peeled back a section of coarse fabric over his heart. The frayed edge crumbled to ash in her hand. Very cautiously, she reached inside and patted the concealed pocket. Something crinkled there. From just the sound of it, she already knew what she would find.

She saw a curled and blackened edge of battered manila envelope peeking from the top of the pocket. "It's fine," she lied. "Safe. You still have it right here. Now let's get out of here before…"

Her words trailed away ineffectually at the sight of someone hurrying towards them, moving to intercept.

An instant later, she recognized Talbott, the Brother Porter, making his way determinedly toward them. At least it wasn't one of the Astors. Although being discovered by anyone at this point posed a serious problem.

As he drew closer to them, a look of concern peeked through the cracks in Talbott's professional composure.

"You are hurt," he said, fussing about them. The fact was so painfully obvious that his words struck Antigone as inordinately funny. She checked a laugh, fearing that, under the present circumstances, it might well come out sounding a bit hysterical. Then again, hysteria might not be entirely unjustified, here.

Talbott gave her a curious look. "I said, come with me," he said pointedly. "This man needs immediate medical attention. I'll summon Master Ynnis."

Antigone watched as he took Felton gently by one arm and glided away from her, back in the direction of the central fountain. She wanted to protest, but words failed her. She felt the full impact of all the evening's trials hit her at once. The sensation was akin to drowning in tar.

"Mr. Felton, isn't it?" Talbott said, as if by merely keeping up a steady patter, he might keep the dark wings of death from his commandeered charge. "I remember the day you came to us, sir. You had a friend with you, didn't you? What was his name, now. Let me think."

"Charlie," Felton rasped, a hollow broken sound. "His name's Charlie. But I don't want him mixed up in all this. I..."

"There, there," Talbott soothed. "We'll just keep it between the two of us then, won't we. Charlie can come and see you in a few days, once you're feeling a bit better. The intercom is on the blink just now, so we'll just make you comfortable here while Antigone goes for the doctor. How does that sound?"

He glared at Antigone who still stood exactly where he had left her. He gestured sharply with his head to indicate that she should go quickly.

"My papers..." Felton said.

Talbott's eyes never left Antigone. "Shh. No need to worry yourself about that. Antigone has it all taken care of, don't you, dear? Of course she does. You two can talk more about it after the doctor has a chance to look you over. All right? You're going to be just fine."

To Talbott's irritation, Antigone still did not run for the doctor. Instead, she moved calmly towards them. "We won't be waiting to see the doctor, I'm afraid," she said, steeling herself to the occasion. "We have to leave here. Quietly. And right now. I trust you understand me?"

Talbott's eyes widened. He could hear the steel in her tone. "You are in no condition to travel," he pointed out reasonably. Then his voice regained its former tone of aloof competence. "And I have orders to see that Mr. Felton gets the reading materials he requires and to see him safely back to his cell. Those orders came from the regent, herself."

"The orders have changed," Antigone said, wondering what orders he was talking about. "We have a security breach in progress. I've got to get him out of here. Right now."

"For his own safety?" Talbott challenged, his voice pitched low to maintain the appearance that he did not want Felton to overhear him. "You take him out there now, like this, and you may well kill him."

"Listen to me, Talbott. If we stay here, he won't last through the night. Do you understand me? They're going to kill him. It's up to me to keep him safe. Sturbridge said to take him to—"

Talbott held up one hand and curtly interrupted. "Please. You must have a care not to tell me things that it would be better that I not know. I have known you these forty years. Do I have your word that the regent has charged you with getting this man out of the chantry?"

"I swear it."

"Fair enough. Then I think I understand the regent's curious orders now. I had wondered why she should send our guest to me for reading materials when Brother Jerome could easily have acquired them for him, as was his wont. She must have anticipated the need to get Mr. Felton out of the chantry."

"Thank you, Talbott. I won't forget this." She turned to Felton. "Come on. We're getting out of here while we can."

He could only nod as she helped him to his feet and together they set their backs to the shelter of the Tremere Pyramid.

Chapter 24
Delusions of Competence

"Sure I see them," Donatello hissed back. "So how can you be so sure that's him? That guy looks pretty roughed up to me."

"You're one to talk," Caleb shot back, barely suppressing a snicker. In return, his companion elbowed him sharply in the ribs. From their vantage point atop the roof of the science building, they had a clear view of Millbank Hall, the most public rabbit hole leading into that subterranean realm of the warlocks—the Chantry of Five Boroughs. The couple below, staggering arm in arm from the shadow of the administrative building were obviously no tipsy late-night revelers. They kept as best they could to the shadows and picked their way with care.

From his perch, Donatello had already seen more than his share of students, still decked out in the remains of the previous evening's finery, engaging in the traditional morning-after walk of shame. This, however, was not one of those occasions.

"Look at him!" Caleb insisted in emphatic whisper. "That's him. I'd swear that's him. I've seen those security tapes at least a hundred times. You're just sore 'cause I saw him first."

Donatello peered more closely. The guy was about the right build, but the Nosferatu sentry was not convinced. "Nah, the guy we're looking for is a white guy. This is just more wishful thinking on your part. Like when you thought you saw Sturbridge the other night."

"I did see her," Caleb insisted in a hurt tone. "It's not my fault that you're lousy at this. And that guy is white, look at his arms. There!"

The tattered garment did a poor job of covering the man below. Its ragged edge flapped as he walked. Now that he was looking for it, Donatello could make out the line of pale flesh revealed intermittently beneath it. "I'll be damned. Well, it looks like the Tremere did a job on him, whoever he is. He's about burnt to a crisp. You think that's really him? The mad bomber, I mean."

"I'm telling you it's him," Caleb said. "It figures the damned warlocks got to him first, shifty bastards. But he's not going to give us the slip this time. No sir, no more stupid stakeouts for Caleb. You play your cards right and I'll tell Emmett that you helped bring him in."

Donatello rolled his eyes. "You've got delusions of basic competence. You don't even know for sure that it's him yet. And you are not taking anybody in. We've got orders, remember? A fly on the wall, Emmett said. Just watch the entrance, he said. No unauthorized contact with the Tremere, period. Nothing short of emergency medical interven—"

Caleb cuffed him ungently on the back of the head. "Now you're thinking, da Vinci! That guy's pretty roughed up. You said so yourself. So how about we go and have us a little emergency medical intervention?"

Donatello shoved him away. "Yeah, you're a regular angel of mercy. Asshole. All right. We'll go give them a closer look. Just to prove that you're an idiot. Only, try to be cool this time. That last couple you swooped down on…"

"That wasn't my fault. They freaked. How was I supposed to know that they would have this thing about open sores and stuff?"

"Dumb-ass. Just be cool, okay? And keep your face on."

Caleb mugged a hideous grimace at him, clawing at his own eyelids with crusted talons, as if he would tear the top half of his head off.

Donatello snorted in disgust and turned away. "Who the hell did I piss off to get stuck with you?" he muttered.

Caleb scrambled to catch up as Donatello bent double, grabbed the end of the gutter in one hand, and hopped over the edge of the roof. It was a good thirty feet down.

"Emmett. Duh!" Caleb replied and followed his companion over the side.

Antigone noticed that their unlikely party had acquired quite an entourage during their trip into the undercity. That didn't bother her. It was better that everyone here should hear what she had to say to the prince.

The two Nosferatu who had intercepted them outside the chantry were more taken aback by their quarry than Antigone had been by them. They had expected resistance, certainly. Or a denial at least. Perhaps they secretly hoped for some pyrotechnics from the prisoner's Tremere escort. In all these hopes, they were disappointed.

They looked so crestfallen and ridiculous that it had been difficult for Antigone to resist the temptation to demand that they take her to their leader. If the truth were known, she found their sudden arrival something of a relief. She had not been looking forward to returning to the scene of the most recent bombing at the high school. At this point, the last thing they needed was for someone from the media or, worse, the police to recognize Felton and start asking uncomfortable questions.

Far easier to surrender to the Nosferatu and have done. They would take her where she needed to go, and pat themselves on the back for having tagged the man that all of their people had been desperately seeking these last nights. Hell, they might even get a medal. She more than half hoped that they would. She might give them one herself.

She had done the next best thing. When their assailants descended upon them, she had been so happy to see their misshapen faces that she had muttered an emphatic, "Thank God," thrown her arms around the nearest of them (whom she latter learned was called Donatello) and kissed him.

He had nearly tripped over himself in his hasty retreat, much to the amusement of his companion. "You'll have to pardon him," Caleb guffawed. "He's got a way with the witches." This sent him into redoubled fits of laughter at his partner's expense and it took some doing to coax the embarrassed Donatello back out of the shadows.

So much for their daring attempt to arrest the notorious bomber.

Only later did Antigone find out that she was not Donatello's first encounter with the mystic Tremere sisterhood. Some years ago, in the course of investigating the death of a young mortal artist, Regent Sturbridge and Donatello had crossed paths. On that memorable occasion, the regent had supposedly said that he was beautiful. Word of this exploit had won the Nosferatu a romantic reputation among his socially retiring kinsmen. He had never quite gotten over that experience, and wasn't entirely certain that he wanted to. It was unlikely that he would be able to live down this latest interlude. During the trip back to the warrens, he mostly kept to himself and to the company of his own thoughts.

Looking at Caleb, it was clear that he was just bursting to relate this little tidbit to the growing crowd that flocked to the curious party as they descended. But for the time being, he was well content to bask in their admiration for his single-handedly apprehending the fugitive. Donatello seemed loathe to contradict the grandiloquent story—which grew more elaborate at each telling—and so draw more attention to himself.

Antigone didn't pay her escorts much mind. She knew she could handle them. It was Felton she was worried about. He hadn't spoken since they'd left the chantry. He hardly seemed aware of his surroundings at all. When the pair of Nosferat had jumped them, there hadn't been so much as a flicker of alarm on his face. He merely shuffled forward, one hand inside the breast of his robes, clutching at the bundle of burned papers. He stopped when she stopped, and started forward again when she started. For all practical purposes, he was little more than an ambulatory corpse.

An ambulatory corpse. Antigone smiled at the thought. That's all that they all were, for that matter. When it came right down to it. Ambulatory corpses. Bodies without the good sense to lie down and stay dead.

But she would have thought that the sudden appearance of the prince's men would have sparked some reaction from him. That it might have penetrated through to that inner sanctuary where Felton had retreated, clutching tightly to his precious papers, the evidence that would clear his name. Retreating from the blackened parchment-thin shell of his body.

And then she found that their little procession had come to an abrupt halt. There she was, face to face with Emmett, the prince's broodmate and right-hand man. *The one Foley was sent to kill,* she thought. *No, the one I was supposed to be sent to kill.* The irony was not lost upon her.

Close up, he did not look like the iron gauntlet of the prince's oppressive regime. Nor did he look like the steel girder that supported Calebros' teetering and corrupt reign. *To tell the truth,* she thought, *he looks a little doughy. And a bit sad. And weary, so very weary.*

Emmett was garbed in a surplus army blanket wrapped around his shoulders. His own right arm was withered and horribly burned. He kept it clutched tightly to his chest. The hand, or what she could see of it, was little more than a shapeless mass of melted flesh and fused bone.

"And here you are at last." He almost sounded relieved, as if an onerous duty that he had found himself unequal to was at last brought to completion. Despite his own failings. "So you are our mad bomber?" He looked Felton up and down, hoping perhaps to find something to arouse his own rage and indignation. What he found was someone who had been broken and burned almost beyond recognition. Far worse than even Emmett himself had.

"You looked so much bigger on TV. But everyone looks so much bigger on TV. No, you are not at all the monster we were led to expect. But you will do. Yes, I think you will do."

Emmett scanned the crowd of expectant faces. "Caleb?" he called. "Where is Caleb? There you are. Come here. Give the man some room. They tell me it was you who brought in our friend here." It was not a question, but Caleb was not one to shy away from an opening.

"That I did. I apprehended him myself, both of them really, if you must know. After the witch had struck down Donatello — after the treacherous fashion of her kind." He turned to his companion and beamed at him, grinning ear to ear.

Emmett turned as well. His attention was not focused on Donatello but on Antigone, as if seeing her for the first time. He regarded her warily. "And you say you nabbed them just outside the chantry door. Tell me, were they on the way in, or on the way out?"

"Why, they were departing. And surreptitiously at that." Caleb seemed inordinately proud of the word. He rolled the word around in his mouth, savoring the taste of it. "If I hadn't been keeping such a keen lookout—"

"I see," Emmett interrupted. "And how long were they inside, before you apprehended them?" 'Apprehended' was only a four-syllable word, but it was the best he could come up with at short notice. He pronounced each syllable separately and distinctly, parroting back Caleb's affectation to the amusement of those gathered.

"Well, I don't know," Caleb huffed. "But I know they hadn't snuck past me earlier in the evening. I can tell you that! Otherwise I would have nabbed them then and there. And we would all have had a drink or two on it already and been well on our way to bed by now."

"I want a full report by tomorrow evening. But for tonight, humor me." He waited for Caleb's nod. "In your opinion, our quarry here must have been holed up in the Tremere chantry for at least one night, right? Maybe two."

"Well, yeah. It does look that way," Caleb admitted grudgingly.

"Maybe our other guest would like to shed some light on this topic?"

"What is it you want to know?" Everyone turned at the sound of Antigone's voice. It was sharp and defiant.

"I want to know how long the Tremere chantry has been harboring this assassin?" Emmett roared. Antigone's tone was something his pent-up anger could lash out against. Much more so than the pathetic husk of a man who had done this to him and to his prince.

"We've come," she said coolly, "to talk to Calebros. Now, would you like to take us to him? Or do you plan on spending what little time we have left before sunrise rehashing old times?"

"Terribly sorry," Emmett said, grinning through oversized tusk-like teeth. "The prince isn't receiving any further guests tonight. I'm afraid you will have to spend the daytime hours here. Not to worry. We have made suitable arrangements. Donatello will show you to your quarters." He grinned down on her benignly.

"I have an urgent message for Prince Calebros," Antigone insisted. "From Regent Sturbridge. It will not wait until the morning."

Emmett shrugged apologetically. "That does not change the fact that the prince is unavailable. Goodnight."

Donatello advanced a half a step, but the fire in the glance that Antigone shot him brought him up short. "If the prince is unavailable," she said, "then I suppose I must deliver my message to you. I am instructed to say to your master, Calebros, Prince of New York, that Regent Sturbridge commends into his care these two supplicants. I am to tell him that she asks that he keep them safe, at all costs. And that he is to do this for the sake of the bones that lie beneath the regent's blood. She has told me that if I do this faithfully, that Calebros will not refuse us sanctuary."

At her words a uneasy hush fell over the assembly.

Emmett seethed. "I will know the truth of this." He made no attempt to mask the threat in his voice. "Make no mistake, witch. If you are deceiving us, you will die alongside this man. And do not think that you have won here, that he will escape us so easily. We honor our debts, oh yes, let no man challenge that. But we also collect what is owed us. We may chose to delay that final reckoning, but we do not relinquish our right to it. Remember what we have spoken here tonight."

Antigone opened her mouth to answer him, but was drowned out by the chorus of voices giving the ritual response. "We hear and remember," the crowd murmured.

Chapter 25
A Little Birdie

"How can you know that he is already inside?" Felton asked, readjusting his binoculars. He lay on his stomach, his elbows propped up on the very edge of the rooftop. The tar and gravel surface was still warm, a lingering memory of the afternoon sunlight. Felton shifted but could not get comfortable. The heat brought back unpleasant memories, memories that a full week of blood and bed rest had not been able to erase.

The Nosferatu had proven as good as their word. They had made both Felton and Antigone as comfortable as possible. They had nursed them back to health, shielded them from any uncomfortable inquiries—from either the chantry or the mortal authorities. And when it was time for the two to leave their care, they had provided the necessary weapons and equipment.

They had not all been happy about it. But they had done what Sturbridge said they would do. By the week's end, however, Antigone could sense that their hosts' patience was growing thin. They departed just as soon as she thought Felton was well enough to carry out his part in the delicate task that lay before them.

"A little birdie told me," Antigone replied.

Felton lowered the binoculars and glared at her. He already had enough misgivings about this little operation. Her plan for him to return to the Conventicle, to confront the Bonespeaker directly, didn't sit well with him. And her attitude here wasn't helping matters. "Not good enough. That kind of advice is what landed me in this mess to begin with. Either you come clean with me or…"

"Or what?" she interrupted. "You take your toys and go home?"

His voice never raised above a whisper, but there was an edge to it. "Or that guy is going to pick us apart. You're the outsider here, remember. You haven't seen him in action. I have. The only thing we've got in our favor is that we both know what's going down. You start holding back on me now and that blunts our only edge."

She shrugged dismissively. Felton was right, of course. There was still a good deal she was holding back. She had not confided in him that the source of her information about the Conventicle was not some arcane thaumaturgic rite, but rather something more mundane. She wasn't sure how Felton would react to the revelation that she, herself, was a member of their little cabal. And that she had been for some time. She had been there the night he had "drawn the dragon" and then found himself in the precisely the wrong place at precisely the wrong time.

Hell, she had organized the Dragonrite that night. But Antigone was not to blame for what had happened to him. In fact, if anything, it was Felton who was to blame that it was he and not Antigone herself who was now on the receiving end of this interstate manhunt.

"All right," she admitted. "I saw a face at the window. Bone white like that mask you told me about. He's worried. He's afraid they won't come."

"Yeah," Felton snorted. "And I'm worried that they will." He checked his watch. "It's still way too early. It's stupid of him to show himself at the window. He's not going to see anything.

Except maybe an apparition on the rooftop. I wish you'd keep your head down. You're only about as obvious as a visitation from the grave."

Antigone turned, the wind blowing a tangle of long black hair across her face like a veil. The skirts of her dark gown rippled out behind her and cracked like a sheet hung out on a clothesline. She cocked her head to one side and regarded him curiously. The expression was undeniably avian. "Why? I am supposed to be here, remember. I am expected. Or at least I am expected to haggle over your ransom and assurances of your 'safe' return to the Conventicle." She smiled, but there was no warmth to it.

She watched him closely to see how her story was holding up. He did not challenge her further, nor did his face betray any sign of doubt. The Bonespeaker was expecting her, that was true enough. True enough to carry that note of authenticity that made even an audacious lie plausible.

She was not about to confide to Felton how closely she and the Bonespeaker were already acquainted. Felton could not have known that the trap at the Empire State Building had not been intended for him, but for another. If he believed that this little meeting was arranged solely for his benefit, however, so much the better.

"Damn it, I don't like it," Felton said. "I don't like it at all. I'm surprised he even bothered to show up. The whole thing screams *ambush*."

"That's why we let him pick the time and the place. We do it all on his home turf. Let him feel as comfortable as he'd like, as if he's holding all the cards. Now all you've got to do is make sure that he never gets the backup he's counting on."

"I've got that covered," he said. "But how do you know he doesn't already have all the backup he's going to need in there with him now?"

"I don't," she admitted. "I think it best that we assume that he does."

"Did I mention that you're lousy at this whole pumping-up-morale thing?" he asked.

"Morale is your field, Mr. Felton, not mine. If you feel your resolve needs bolstering, I'll trust you to see to it. Your primary responsibility is to make sure that the cavalry never shows up. Anything beyond that is a windfall. I can hold off whatever is lying in waiting for us in there for at least ten minutes or so. Is that going to give you enough time?"

"You're full of it," he said. "You've got absolutely no idea what's waiting for you in there, much less whether or not you can hold it at bay for ten minutes. I'll be there in five."

"I'm not having you busting in early and showing our hand while his reinforcements are merrily kicking their way through the front door behind you."

"I've got it covered," he said for the second time.

"It would be well, however, if you were to keep out of sight for the present. As long as he believes that I have you safely tucked away back at the chantry, it dramatically increases our bargaining power."

"This whole thing stinks. You really think you're just going to waltz in there and fluster him? Get him to slip up? Hell we're not even sure that he knows anything more than we do."

"He knows," Antigone replied. "If he didn't, he wouldn't be so anxious for your return. It would be far better for him, for the Conventicle, if he never saw you again. If you just turned up quietly dead somewhere. The less evidence to link the bombing back to them, the better."

Felton shook his head. "I just can't help thinking that we're both going to end up 'quietly dead' because of this. I've waltzed into one set-up too many for my taste."

"Too late for second thoughts now," Antigone said. "See you in ten minutes." She laid a hand on his shoulder and squeezed before vanishing down the fire escape.

Chapter 26
Whispering Through Bones

F elton watched her pick her way across the darkened street and vanish into the shadow of the building opposite. He'd be damned if he was going to give her ten minutes. She might be killed twice over in that time. He gave her five and then went over the side. It would take a concerted effort for her to get herself killed in five minutes.

Felton clung to the lip for just a moment, enough to break his momentum, before dropping to the street below. From the roof's lowest point, it was no more than a two-story fall. He hit and rolled; the impact still knocked the stagnant air from his lungs. It didn't slow him. He came up running and cut a zigzag pattern across the street that Antigone had so calmly strolled across just minutes earlier.

He darted to the short flight of stairs at the side of the old theatre. So far so good. There was no sound of gunshots either from the street or from within. He pressed his back into the brick wall. It steadied him.

Stooping, he unwrapped a bundle from his jacket pocket and scattered its contents on the lowest step. The skeleton of a bird. That sign should serve to warn off any other members of the Conventicle. It didn't take an oracle to read omens in the fall of the bones. Their message would be clear enough. *Danger: Meeting site compromised. Await further contact.*

Felton bounded up the stairs two at a time. The brass plate above the door read, "Service Entrance." It mostly obscured the scars where the older flaking paint peeked out from beneath it. He could still pick out the arc of the initial "C" and the angry line of the trailing "d." *Colored,* he thought. The sign was a lingering reminder of a less enlightened age.

Quietly he tried the door, and then rattled it a bit more determinedly. Locked. That meant trouble. He cursed under his breath. Antigone surely would not have locked the door behind her. Either someone had met her at the door or some unseen pursuer had already followed her inside.

They hadn't been planning on either of those contingencies. In fact, one of Felton's main responsibilities was to make sure that nobody got behind Antigone. That she would not only have time enough to find out what they needed—without any unpleasant interruptions—but she would also have a clear avenue of retreat when she needed to break away.

He swore again and pulled a long, wide knife from his jacket. He studied the door for a moment, appraisingly. There. He inserted the blade into the crack in the jamb and was satisfied to feel it scrape against the deadbolt. He balled one fist around the pommel and brought the heel of his other palm smashing down upon it. The blow would have felled a bear. There was a splintering sound and the gap between door and jamb gaped.

Felton kicked the door open hard and it rebounded with a crash that sounded ominously loud in the stillness. By the time it swung back, he was lying prone upon the narrow landing just inside the doorway. The door caught him in the side, but the bullets missed him, flying overhead. He answered in kind.

"You're early, Ms. Baines," said the Bonespeaker as Antigone peeked through the crack of the door. "But forgive me. I have startled you. I heard your footstep on the stair."

"Not at all," she replied. "I was actually hoping to find you here. I had thought we might talk before the others arrived." Antigone had the advantage of Felton in that she knew exactly where and when this next meeting of the Conventicle would be held. She did not need to arrange with the Bonespeaker in advance for some private interview to discuss Felton's case. She just had to show up early and make sure that no one else did.

She pushed the door fully open and took one careful step into the darkened loft. She knew that this was not the same theatre where they had last met, but someone had gone to great pains to make the interiors look identical. The room's focal point was the same circle of grisly chairs—made by human hands, from human skin. It was their Round Table. Its highest ideal was a twisted sort of egalitarianism—its common thread, man's inhumanity to man. It was the justification and the first tenet of the Conventicle.

"I am glad you are here," he said, his voice somewhat muffled, distorted by the elaborate avian mask. "I more than half expected that no one would show up tonight. Not after this recent unpleasantness."

"Not after the bombings, you mean. There is no reason to couch it in euphemisms for my sake. I'm a big girl now, I can take it." She smiled without warmth. "But I can certainly understand your concern. I was more than half hoping that no one would show up myself. I figured we could have a private chat."

"By all means." His tone was calm, accommodating, but Antigone caught his furtive sideways glance. She could not pick out any others present in the darkened loft, but his gaze told her what she needed to know. They were not alone.

It might have been a slip, but it could just as easily have been a warning: *Have a care what you say. Even here, there are ears.* "What's on your mind?" he asked.

She wasn't pulling any punches. "Blowing up the Empire State Building. That wasn't part of the plan. It was supposed to be a clean hit. In and out fast; no complications, no entanglements. Take down the prince's right-hand man and kick one of the last remaining props out from under the faltering regime. When exactly did all that change? When did this become some terrorist-attack, media-circus bullshit?"

He motioned her to calm with both hands. "Believe me, Ms. Baines, I am as alarmed at this unforeseen turn of events as you are. Some of our operatives, they become a bit...overzealous in carrying out the missions we entrust to them. Some become a danger to themselves and others. Some even threaten the continued existence of this Conventicle with their brash exploits. I must admit, I have been a mass of nerves all week. I am quite anxious to hear your report as to what has been done about our over-exuberant comrade."

There was a slight sound in the shadowed corner behind the Speaker and to his left. It sounded like a rustling of leaves, or the passage of a serpent over the rough planked floorboards. It seemed the Bonespeaker was not the only one who was anxious about this issue. She took her time and chose her words carefully.

"I've seen him," she said at last. "He had to break from cover eventually. Showed up at the house of...of another of our number. Tried to convince him that he didn't set the bomb, that it was all a setup."

"Whose house would that be?" The Bonespeaker was a touch too anxious, but his voice carried a clear tone of command. He swooped down upon her words, fierce, predatory. The skeletal bird mask pressed close to her face. She could almost smell the sharp pungent stench of decomposing carrion and feathers. With an effort, she shook off the force of his demand and staggered back a pace, her nose wrinkling in undisguised distaste.

Immediately, the impression passed. His manner was polite once more. Controlled, formal. "We must make sure this benefactor is on hand tonight to give witness to what he has seen and heard."

"That's not going to be possible," she said. She hoped he would leap to the obvious conclusion—that there had been a falling out, a violent one. She pressed on. "What do you make of these wild claims of his? That he didn't blow up the building, that he was set up."

The Bonespeaker snorted and began to pace, thinking aloud. "That's all a bit hard to credit, I'm afraid. It seems to raise more questions than it answers. Who would set him up? And—I trust you will forgive my frankness—why bother? Our associate is hardly the sort of major player who invites such Machiavellian plotting against his well-being. He is a man-at-arms, nothing more."

Antigone opened her mouth to object, but he turned upon her and raised his voice to speak over her. "Don't get me wrong, he's very competent at what he does. He'd have to be to still be around in his line of work after all this time. But he is hardly worth that sort of trouble. No, it has been my experience that in dealing with these soldiers of fortune, that the simplest explanation is usually the correct one. Our friend was just a bit too gung-ho that night. And now we must all pay the price for his excesses."

"Occam's Razor," Antigone muttered. Her hand strayed to the reassuring weight of the folded steel blade tucked away in the inside pocket. It was cool in her grasp.

"Excuse me?" he said.

"It's nothing. Someone once said much the same thing. A Franciscan monk. In the fourteenth century. He said..."

"Ms. Baines, where is Mr. Felton?"

Well there it is, she thought. *Out in the open, names and everything. So much for the polite preambles.*

She could not answer him truthfully and she was convinced that the absolute worst thing she could do in the present situation—the surest way to guarantee that she never walked back out of this loft—would be to start lying now. All the signs and portents seemed to focus on this one point. Occam's Razor. Diogenes' Lantern. Aquinas' *De Veritatis*. The Feather of Truth. The Blade of Damocles.

Discerning truth only got more complicated once you started muddying the waters with your own fabrications. It was too easy to slip, to betray yourself inadvertently. Or worse, to fall into believing your own lies.

She had a momentary vision of herself back home in Scoville, suddenly back on the Widow's Walk. But now the gulf in front of her was not the vastness of the sea. A chasm of deceit yawned below her. The way forward was narrow and treacherous. One misstep in either direction would precipitate her off the path. *One foot in front of the other*, she thought. *You've done this a hundred times before.*

But it never got any easier. The straight way between truth and falsehood. The blurred line between the living and the dying. She locked eyes with the Bonespeaker, as if to anchor herself. She steadfastly refused to look down, to look at her feet. Slowly, she took a single step forward. She tested the ground beneath the ball of her foot. Solid. She exhaled soft and slow in relief, but otherwise kept her stony silence.

Seeing her reluctance, he tried another tack. "Surely you're not having second thoughts? You cannot believe this ridiculous story about his being set up?"

"No, Felton wasn't set up," she said. "That doesn't make any sense. Felton wasn't even supposed to draw the dragon that night. You know that."

His eyes behind the stark white bone of the mask widened, but his voice remained steady. "Of course. It is obvious that he concocted the whole ridiculous story. Let us talk no more of it. Felton needs to be dealt with and swiftly—before the authorities trace him back to us. If you have any knowledge of his whereabouts…"

Antigone seemed lost in her own private thoughts. She spoke over him without seeming to be aware of the fact. "It's funny though, Felton wasn't entirely wrong, was he? I mean, it was a set-up. It's just that he wasn't the intended fall guy."

The Bonespeaker stiffened. "I don't think I follow you." He enunciated each word slowly and precisely.

"Well, Felton wasn't the one who was supposed to draw the dragon that night, was he? *I was.* It was my mission. We had a deal."

He tried to speak but she cut him off. She advanced upon him, pressing closer until she was right up in his face. "Tell me what it was, how I got fingered to take the fall for this one? The old-boy network again? Because I'm too female? Because I'm too young? What the hell makes you think that you could hang my ass out there like that and even hope to get away with it?!"

"I assure you, Ms. Baines, I did no such thing. You must calm yourself. You must think. Why should I—"

This time it was not Antigone that cut him off, but rather the sound of rapid gunshots.

Antigone cursed. Damn that Felton. Ten minutes! He had promised her ten minutes. She really hoped he hadn't just got his sorry ass shot all to pieces—not that it wouldn't serve him right. If he had… If he had, she thought angrily, she hoped she could still find a big enough chunk that she could kick what was left of his worthless lying butt. She was already moving towards the door.

Out of the corner of her eye, she caught a slight gesture of annoyance from the Bonespeaker. In answer to his unspoken command, two shadowy blurs, one from either side of him, peeled away from the walls and shot toward the door.

It was almost too fast to follow. Antigone half-turned to avoid the nearest streak of shadow. Her hand came up defensively, but the motion seemed too slow, almost languid. Her arm unfolded in sections, like the wing of a bird unfurling. First the elbow locked, then the wrist, and finally the hinge of the straight razor.

She was rewarded with a gurgling cry from the onrushing guard, who clutched at his throat. The heavy, misshapen body teetered precariously for a moment and then crumpled noisily to the floor, choking on invectives and his own blood.

Antigone pivoted gracefully like a dancer. The motion flung an arc of blood from the dripping blade, leaving an angry red graffitied weal upon the nearest wall.

The second guard, startled, turned to face this attack from an unexpected quarter. It was a mistake. Antigone should have been able to take advantage of that opening, were it not for her own error: She met its gaze. It was no human face. The creature's two small beady eyes were set vertically, one on top of the other. It had neither nose nor mouth, but a mucousy rasping noise emerged from loose flaps of skin under its rolling jowls. She didn't know how it fed, and she didn't want to know.

The creature, however, seemed keenly interested in instructing her on this very point. She shrank back from it, trying to keep the Bonespeaker in view at the same time. She could spare him little more than a momentary glance just now, but she wanted to know about it if he tried to circle around behind her.

The creature pawed at her, but she managed to rebuff its advance with a desperate downward slash of the razor. Her blow connected and, for the second time tonight, the ancient blade tasted blood.

Antigone tried to shut out the warbling howl that erupted from the wounded monstrosity. She fell into a more defensive posture as the creature hurled itself at her, launching a flurry of blindingly fast attacks. Antigone was sorely pressed. She barely had the breathing space to realize that the overwhelming rain of blows was not really intended to connect, only to test her defenses, to probe for weakness. The creature was sizing her up. It was very systematic about it, and it did not seem at all discouraged by what it found. Antigone felt her resolve begin to falter before the machinegun-fast onslaught.

It was the feint towards her off hand that got her. Stupid, really. She overparried and, before she could recover, she felt the viselike talons close over her wrist. The same wrist she had broken in the fight with Helena just weeks before. Its touch was cold, scaly and slimy, like that of a bottom feeder. Antigone squirmed in its grasp.

The creature could just as easily have used the opening to gut her, she realized with a curious detachment. It was still holding back. But then the driving pain forced all such concerns from her thoughts. Distantly, she heard the razor clatter to the floorboards.

The noise echoed jarringly in the cramped confines of the theatre loft. A resounding boom like a door slamming open.

She expected the beast to snap her forearm like a twig. She stiffened, bracing herself against the anticipated wrenching blow. But instead she felt only a series of short, quick jerks as the creature's body writhed under a long burst of bullets.

Antigone curled and dropped, rolling away from the deadly spray of projectiles. She kept a firm grip on the creature's arm as she went down, hurling its ponderous bulk up and over her. The stream of staccato impacts doggedly followed the body's flight, carving away chunks of the cold and decayed flesh. Even after the creature had crashed into the wall and slumped motionless to the floor, the quick patter of gunshots continued to rip into it.

And then silence. There was no further hint of movement from either of the felled guards.

"Nice throw," Felton said. "No, it's all right. You don't have to thank me. Where's the Speaker?"

"Thank you?! You'll be lucky if I don't stake you!" Her voice was a sharp whisper. She was still acutely aware that the danger was not yet behind them. She crouched and scooped up the straight razor. "That was not any kind of ten minutes. They didn't teach you to tell time in that school of yours?"

Antigone cast about worriedly for the Bonespeaker, but could see no sign of him. She cursed aloud and stooped to retrieve the blood-streaked straight razor. "I can't believe you. If you hadn't busted in here I would already know—"

There was a sharp crack and a delicate red bud unfolded in the exact center of Felton's forehead. Antigone took one involuntary step towards him, but his body had already collapsed to the floor. Stunned, she turned in the direction from which the shot must have come. She felt a nagging itch on her brow and absently smoothed aside a stray strand of hair. Then she realized the source of her irritation and exactly how fine a target she had just made herself.

Shaking out of her initial shock, she dove behind the circle of chairs. As she threw herself down, an angry buzzing streaked past her. A close call. She hit the floor hard and rolled. Her free hand went to her ear to try to clear the ringing. It came away covered in blood.

More shots fell around her, burying themselves deeply into the wood of the chairs and floor. She checked her path to the door. Other than the obvious obstacles—the bodies—the way was clear. If Antigone could not pick out her assailant soon, she would have to make a break for it.

She wiped at her forehead unconsciously with the back of her knife hand. As the razor came up, she caught sight of its edge, still streaked with blood. The scent of it was heady, sweet, nearly overpowering.

Yes, there was a power in the blood. But she, for one, had absolutely no idea how to unlock it. There was a hint of movement beyond the circle of chairs and a sound like stealthy footfalls upon the metal rungs of a ladder. She squinted past the razor's edge, trying to make out the source of the disturbance, the form of the fleeing Bonespeaker. A pinprick of moonlight from the window caught the line of the raised blade and gleamed like a red star in the darkness.

Antigone was suddenly dazzled. The light reflecting off the razor seemed to pick out every bit of metal in the room. At each point, the gathering illumination was mirrored back, redoubled in intensity. Each of the polished brass rivets on the chairs blazed like a sun. On the wall opposite, a fiery ladder ascended towards the heavens.

She traced its course with her eyes, disappointed to find that it terminated only in a catwalk near the high, vaulted ceiling. The rails of the catwalk shone like gouts of flame. Nor did she have any trouble picking out the blackened gunmetal of the pistol that was leveled directly at her.

Three quick shots. One went high, the second caught her upraised forearm. The third sank deep into the hollow of the same shoulder. All the strength went out of her arm. She could not keep her grip on the razor, and it fell to the floor with the inexplicable sound of glass shattering.

She dropped prone, hoping the high-backed chairs would shield her from the Bonespeaker's line of sight. *Glass shattering?* Willing the flow of healing blood to the gunshot wounds,

Antigone groped around on the floor. She was rewarded with a deep slash along the heel of her palm. A jagged shard of glass, three inches long, protruded from her hand. She wrenched it free, but in doing so, her elbow hit something in the dark. It rang and overturned. A renewed flurry of shots homed in on the sound.

Antigone picked up the object. It was a cast-iron lantern. Two of the glass panes had been shattered. Inside was the stub of a soft tallow candle, its wick still smoldering.

She righted it and blew it to life. *Fiat lux*. More shots rained down upon her, these more precise. Her opponent must be making his way along the elevated walkway, maneuvering for a clearer shot.

There was no sign of the razor in the wreckage about her. *Must have slid beneath one of the chairs*, she thought. The truth of its unexpected transformation never crossed her mind.

The gunshots had fallen silent for the moment. Antigone knew, however, that it would not be long before they were renewed and from a more promising angle. She needed a quick diversion.

She put one hand on the lantern and, muttering a hasty invocation to Diogenes, shoved hard. Before it had slid to a halt in the center of the room, Antigone was moving. She scrambled around the ring of chairs in the opposite direction. Making for the ladder.

Her progress was checked by the most unlikely of sources. A slight, but unmistakable groan from the direction of the door. Felton.

Unwisely, she stopped and turned towards the sound. Felton lay just at the outskirts of the circle of illumination cast by the lantern. His hand came up to shield his eyes from the piercing light. He shook his head as if to clear it, a gesture which he must have instantly regretted.

She could pick out the movement clearly enough from her vantage point, but from the Bonespeaker's elevation?

Shots thundered. The light went out amidst the tinkling of broken glass and the tin-can clatter of the lantern bouncing across the floor.

Cursing, she broke away and dashed back towards the ladder. There was little enough time, and even less she might do for Felton at this point.

Nothing except take out the Bonespeaker.

In the dark, her groping hand found the rung of the ladder. She began to climb.

She feared that the sound of her ascent would betray her and guarantee that all that awaited her at the top was the wrong end of a gun barrel. But there were other noises that masked her clumsy ascent. Above her and still some distance off came the echo of agitated pacing. From below, there was a sound of something heavy—one of the chairs, perhaps—being dragged across the floor. She felt a wave of relief wash over her at the thought that Felton might still be among the living. Almost immediately, however, she realized that the sound could just as easily have come from one of the two guards. Or maybe even the antagonist—antagonists?—that had traded shots with Felton downstairs.

What she did not hear, thankfully, was the retort of further gunshots. Single-mindedly, she clawed her way up the ladder. She did not even realize she had reached the top until her outstretched hand found, not another rung, but the boards of the walkway.

She pulled herself up and onto all fours. Gingerly. Afraid that her weight upon the walk might be enough to warn the Bonespeaker that he was no longer alone on his perch. She tried to keep low and quiet.

230 / Eric Griffin

A single shot zinged off the railing right next to her head. She instantly flattened. Her impression was that it had come from below. Somehow, that did not reassure her.

She started forward again, slowly—acutely aware that she was unarmed, crawling on all fours, without benefit of cover, towards a man who was, in all probability, going to shoot her. Repeatedly.

At the sound of the latest gunshot, the Bonespeaker's agitation became more pronounced. He had, however, apparently given up on taking wild shots in the dark. To her mind, this spoke of conserving a dwindling supply of ammunition.

There was a mournful wail of distant sirens, but for Antigone they carried little hope. Probably even less so for Felton, if he were still aware enough to hear them.

A glaringly bright flash momentarily illuminated the room, accompanied by a resounding roar. The entire catwalk lurched drunkenly. If she had been standing, she would almost certainly have been precipitated over the edge. As it was, her center of balance was low and she was able to catch herself on the railing.

Antigone rose unsteadily to her full height, struggling to regain her balance. The once level walk now slanted down sharply away from her, descending in the direction she knew the Bonespeaker had taken. Abandoning all thought of stealth, she pounded forward and down the steep planked incline, sliding her hands along the railing as she went to steady herself.

It soon became apparent that the entire support structure for this section of the walk had been suddenly cut out from underneath it. The fact that the walkway still swung from side to side with the force of that cut put her in mind of demolitions. This also did nothing reassure her.

At the end of the incline, she saw a dark form dangling from the railing. More accurately, it seemed to be pinned between the tangle of walk and railing and struggling to free itself. The Bonespeaker.

He hung head-downwards, suspended and inverted. The walk here had sagged so low that the fall would not have been anything to speak of, certainly no more than ten feet. Below, Antigone could see a form stalking towards them out of the darkness.

She froze, expecting more gunshots.

For the first time this evening, she was pleasantly disappointed. In the dim light from the window, the approaching figure gradually took on the familiar shape of Felton. His visage was grim. Most of the flesh of his forehead had been clawed away, apparently in the effort to extract the bullet. It did not look as if the operation had been a success. Much of his face was covered with angry-looking flash burns. He walked with a decided limp, his pants leg shredded by a veritable strafing run of bullet wounds.

Without ever taking his eyes from the Bonespeaker, Felton let the detonator drop to the floor. He came three paces closer, stooped, and picked up a large-caliber automatic pistol that had fallen from the Speaker's grip when the explosive charge went off below him. In Felton's other hand, he held a bloody straight razor.

Antigone hardly recognized it. Like Felton, the blade had not suffered the rain of bullets gracefully. It was badly bent, nicked, its handle shattered.

Felton raised the gun and leveled it at the Bonespeaker's head. From these close quarters, Antigone could see that the pistol looked to have escaped in much better condition, which was not surprising as it had been on the giving rather than the receiving end of most of the carnage. "Stand clear, Ms. Baines.

He's mine. He's got it coming to him. And I'm going to finish this, right now."

"Nope," she replied planting one foot firmly on the Bonespeaker's sternum and digging in. "Think a minute, Mr. Felton. You kill him now and we're never going to find out who set me...who set *you* up."

The change of emphasis was not lost on him. Slowly, the pistol lowered to his side. "So that's what this is all about. I should have known better than to think that the damned Tremere would just help me out without having some personal stake in the outcome."

The Bonespeaker laughed softly. The sound bubbled out of him like a spring. There didn't seem to be any end of it. "The Tremere? A personal stake in this matter? Our Ms. Baines really has kept you in the dark, then, hasn't she?"

"And you, shut the hell up!" Felton yelled. "I'm serious, I'm not going to tell you again. You think I'm going to hold back because *she* might get caught in the line of fire? You're fooling yourself. I said, shut up already!"

Antigone put the whole of her weight upon her one heel. It ground all the air out of the Bonespeaker and the laughter with it. "Felton," she interrupted gently.

"What?"

"I'd like to get out of here, preferably before the police arrive. We can't go anywhere until I get a certain answer out of this man. I would already have gotten it, if you hadn't barged in here five minutes early and nearly gotten the both of us killed in the bargain. So if you would just hold off on killing this bastard for a minute, I think we can all get what we want. Okay?"

"Did I mention you're starting to piss me off?" he said. "Now I remember why I work alone. The sooner we get this over with the better as far as I'm concerned. Here you go. Ask away. I'll be right here if you need me." He tossed the razor up to her.

She caught it, seemed about to make an angry retort and then thought better of it. Instead, she stooped over the Bonespeaker. She held up the blade for his inspection.

"Okay. It's all up to you now. We can kill you, or we can cut you first and then kill you. I want to know why. That's all. Why you went to all the trouble to set me up. I already know why you blew up the building. To take down the prince. That's what this whole damned takeover of the Conventicle is about, isn't it? But what I want to know is, why me?" The blade nuzzled up against his throat.

"You still don't understand, do you?" he said, his voice rasping through the stark white avian mask. "Put the knife down and think for a minute. I didn't blow up the building."

Below Felton cursed and began pacing.

"Like hell you didn't!" Antigone shouted directly into his face. With an angry slash, she wrenched the blade down and around in a tight arc.

His head fell back, dangling over the abyss as if suddenly deprived of all visible means of support. A frail gurgling noise bubbled up through the mask as he clutched as his throat.

Felton, standing exactly below him, met his eyes. He could see the fear and confusion there as the Bonespeaker's hands came away, not covered with his spilling lifeblood, but perfectly dry.

"Oh shit," Felton said sadly, shaking his head. "Now you're in for it. You know what that is, don't you? It's blood magic. Thaumaturgy. I've seen her perform this little trick before and it's pretty gruesome. My advice to you is to answer the lady's questions as quickly and accurately as possible. You should've stuck by me, pal. I would have just shot you."

Antigone balled a fist into the front of the Bonespeaker's robes and hauled him back to a sitting position. "Who blew up the damned building?" she demanded.

"I...don't...know."

"Damn, he sounds bad," Felton said. "Like his vocal chords have been severed or something."

"Shut up, Felton," she barked. Her eyes never left the bone-white mask. "You. Listen to me. Was it any of our folks? Anybody in the Conventicle?" Antigone was thinking of the dark woman who had picked up the redress—who had set off the explosion at the high school in an attempt to kill or silence Johanus.

"No," he rasped. He tried to clear his throat, coughed and spat bloody phlegm down over the side of the swaying walkway. Felton scowled up at him.

The Bonespeaker tested his voice again and it sounded steadier this time. "If you had any idea what you have blundered into, Ms. Baines, you would not be so eager to cut yourself off from all of your allies. Yet you systematically alienate yourself from anyone who might protect you—from the Pyramid, from the Conventicle, and now even from your last fawning supporter, poor deluded Mr. Felton."

"Just waste this bastard," Felton said. "He doesn't know anything."

"I'm a big girl," Antigone answered the Bonespeaker. "I can watch my own back. So how about you tell me why you, my so-called benefactor, set me up? You knew the building was going to blow. You even knew when it was going to happen. And you arranged things so that I would be there to take the fall. Why?"

The Bonespeaker laughed quietly. "You don't know. You really don't know. And I thought you were just stringing our Mr. Felton here along. You don't see why it would alarm me to have another Tremere infiltrating the Conventicle at this point? *Especially* a member of the chantry security team."

"What the hell do you mean 'another' Tremere?" Antigone asked. "Jeezus, there are other novices from the chantry inside the Conventicle and you didn't even see fit to tell me?!"

The Bonespeaker shook his head. "Of course there is another. And your presence—not to mention your determination to force your way up through the ranks—put the infiltrator in a rather tenuous position."

"I need a name," Antigone growled.

"And you'll have one," he said. "If you will see reason. Surely you realize that you cannot go back to the chantry now. Not even Helena could protect you. So where will you go? Your only hope is the Conventicle. I can hide you from the prince and the Pyramid. We will lead the Conventicle through this crisis together. I am willing to make a blood-compact with you."

"You tried to kill me before," she reminded him.

"No, I tried to get you out of harm's way. To get you to leave the city. I knew that if you kept on the way you were going, you would get us both killed. I couldn't let you jeopardize all I have built here. The Conventicle is my House, Antigone. My chantry if you will. You of all people can appreciate what that means. I am offering you the protection of my House."

She shook her head. "It's too late for all that now. You should have offered me that weeks ago, before this whole mess started. Then none of this would have happened. And you wouldn't be about to die. Now, one last time, how did you know the Empire State Building was going to be blown up? I need a name."

"If I tell you that, we're both as good as dead."

"You're already good as dead, and I'm willing to take the chance. Now tell me! Who tipped you off?"

The Bonespeaker fidgeted uncomfortably but saw no other way to escape his present predicament. "His name is Graves. Adam Graves. He's…"

Antigone knew very well who he was. His face had been plastered all over the news of late.

"Lying son of a bitch," Felton muttered from below. "I've seen that guy, Graves. On TV. *Daytime* TV. He's not even one of us."

Antigone ignored Felton's outburst. She knew that if the Bonespeaker were lying, she'd know about it immediately.

"Look, you remember the last time we met? When you sent me out to kill Felton?" she said.

"What the fuck?" Felton demanded indignantly from below.

The Bonespeaker shifted uneasily. He hesitated; he cleared his throat. Antigone shook him by the collar. "Do you?!"

"Yes, certainly. I—"

A hot wave of blood slapped across Antigone's face. Felton stepped back hastily, cursing. The Bonespeaker's back arched sharply and then he went limp in her grasp.

"Damn it." She brought her fist down, pounding on his chest, and then pushed him sharply away. His head swung down below the level of the walk. A cascade of blood pattered to the floor below from the gaping slit in his throat.

"Oh, that was great," Felton said, wiping at the splattered blood on the front of his shirt. "Very effective. Can we get out of here now? Or would you like to cross-examine the corpse?"

"You go ahead," she said, clenching her teeth over an angry retort. "I've got one more question to ask him."

Felton snorted in disgust. "You're crazy, you know that, right? This guy's answering days are over. He's… Never mind. It's not worth it. You're not listening anyway. Look, I'll wait downstairs for you, if you want me to. I figure, you did help me out when I had nowhere else to go. And you came back for me, back at the chantry, and pulled me out of that inferno. And even if your motives weren't entirely altruistic, you deserve something. At least for somebody to give you a heads-up before the cops bust in."

His unanticipated offer brought her up short. "That's very considerate of you, Mr. Felton. I'll see you back in the warrens then."

"Jeez, you are crazy. I'll see you around, Blackbird."

Antigone looked after him until she heard the street door bang shut. Then she tugged the limp body back up onto the remains of the walk. The chalk-white mask was streaked with blood. The pattern caught her by surprise. Like the counterintuitive course of the Nile, the ruby lines ran *upwards*, south to north—a side effect of the body's dangling upside down.

Antigone stared at the alien, bird-like features a long while. Felton's words of a week before kept running through her mind. *"All of the bosses are interchangeable."*

The Bonespeaker had failed the razor's test. He had been caught out in a lie. *But it wasn't a lie!* Antigone silently raged. He had merely admitted to sending her to kill Felton at their last meeting. Or had he?

The troubling thought struck her, remembering how the Bonespeaker had hesitated when she had put the question to him. *What if that hadn't been our last meeting?*

With growing apprehension, she hooked her fingers under the edge of the mask and pulled. It refused to come away, as if the surface tension of the blood film had sealed it to his face. She tugged harder, but to no avail. Frustrated, she grabbed the object that was closest to hand. Occam's Razor. Inserting the blade through one eyehole, she insinuated it between the mask and the underlying flesh. Then she bore down hard, using the razor as a lever.

238 / Eric Griffin

The blade bent nearly double. Antigone sat back on her heels, staring at it in open incredulity. Instead of a straight razor, she found that she clutched a long black feather. She recognized it instantly—the feather of Ma'at. The jackal god's standard for taking the measure of the dead.

She remembered his parting words to her—about the inherent interchangeability of the symbols of truth. About his allowing her to go back and be judged by the symbols of her own people—by the standards of her own peers.

At the time, she had been afraid that he had meant she would be returned to face the inquisition of the Astors. But it seemed that the Laughing Guardian of the Dead had picked out three very different judges for her from among her brothers and sisters of the Tremere Pyramid.

She thought back to her encounters with Johanus, with Jervais, with Helena—and of the trials and the accusations that each had laid before her. Some of them she had met well, with honesty and compassion. Others, not so well.

She hadn't found any easy redemptions, nor earned the absolution of even a single one of her tribunal of judges. If this feather was a summons from the Jackal, a sign that her time here was drawing to a close, she was afraid she had nothing to show him for her sojourn here among the living. Even with his second chance, she hadn't managed to do any better this time around. She had tried to help some people, she had hurt others. She had shed blood and drawn blood. She had sought after the truth, and she had been willing to bend the truth to do so.

So where did that leave her in the final reckoning? She feared that, if she were to face the Jackal's golden scales again now, the verdict would be no different than it had been before. She was no monster, although her very existence had become monstrous. She was certainly no saint, although she acutely felt the weight of the twin burdens of truth and compassion. She knew she had been given gifts both beautiful and terrifying—and that because of them, she would be held accountable to a higher standard.

She was empty of all desire now, but also curiously free of all fear. There was nothing left to her but the inevitable. She moved a hand through time and eternity danced upon her fingertips. Confidently, she reached out and laid the feather on her side of the balances, for a change.

Antigone laid the Feather of Ma'at gently across the sharp avian contours of the Bonespeaker's mask. Like a shroud, drawn up to cover the staring eyes of the deceased.

The skeletal bird mask cracked neatly in two vertically, the pieces falling away to either side.

Antigone glanced only briefly at the familiar face that was revealed there. The face of one of her judges—the one she had most failed.

Jervais.

She had abandoned Johanus to deal with the aftermath of the explosion alone. To drag the bodies from the wreckage, to tend the wounded and dying, and to hide the evidence from the authorities.

She had left Helena to the mercy of the Astors. To bear the brunt of their inquisition, to comfort the novices, to try to hold the crumbling chantry together by force of will.

But Jervais she had failed most of all.

Carefully, Antigone gathered up the halves of the mask. She cradled them in her arms, like broken eggshells, as she descended from the walk.

A gunshot sounded in the street outside. *Felton's warning,* she thought. Already she could pick out the wail of sirens drawing closer. She knew she must hurry now. But still she stood, rooted to the spot, listening. Waiting to be called back to face the final judgment. In the baying of the sirens, she thought she could detect the faint mocking laughter of the Jackal.

He was laughing at her. It was not until that moment that Antigone realized that she was not going to be suddenly whisked away. She could no longer dance the fine line between the living and the dead and walk away unscathed. If she were going to walk away from this room at all, she would have to take responsibility for her own redemption. To become her own judge—self-accused and, hopefully, self-vindicating.

Slowly, she raised the shattered mask to her face and, for the first time, looked out through the impassive avian eyes of the Bonespeaker.

Chapter 27
Widow's Weeds

Sturbridge's memories of her previous trip to the Fatherhouse were disjointed, almost feverish. The edifice had a weight of history and tradition about it unlike anything she had experienced anywhere else. It was simply too much to take in at once. Being here always felt a little like drowning. Of being thrown into a dark well, a thousand years deep—while yoked to a great pyramid-shaped stone.

The walls of the old manse had once, no doubt, been white, pristine. But the centuries of dark rites enacted within them had taken their toll on the place. The antique hand-painted wallpaper had turned a uniform dark sepia, as if it had soaked up some sanguine essence from the rivers of life that had been spilled here.

Sturbridge passively allowed herself to be guided through the half-familiar galleries and balustrades. She peered down upon the formal ballrooms and conservatories, her eyes and ears filled with the ethereal afterimages of legendary performances of bygone eras. Performances that had risen to greatness unaware of—and actually making—the wailing of the afflicted from the labyrinthine cellars.

Sturbridge could feel eyes upon her as well. Luminaries of her Order regarded her curiously at her passing. They whispered behind their hands at the sight of anyone in these halls—much less a lady of such regal bearing—attired in the humble black robes of the novitiate. The Widow's Weeds were tolerated here, but it was expected that they should be relegated to the churchyard, not ushered within the halls of power.

But there were other eyes here as well, eyes more penetrating and more vigilant. Sturbridge could feel their scrutiny like groping hands. Ghosts, daemons, guardian spirits, gargoyles frowned down at her from every cornice, capital, buttress and rainspout. The stunted servitors of the old manse craned down towards her as she passed, hungering.

Sturbridge could evade the need in their eyes, the silent pleading. She closed her own eyelids against them, only to find herself confronted by other faces. Faces of the twisted and the lost, rising up to greet their counterparts. From somewhere deep within her, eyes as round and bright as moons broke from the surface of the dark waters and peered curiously out at these other victims, those still clinging to the world of the living, trapped on the far side of the chill, rippling mirror.

She could feel Dorfman's hand upon her elbow, but there was no comfort in it, no warmth. At times it seemed that she could barely see him through the haze of rippling victims that pressed her from all sides, from without and from within.

"It was a mistake to come here," she said with certainty. "You see how they titter? How they talk behind their hands? The words of my accusers have preceded us. They have already hardened their hearts against us."

"It's all right," Dorfman said, his voice tight and pitched low. "Ignore them. The only person we've got to convince is Meerlinda. We talk to her, we find out what we need to know, and then we're out of here."

"You still think they're just going to let us say our piece and walk out of here alive?" Sturbridge demanded. "Look around you. Do these strike you as the kind of folks who suffer any kind of shake-up gracefully?"

"Look, it's been a long night," Dorfman said. "We could both use some rest. Tomorrow night we'll see Meerlinda. We will make her understand. I've got everything taken care of."

"Oh, you do not." But she smiled at his attempt. They walked for a while in silence, but a dim sense of foreboding was growing on her, fueled by the whispers of this old manse and its many victims. "This place is so cold, so empty. Can you feel it? It is an overwhelming sense of…absence. He is not here," she said with sudden certainty.

"What are you talking about? Who's not here?"

Sturbridge's tone was very calm, conversational, belying the growing horror of her realization.

"He has abandoned this place, shrugged it off like an old and ill-fitting garment. Shed it like a skin. Can't you see, Peter? He has freed himself from the Children, from their mute reproaches. He has freed himself of his childer, from the ceaseless feuding and bickering of his blood descendants. And now there is no telling what he might be capable of. How can they stay here? How can they stand it? Going through the same sad pantomime, night after night. Pretending that nothing has happened. These harlequin magi. These hollow men. Oh, it was foolish to have ever come here."

Dorfman smiled. A radiant, authentic smile. Something about it, its tangibility, broke in upon her dark musings and pulled her back away from the brink of that dark inner well. It seemed to encompass everything about them at once—the inspiration that breathed from the very architecture, the anchoring weight of history and tradition, the company of keen centuries-old intellects. And the certainty, the surety he could feel in his very blood, that this was home.

"I was just thinking," he confessed, "that I was a fool ever to have left it."

About the Author

Eric Griffin is the author of the Tremere Trilogy (*Widow's Walk, Widow's Weeds, Widow's Might*) as well as the novels *Tremere* and *Tzimisce* in the original Clan Novel series.

He is currently co-developer of the Tribe Novel series for **Werewolf: The Apocalypse**. His work on this series includes *Get of Fenris, Fianna, Glass Walkers* and *Black Spiral Dancers*.

His short stories have appeared in the *Clan Novel: Anthology, The Beast Within, Werewolf: The Apocalypse* and *Inherit the Earth*.

Griffin was initiated into the bardic mysteries at their very source, Cork, Ireland. He is currently engaged in that most ancient of Irish literary traditions—that of the writer in exile. He resides in Atlanta, Georgia, with his lovely wife Victoria and his three sons, heroes-in-training all.

(

Curious about other Crossroad Press books? Stop by our
website: http://crossroadpress.com
We offer quality writing
in digital, audio, and print formats.

Subscribe to our newsletter on the website homepage and
receive a free eBook.